Head Wound

Head Wound

JUDITH CUTLER

Allison & Busby Limited
11 Wardour Mews
London W1F 8AN
allisonandbusby.com

First published in Great Britain by Allison & Busby in 2018.

A CIP catalogue record for this book is available from
the British Library.

First Edition

ISBN 978-0-7490-2330-0

Typeset in 11/16 pt Sabon by
Allison & Busby Ltd.

The paper used for this Allison & Busby publication
has been produced from trees that have been legally sourced
from well-managed and credibly certified forests.

Printed and bound by
CPI Group (UK) Ltd, Croydon, CR0 4YY

For my dear friends Jill, Jerry,
and the inspirational Jeffrey

CHAPTER ONE

'I think she's still alive!'

A girl. Yes, still alive – but not for much longer.

She was nailed, hands and feet, in a parody of the crucifixion. She was gasping for breath – hadn't enough to scream, though the pain in her hands must have been excruciating as the weight of her body pulled against the nails, leaving trenches in the flesh.

A bleak February day. An east wind apparently straight from Russia hurtling across the grey fields of Kent to sling horizontal rain at the windows. What does everyone want? A quiet evening at home. What do I get? An emergency meeting with the school governors.

In fact, since I was head teacher of two schools, Wrayford and Wray Episcopi, I had two sets of governors to contend with. They had agreed to have a joint session since the

7

problem was one that would affect both schools equally – proposed changes to school funding throughout the country. For once we were all pulling in the same direction. We were desperate to avoid staff redundancies and any reductions to the curriculum. So – after much depressed discussion – we had agreed what I had actually told them at the start: while we appreciated the huge efforts everyone put into Christmas and summer fairs, and spin-off raffles and refreshment sales from the play, we needed to raise a lot more money than they produced to support all the activities that broadened the children's horizons. It wouldn't stop at funding things like sports equipment and school trips, no matter how educational. It would mean buying books for the library and for the classroom. Even then we'd have to recruit volunteers for appropriate tasks – in other words, anything that didn't need properly trained teachers.

'I'm sure we can rely on the parent–teacher groups at both schools to step up to the plate,' the chair of Wrayford governors declared, leaning heavily forward and eyeballing each governor in turn, as if challenging them to object to the cliché. Not just because of his physical presence – his thick neck and heavy shoulders – Brian Dawes was a man hard to stand up to, though he could be charm itself. He flashed me a disconcertingly conspiratorial smile even as he spoke.

Hazel Roberts shook her head. In her seventies, she was a little older than Brian and was actually chair of the Wray Episcopi governors. She had graciously – or sensibly – allowed Brian to take the lead in the meeting. Others might say she had been elbowed out, though with a great deal of persuasive courtesy. 'Our Parents' Association – which pointed out that the teachers don't get much involved—'

'Not through lack of interest,' Colin Ames said quickly. He'd drawn the short straw, as the secretary of the Wray Episcopi governors, the job of taking the minutes. 'Lack of time. It's even worse than when I was in the profession. I can't believe the amount of paperwork teachers today have to deal with.' He looked at his own reporter's notebook, as if expecting it to sigh in sympathy. He'd certainly covered a huge number of pages, taking conscientious note of everything – though I would have thought nice succinct resolution minutes would have been enough.

Brian was ready to leap in, but Hazel was there before him. 'Exactly,' she said firmly. 'More importantly, there's been something of a schism within the Parents' Association, largely because of the disruptive presence of one parent whose politics and manner of expressing them were offensive in the extreme.'

I could see Colin's pen move.

. . . in the extreme . . .

'Sadly, as things stand, it's impossible for us to force the man to resign. It would be worse if he was a parent governor, of course, because . . .'

Which was true but not to the point. At last Hazel pulled herself up short, continuing more relevantly, 'We also lack the village infrastructure so helpful to Wrayford. You have your playing field and the Jolly Cricketers' garden. We have neither field nor pub. Lady Preston used to allow us to use her grounds for our fete but while she's not in residence at the Great House, nor likely to be for some time' – she coughed with delicate irony – 'we can hardly expect the same privilege this year.'

'The greed of the woman!' someone put in. 'Owns all

that lot and still wants to make money by exploiting others!'

'That's a bit strong. She did a lot of good in the village.'

'Once upon a time! And now she's a convicted criminal doing her time, quite a lot of it, in jail. Don't waste your sympathy on her and her like.'

'It's because our resources aren't quite equal,' I put in, hoping to draw things to a close so we could all go home, 'that I suggested that the schools and the parents acted together for the common good. United we may stand; divided we will almost certainly fall. If we can't run the schools "properly" – in the eyes of Ofsted, that is – I'll bet my pension that someone will decide to put them in special measures and then quite coincidentally close them. The villages will be a great deal poorer in every sense if they lose their schools and the children have to go to bigger ones in towns that may be some distance from their homes. What I'd like to suggest, Chair, is that we reconvene next week, each of us with a list of ideas for heavy-duty fundraising that the schools with their PTA or PA will do together. If we don't raise funds we might even lose teachers. It's as serious as that. Now, it's unlikely we can all be present, of course – but if we email each other our ideas, even non-attenders will be making a significant contribution. I'd also like a subcommittee to be set up to evaluate the ideas that seem to have the greatest potential . . .'

'And to organise a search party at Wray Episcopi for Lady P's mythical missing masterpieces,' someone added, to general laughter. By now everyone knew about her ladyship's strange insistence that one of her forebears had donated paintings to the school and that she now wanted them back. There were two problems: firstly no one could

10

find them anywhere, and secondly the county council archive's search for any documentation stating that they had been loaned, not simply given like the school itself, had so far been fruitless. More to the point, no one could find any references at all to the paintings. But her ladyship's lawyers, when not trying to get her a reduced jail sentence, were threatening legal action if they were not returned.

I wasn't surprised when Brian dawdled at the end of the meeting, falling into step with me when I walked back to the office I shared with Tom, my deputy.

'Will you be eating at the Cricketers this evening?' he asked. 'Would you mind if I joined you?' This comparative humility was new. The behaviour of the said Lady P – Cassandra Preston to her intimates, one of whom was Brian – had rocked the village. Brian seemed to have been hurt more deeply than most by her fall from grace: his shoulders slumped from their previous quasi-military straightness, his face had sagged into deeper lines. A man who valued trust had had his betrayed. He added, 'I could use a really stiff drink.'

'Me too.' There was something in his voice that stopped me reminding him that I was driving. Perhaps I could simply leave the car locked in the school car park and indulge after all.

We set off, leaning into the wind, which might have been exhilarating. But in fact it was simply unpleasant, though at least the rain had stopped. Refuse from the collection earlier in the day was blowing round the playground: lit by the security lights we both gathered handfuls and shoved them into the bins.

'It's worse in cities where they use black refuse sacks,' I

11

observed. 'You should see the mess when people leave the bags on the pavement the night before a collection.'

'At least we have wheelie bins – almost impossible to blow them over,' he said confidently.

Usually, brisk though I am, I have to work hard to keep up with him. Now I was already a metre or so ahead. Was he dawdling because he was planning to ask me something? I risked a sideways glance, but out of the lights' range, the village's lack of street lights made it impossible to detect any subtle changes. In a sudden lull, the wind dropping almost to stillness, his breathing sounded laboured. Was there a problem? But there was a limit to the personal questions I could put to a man who was not only the chair of governors but also my landlord, and I certainly couldn't demand that he turn back so I could inspect him under our security lights. Then the wind, as if it had paused for a greater effort, let rip again. Waving the stiff drink goodbye, I turned towards the car after all. Brian sank on to the passenger seat with a deep sigh, forgetting his seat belt till I prompted him.

Perhaps I shouldn't try any conversation till we'd reached the pub.

He was already well down his first glass of wine and we were ready to order when he muttered, almost as if he was hoping I wouldn't hear, 'When you're walking against the wind like that and it's cold, do you ever feel as if – well, as if you've got something tight – like a belt – round your ribs? So you can't breathe?'

I put my hand over his glass. 'Leave that. I'm taking you to A & E right now.'

He shook his head dismissively. 'No, no. It's not an

emergency. I've had the feeling before. Several times. I was just wondering . . .' His hand went to his ribs.

Conversation in the car was a bit stilted, because I was pretty sure no one had ever ordered him about so much and because I was having to concentrate very hard on my driving. 'Are they making progress on your new house?' he asked, with an obvious effort.

'Yes. At last. The builders and architect have managed to persuade the powers-that-be that it's not interesting enough to be listed – which took far longer than any of us anticipated. So long as the police don't keep wanting one more look at the garden – just in case it's still a crime scene.'

'But they haven't found any more . . . remains?'

'No. Nor anything else of forensic interest. Nothing in the house, either. Yet,' I added dryly.

'And is that neighbour of yours any friendlier? The one who looks like a fashion plate? Hair cut like a Frenchwoman's?'

He was spot on. She always looked as if she'd stepped from the pages of a chic magazine for the older woman – *Saga*, *Vogue*, maybe. 'Joy Penkridge? Much friendlier. She really improves on acquaintance. She's stopped peering over her garden fence all the time to complain about the building mess. In fact, she invited me to Christmas drinkies and I've been to coffee a couple of times. We have a shared interest in her granddaughter, who started school in September. Charlotte Bingham. Nice bright kid.'

'I still think the location is too isolated for a woman on her own. It would have been better to find a property in the village' – he smiled almost apologetically – 'had there been any on the market, of course.'

Had people like him not snapped up every single one before the public even knew they were for sale in order to turn them into highly profitable holiday cottages or second homes. I couldn't bitch at him because he'd been prompt to offer me one of his properties – more accurately, another of his properties, a mishap having occurred to my last one. In fact, the whole row had had to be demolished and work was about to start on new ones. The present one was a four-bedroom family house in Little Orchard Close. This was a pleasant little enclave of forty or so dwellings, mostly houses though there were some bungalows, in a variety of sizes and shapes built in the 1980s a couple of hundred metres from the main part of the village. Apparently the hotel originally occupying the site had been gutted in a fire that everyone – except Brian – assured me was an insurance job. That was village life for you.

'Might I ask how that police officer friend of yours is? Will? Is there any change in his condition?'

Personally, I didn't think there would be, ever – until a merciful death claimed him. I said quietly, 'Thanks for asking. He's still deeply unconscious.' Persistent vegetative state. What a terrible way for a life to end. Or had it ended before I even tried to resuscitate him?

'All these months after the attack on him. Yet they say you still go and talk to him all the time.'

Did I detect a strange sort of jealousy? If he hadn't been so worried about his own health I would have challenged him. As it was I said quietly, with only the slightest emphasis on the noun, 'All his friends do. And we all read to him and play his favourite music. Jo – you know her: she's the part-time maths teacher – she and her husband are regulars. There are other people I only ever meet there. Some talk to him; some talk across him. Now things are so tough at work I can't go as often as I'd like, of course. Plus training the new women's cricket team takes time,' I added, not admitting that one of the reasons I didn't go so often was because I couldn't deal with all the unresolved emotion.

It was time to change the subject.

To my amazement, A & E was relatively empty – it was, as the receptionist observed, before the pub-closing rush. Waiting time now was about an hour; later it would grow, exponentially.

It was my time to accept Brian's instructions. I was to go home and leave him in these safe hands. He'd probably be subjected to a battery of tests, all of which would take time. 'Please, before conditions get any worse. I'm sure you have a mountain of work to get through.'

'I won't argue,' I said, adding with a smile it took him a moment to reciprocate, 'because it'll only add to your stress levels.'

And it would only add to mine if I called in on Will. Resolutely, I turned my back on the pair of them.

Weather like this always rattled the kids – kids everywhere I've taught – and I have to admit I found it hard to settle into the work I was supposed to finish before school next day. It might have been concern for Brian, or perhaps it was the drive home: there were twigs and full-size branches everywhere; I'd had to move two wheelie bins out of the main road (yes, Brian!) where they lay helplessly on their sides, like beached porpoises. In Little Orchard Close there was a smattering of smashed tiles, though my own – Brian's own – roof was intact, as far as I could see. So it was time to draw the curtains, turn up the heating, make a sandwich and get on with it. I might even treat myself to a glass of wine once I'd finished.

I'd hardly opened my laptop when my mobile rang. Drat.

'Jane? Joy here.'

Joy Penkridge? Oh dear, I really didn't have time for a nice girlie gossip. I looked at the pile on the desk. All that work to get through! All the same I tried to sound polite, enthusiastic, even. 'Hi, Joy. Everything OK?'

'Yes. No. Not really. Ken's away with his wretched model boats, and I didn't know who to ask.'

Feeling in my thumbs I was going to get involved, I tried to stop the question, but it came out anyway. 'What's the problem, Joy?'

'Tiles. I can see them on the drive. Quite a lot. Do you think you could ask your builders to fix them when they come tomorrow?'

Were roof repairs as simple as that? 'Of course. And if they can't they'll know someone who can. Don't worry.' I could relax after all.

'I'll do my best. When do you think you'll move in? It'll be such a relief to have a neighbour like you.' Which was not what she'd said at first, but I'd be the first to admit I couldn't blame her for her original hostility.

'Easter, all being well. What was that noise, Joy?'

'The fence, I think. What should I do?'

'Go and have a quick look.' Oh dear. I was implying

something, wasn't I? But no way could I go and sort it out for her myself. Not at this time of night.

She was back. 'Yes. It's all over the front garden. What should I do?' she repeated, this time quite desperately.

'The big larch-lap one the other side from me? That's far too heavy for us to lift, Joy. The builders will be able to shift it in the morning. Now do as I've done. Draw the curtains and turn up the volume on the TV. See you soon.'

'Do you think I should phone Ken?'

Yes! 'I think he'd want to know, don't you? Maybe he can cut short his trip and help organise the repairs.'

'What a good idea. Men are so good at that sort of thing, aren't they?'

'Absolutely,' I agreed through gritted teeth.

I was just getting ready for bed when the phone rang again. Calls late at night always make me panic. Had my ex-husband escaped? Had Brian been taken really ill? Had Will—I couldn't complete the sentence even in my thoughts.

But I simply wouldn't let my voice quiver.

It was Joy again. 'Jane, I'm so sorry. But I'm really worried about the tree next to the house. I'm so afraid. I think it's going to come down.' Her voice was rising in a crescendo of panic – and why not? 'On top of the house!'

What could I do? Go and prop the damn thing up? But she was right to worry. I would, in her situation. 'Listen, Joy: pack a bag quickly and come over here for the night. Just in case. I'll air the spare bed. No, don't argue.'

To my amazement she didn't.

I was even more surprised when she brought in her own towel, pillow and duvet. 'I don't want to put you to any trouble . . .' In fact, she didn't. We had a companionable glass of single malt and headed to bed. The wind seemed to ease. I slept like a log.

To my relief, Joy declined my invitation to stay for breakfast. I might have been working on the computer since before six, but that didn't mean I could afford half an hour to be sociable over toast. We left the house together, tutting at the debris all over the road, and thanking goodness that neither car had been damaged. Waving cheerfully, we set off in opposite directions.

I'd barely switched off the Wrayford School alarm when my phone rang.

Joy again.

'You'd better come over,' she said. 'Straight over.'

CHAPTER TWO

Her tree. Her responsibility. Joy said it over and over again.

Damage to my house.

Actually, not to very much of my house. Some of the roof had been swiped by the branches as the great tree descended, but the harm seemed to my untutored eyes to be fairly superficial. The media were gathering already, of course. And departing. It seemed they wanted footage of damaged homes to add to footage of other damaged property, which would be shown on the lunchtime news. One to miss, then. At least, as one of the reporters pointed out, I was lucky – there had been at least one death and several injuries as the wind had beaten up other innocent premises.

I had to agree to the interviewer's suggestion that I was more than lucky, especially as two of the builders working on the place hove into view. Paula and Caffy: PACT – Paula and Caffy's team – was their all-woman business. I knew they always made early starts but this seemed above and beyond the call of duty.

'He's right. You're not just lucky but very lucky indeed,' Paula said briskly, donning her hard hat. She wasn't officially the boss but always behaved like one. 'We can see what's what as soon as someone's dealt with the branches, but I'd say that though you won't be able to move in at Easter it should be possible early in the summer.' She seemed to have lost interest, and was pacing back the length of the tree to where it lay on the garden fence – which had fetched up several metres into my patch. Stepping carefully over the detritus she came to a halt by the great crown of roots, inspecting them arms akimbo.

'Why your neighbour didn't put the poor tree out of its misery years ago, goodness knows,' Caffy said.

'I've an idea it was protected,' I ventured.

'By someone who didn't know his acorn from his elbow. OK, I'll draw up some estimates so we can have a happy haggle with your neighbour's insurance company. And then we'll be off – we've got a church roof, two cottages and three garden rooms to assess,' she said.

'Sounds like part of a Christmas song, doesn't it?'

'I'll let you know if we come across any calling birds. Hello, what's Paula found?' Caffy donned her hard hat too, holding up an authoritative hand when I attempted to follow her. Almost at once she was back, darting into their van and returning with two more hard hats, one of which she threw to me by way of an invitation.

The other was for Joy, who was arguing with Paula – generally a futile exercise, as I knew to my cost.

'I can't possibly move out. Possibly. Whatever would Ken say?'

'That you should.'

'I have to say, Miss—'

'Paula. I have to say this, that this property is unsafe. You can't stay in it. I shouldn't even let you go in to collect a suitcase, but I can't stop you if you insist. Put this on first. Jane – look at that!'

I looked. There was a huge hole – the depth and circumference of the roots. Bigger. It started well under the foundations, which already had one big crack spreading up into the front wall of the house. It had reached a window, dodged round it, and was continuing upwards. As we watched, the frame moved, shattering the glass.

'Talk some sense into her, Jane. I'm getting some plant moved here in the hope we can underpin it and stop the whole place collapsing.' As she tapped her phone, she said, 'Caffy – will you try Herbert's? After Big Sid they're our best hope. Jane – make sure she stays the far side of the house. OK? You've got ten minutes absolute max. And put that hard hat on straight, Joy – this isn't the time for looking cute. Ah, Sid—' She made little shooing gestures at me.

I obeyed her instructions: 'There's no point in arguing, Joy. We do as she says and scarper. Thank goodness your bedroom's the other side.'

'But my cases – they're in the attic.'

'Then we'll bundle everything into sheets or towels. No marks for being neat and tidy. No time, more to the point.' We were upstairs by now. 'You grab what you need: jewellery and any other precious items first – your insurance will cover clothes and such, if necessary. Throw me some towels and sheets and I'll stow the stuff you pass me.' Did I hear creaking as the house settled? I told myself I was imagining it. But maybe I wasn't.

I'd never have expected Joy could act so quickly and deftly. Soon we had three good bundles which I dropped gently out of the window. Then some smaller ones.

'Address book? Insurance contact details?' I prompted.

'Ken has those in his den. At the back. Downstairs.'

We ran down. Definitely there was creaking. The den was the same side as the crack. 'Two minutes – what you can't find you leave,' I said, channelling Paula. 'I'll be outside, loading the cars.'

'What we do now is this,' I said firmly, taking her arm as if she was an old duck rather than a Mercedes-driving woman whose chic Brian had noted. 'We go back to my place and have a cup of tea and a biscuit. You phone Ken and tell him what's happened. Then he can come and look after you.' The words stuck in my craw.

She stared at me in apparent disbelief, shaking her head. 'He can't. Didn't you listen to the news? The Severn Bridges are both closed because of the wind. Even if he drove north to come south, there's been a pile-up on the M40. Two overturned lorries are blocking the M4. God knows what'll be happening on the M25. He's stuck, Jane. And not just him: the storm has wreaked absolute havoc. All over the country.'

I promise I didn't sigh. I didn't even think of consigning her to a hotel. 'It's a good job you'll be safe and sound at mine, then.' On the other hand, she was now shaking with either cold or, more probably, shock. 'You're sure you're OK to drive? OK. Let's go. Follow me.'

Joy looked around bleakly as I set the heating to override.

Putting on the kettle, I confessed, 'There's nothing much in the way of food.'

'No problem,' she said briskly, though I suspected a lot of effort was going into her can-do demeanour. 'I'll do a supermarket run.'

'That'd be wonderful. But—'

I'm sure she didn't catch me checking my watch, but she said quickly, 'Jane, you have a school to run. Two schools. You know what those posters say: *Keep calm and carry on.* That's what we both have to do. Oh, a key!' She pocketed the one I threw to her. 'Now, off you go.' She actually spun me round and gave me a gentle push.

I couldn't have argued anyway. Come hell or high water I needed to be in Wray Episcopi School to take assembly before a day of wall-to-wall meetings. Not to mention checking on both schools' fabric.

Then, after a full day's work plus some, I'd come home to find a visitor *in situ*. I was shuddering already. But not visibly, I hoped.

I checked the building, which looked in one piece; thank goodness I'd authorised expensive repairs last term. Now I could safely leave Tom, more head than deputy since the school seemed to run quite well without me, to take the Wrayford assembly. Because it was Open the Book day, he had nothing to do except look on appreciatively. Every week a team from the village church came along to enact a

Bible story. Homespun and amateur they might be but the kids – and, yes, the staff – loved their presentations. Sadly, there weren't yet enough of them to extend their activities to Wray Episcopi School, but they assured me they were working on the problem: it was one thing, they assured me with kind firmness, that I didn't have to worry about.

At last I bustled, with more haste than dignity, into the Wray Episcopi school hall, firing glances at any child with the temerity to fidget, saving a particularly hard stare for a girl looking ostentatiously at her watch. Then I recalled it was her birthday the day before.

'Was that a present, Cecily? Can we all see?'

Clearly it wasn't. Cecily subsided.

In front of a somewhat diminished gathering – no doubt some of the lanes the kids would use to get to school were blocked by trees and other debris – Medway class were doing a presentation about courage. Since they'd soon be going out into the big wide world of secondary education, I thought they'd need some. They talked about the pictures they'd drawn; Hettie read a poem; Jason talked about how he felt every time he faced an opponent when he was a goalie. We bowed our heads and closed our eyes while Hannah read a prayer she'd written about children being forced from their homes. My amen was especially fervent. I was so proud of them all. If only I could spend time in the classroom with them – but I was already late for the first meeting of the day, which Hannah might have cued in: planning for the integration of refugee children in mainstream schools. With luck, debris on the local roads would have thrown up enough problems to make my colleagues late too.

I was just starting my car when a text came through. The

roads were so bad the meeting had had to be postponed. Good news, bad news: I didn't think we needed a meeting to agree that we all wanted to help, that we all wanted to welcome kids who'd seen more suffering in their short lives than anyone deserved – but we needed the finances to support language specialists, classroom assistants and counsellors. But my frown soon evaporated. Young Zunaid, an unaccompanied refugee child who'd simply turned up in school one day five months ago, came swiftly up to me as I strode back to my office: 'How can I help, Ms Cowan? You look so sad.'

That's what teaching is all about. That and hiding your face when your tears are battling it out with your smile. And being amazed that despite all the trauma that had afflicted him he was already leading his class in maths and speaking English fluently with a hint of a Kent accent. Currently he was living with trained foster parents, but we all hoped he'd soon be able to move in with Pam, one of our dinner ladies, who loved him almost as much as he adored her.

'You know what, Zunaid, you've made me feel better – just by asking.'

What had I said? His eyes narrowed, as if he was looking into the distance; he said wonderingly, 'My dad used to say that. Back home. Not home here. Home there.' He gestured at some invisible horizon. '"All I can do to make them better is ask how they are," he said.' Then he focused on me again, and I knew he was going to ask the question we'd all dreaded. 'Do you think I will see my dad again before we meet in Paradise?'

'What do you think?' It seemed a supine response, but was one we'd been advised to give.

25

'I think you would tell me the truth.'

I folded myself down to his level, so I could look him in the eye. 'I know that your dad is looking for you. People here in England are looking for your dad. We are all doing everything we can to get you back together. I promise.' Should I leave the rest to the experts who from time to time would question him delicately about his past? I didn't want to ask anything that might upset him.

'When they blew my mum up, Dad said we'd meet her again in Paradise,' he said matter-of-factly.

'Dads never lie about things like that,' I said as if I believed it absolutely.

'That's what he said.' He smiled and suddenly reached up and kissed my cheek. 'You're like my auntie,' he added radiantly.

An auntie: this was the first time he'd mentioned any relatives. I risked a gentle question. 'How am I like your auntie?'

'You frown like her. And you can be fierce and frightening, like that dragon we read about.' He snarled and made claws.

Me, an old dragon! That was encouraging. But we were laughing together.

'And you both smile with much love.'

'Is your auntie a teacher?'

He shook his head. 'She works in a hospital, which makes her very tired. She is a doctor and tries to make people better. Like my dad.' He stared into my eyes with sudden urgency. 'Ms Jane, what if my auntie is in Paradise too?'

I had to sidestep that. 'Can you remember her name?'

'Auntie Noor. She has another name, but I can't remember it.'

'The moment you do, come straight to me, and we'll start looking for her as hard as we're looking for your dad.' I cupped his face gently: it would have been lovely to give him a proper hug, but I'd been told to leave that to Pam. 'Off you go.'

He started with a carefree skip, but suddenly recalled the school walk-don't-run rule and switched to a proud march instead.

Ms Jane. I liked that name.

Yes, we needed that postponed meeting. We must make things happen, whatever difficulties we had to overcome.

Meanwhile I had an urgent if less fundamental problem. All our gutters had slipped their moorings and were littering the furthest reaches of the playground. There were a couple of cracked tiles. I left a few messages on what were probably overfull answering machines and moved the debris into a tidy heap, which I weighed down with some sacks of compost I'd set aside for the kids' new garden: I dared not risk any rubbish coming loose and hurting a child – or a colleague, for that matter. Oh, for the dear dead days of on-site caretakers . . .

It was lunchtime before I could text Brian. He might prefer to hear real speech but he wasn't going to get that luxury when I was scrounging a few leftovers from the school canteen. Zunaid's best friend Pam was on duty. She knew my tendency to forget breakfast and lack of time to prepare a packed lunch. She also knew that I regarded salad with an enthusiasm still lacking in too many of the kids.

'Numbers are a bit down,' she said cheerfully, adding a little pasta to a plate of mixed greenery. 'So there's even a slice or two of garlic bread.'

'Yes, please. I promise I'll clean my teeth before the next meeting!'

She grinned. 'Shall I get Zunaid to bring some fruit salad along in a few minutes?'

Who could resist? Bad manners though technically it might be, I could text and eat simultaneously. And think about the after-school meeting about one or two problems amongst Stour class's older pupils.

Brian didn't respond immediately, which gave me a niggle of worry, since he was usually very prompt. But I told myself he was probably having a nice business lunch, and I applied myself to the fruit salad – with crème fraiche, no less – that Zunaid placed carefully on my desk.

I checked my phone between meetings, but there was still no reply. At last, as I waved the last child off home, I tried a phone call. Straight to voicemail.

Now I was concerned. No, I wasn't. That's the word everyone uses as a euphemism for worried. I was worried. Very worried indeed.

CHAPTER THREE

Was my relationship with Brian one that meant I could simply pop round to his house and ask how he'd fared at the hospital? On the whole, I thought not. For all sorts of reasons, mostly involving my violent ex, Simon, currently safely in Durham jail for his savage assaults on our dog and indeed on me, I found it very hard to trust alpha males on a personal level. It was one thing to exercise authority over them when I umpired village cricket matches, quite another to put myself in a personal situation with them. I might eat with Brian occasionally in public at the Jolly Cricketers, but knocking on his door with nothing except a possibly intimate enquiry was—no, I couldn't do it. I reasoned (spuriously, as I knew quite well) that staying at my house I had a guest to whom I ought to return: she'd had a terrible shock and might not be as resilient as I'd been in tough situations. Though she was incredibly chic and used the gym, she was older than Brian, and might have health problems I knew nothing about. I often stayed at school till eight or nine, especially on Tuesdays like this one when I nipped back to Wrayford to teach the after-school ball-skills club. Tonight, I must make an effort to get back at an hour Joy would no doubt call civilised.

But I had to pass Brian's house on the way home. I ought to call in. Perhaps all I needed was an excuse, such as some paperwork he needed to see. But in a country battered by Storm Emlyn, as the gales were now officially called, very few people had troubled themselves with high-level policy meetings generating controversial outcomes. No crazy government edicts either – apparently all the ministers who might have made our job even more tricky were either commiserating with their constituents' housing damage or plotting knavery so foul that they didn't dare risk a public announcement for fear of middle-class revolution.

Tom hadn't flagged up any problems for me to worry about. So I was left with my conscience. Even as I turned the car for home I was still undecided. What if Brian took my concern as a sign that I was developing a personal interest in him? Once or twice he'd hinted that he found me attractive. I didn't reciprocate, not one smidgen, especially as I had first-hand experience of his capacity to bully, and didn't want to do anything that might be construed, in the sort of words Joy might use, as leading him on.

His car wasn't in the drive. Apart from the light he always left on when he was out – a good clue to a would-be burglar, that! – his house was in darkness.

All the same . . .

My mobile told me the signal was good out here. I tried calling him again. I didn't bother with voicemail. Home to Joy, then.

I'd always quietly sneered when women described themselves as homemakers, but seeing my place when Joy had spent a few hours in it made me understand that the role might have some value after all. It took me a while to work out what she'd done – subtle changes like moving around the table lamps in the living room. There was also a delicate, subtle perfume from thick candles. Dropping my bags in the small room I used as my study, I headed for the kitchen. There I was greeted by more smells, wholesome and quite strong: two casseroles occupied the oven, the controls of which I'd never quite mastered, and a fresh loaf sat on a rack. Yes, it was still warm. There was also a pile of biscuits.

The author of all these miracles? The sound of her careful footsteps on the stairs reminded me that for all her energy she wasn't young, despite the jeans and cashmere top that showed her gym-using figure was as good as any fifty-year-old's.

I put back the biscuit guiltily.

'Now, a nice gin and tonic,' she declared, opening a fridge that bulged with unaccustomed goodies. 'And if you tell me what time you like to eat I'll see to it that supper is ready. It looks as if you've had a bit of a day.'

'Not as dramatic as yours, though, Joy.'

She smiled and shrugged. 'Your building friends are angels, aren't they, though it's such a strange occupation for women. Paula and Caffy? So very different from each other. Like, like . . .'

'Like ice cream and hot chocolate sauce?'

'Exactly! Or Baked Alaska! Between ourselves, I've never dared cook that. Have you?'

Me? I shook my head. 'But what have Paula and Caffy been up to?' A great deal, most of it with kindness, judging from my own experience.

'They just took over. I dropped in at one point to see what was going on, so I could report back to Ken. I told him to stay where he was until the roads were better, but he'll set out first thing tomorrow. If you're sure about my staying here tonight, of course. Ken'll sort out a place for us both – and all our furniture, of course – when he gets home. Assuming Paula and her team have managed to stabilise it sufficiently. Oh, Jane – my pictures! All the photo albums.' She tried hard not to let her voice crack, but the sip of gin became a veritable gulp.

I gave her a silent hug.

I'd had to learn to travel light. I'd never managed to keep all the domestic impedimenta that had graced Joy's home. Furniture? Simon had smashed a lot. Photos? He'd stood over me and made me shred them. Now my life involved a very few books, some clothes and two teddy bears, Nosey, the larger, a very conventional teddy who reminded of one that Simon had torn apart, and a small floppy one left to look after me when I'd been ill last summer – Lavender, so-called because he was. One day, maybe, I'd fill my new home with treasures. Maybe. I didn't want hostages to fortune. But Joy didn't need to hear any of that, lest it imply a criticism. I'd better be careful when it came to asking any questions, too, because it was clear she was finding it hard to focus on anything specific – perhaps it was too painful.

Yes, I'd been there.

'Have you been in touch with your insurance company?' I asked, ashamed to sound so prosaic.

'Ken always does that sort of thing,' she said. 'I don't even know who we're insured with.'

'Why don't you call him and ask while I have a quick shower? Or make sure he's on to it,' I added, as I headed off upstairs. It was only as I towelled myself off I realised what a bad host I was being. I was dressed and downstairs within three minutes.

She was staring despondently at her phone, but straightened and stowed it in her bag as soon as I appeared. 'He says he'll do it after dinner. But isn't it urgent? I should have done it!'

I'd better avert her tears. 'I forgot to show you how to use the washing machine,' I declared contritely. It had taken me weeks to master.

'Oh, I hope you don't mind my using it,' she added anxiously.

This was the strong, assertive woman who'd once tackled me head on when the state of my garden had annoyed her. But disorientation and grief could do that.

'Actually, I'd quite like a lesson. And on the oven, too. I'm a bit of a technophobe,' I said, with some, if not complete, truth. After all, I could reheat or microwave precooked meals with the best of them. I'd soon learnt which washing programme creased clothes the least, and managed to set the tumble dryer quite competently, so long as I read the little pictures on the dial. But it gave her something to bustle about doing, and I was as happy to learn as when one of my year four pupils showed me how to master a new app. The downside was that it made me feel even more like a guest in my own temporary home.

'There you are – I told you it was simple, didn't I?' she said triumphantly, as without prompting I found the setting best for cooking flans without soggy bottoms. Which I might do, one year. One decade.

'You did. Thank you. Now – you've sorted the cooker and pointed out that the microwave is far cleverer than I'd imagined. Maybe you can fill me in on all the other things I don't know. My neighbours, for instance. I might wave at one or two of them, but unless they're parents or are involved with the church or the cricket club, I certainly don't know them properly.'

'Funny you should say that,' she said, leaning against a work surface, 'because something odd happened. Twice. So maybe that means it's not odd. But I checked – the house numbering's really easy to follow and once you've worked out that there are a few little cul-de-sacs off the main run, then it's all straightforward. Like the edge of an oak leaf. Isn't it nice, the way no house actually directly overlooks another? And that nice green space in the middle for children to play on? I went to a barbecue there once. You know they planned to build eighty properties but one of the local councillors wanted to live there himself and insisted they could only build forty-five? Anyway, when I was leaving the house I saw a white van going really slowly as if the driver was looking for somewhere. Then he saw me – no, maybe I'm imagining it . . . It just seemed as if he didn't want anyone to see him. He accelerated away. Quite fast, actually.'

It took me every ounce of willpower not to show my terror.

However, much I knew he was locked away in a far-distant part of the country, I was still afraid my ex-husband would find me and deal with me, as he would probably put it. As casually as I could, I asked, 'And did you see anything of him?'

'Young. Twenties or thirties. Very dark hair. Bit of a beard. Olive skin – a bit pockmarked as if he'd had bad acne as a boy. Put a cutlass between his teeth and he'd look like a pantomime pirate!' It was good to share a laugh. But her face straightened. 'The strange thing is, later on I was having a bit of a gossip with Marie – do you know her? Number 26? – and Tess from number 27. Ken's Lodge's Ladies' Nights,' she added. 'And we saw another similar van, also driving slowly round. Definitely not the same driver – this one was older. It was as if he was looking for something too. Somewhere, I should say. Tess actually started to walk across to ask if she could help, but he went and drove off in a great rush. Tess said she thought he was casing the neighbourhood – seeing who was in and who was out and who left windows or gates open. She wrote down his number, actually, in case there were any burglaries in the next couple of days and she had evidence that might help.' She registered my expression. 'What?'

'I'm just wondering if it might have been worth her calling 101 with the information. In case the number's on file.'

'I'll phone her now!' She bustled off.

There was only one hope in my selfish head – that these might be nice common criminals only interested in nicking garden furniture: there'd been an outbreak of that in the autumn, supplemented by a raid on planters, some complete with winter pansies. Even taking garden benches only constituted low-level crime, my friend PC Lloyd

Davies insisted. No violence, no injury, nothing the police had time to tackle. Just call your insurance and wait for the hollow laughter.

A Neighbourhood Watch group had sprung up. No, I wasn't involved, because it always met on staff meeting night. I stared down at my empty glass as Joy returned: I'd drained it without even noticing. Damn! It wasn't often I got a G & T as good as this, and I daren't have another, not with all I had to do.

And it seemed that Joy was expecting us to drink wine with our meal.

How did she stay so svelte?

Huge portions of baked potatoes and boeuf bourgignon. Cuisine neither nouvelle nor *minceur*. Classic. Filling. Heart-warming. Amazing with the Cahors black wine she served at just the right temperature.

It dawned on me: I needed a wife.

And now cheese. Her choice was Chaource just the right side of liquefying. A fresh baguette. Another glass of wine. Sod the preparation for tomorrow's meeting. I'd have to wing it.

So why was Joy putting her coat on?

'Just a little evening ritual, Jane. When Ken and I had Toby we always had to take him out last thing in the evening, of course.'

Ah. They'd had a dog, as I once had – much loved, till Simon had killed him before my eyes. Ironically, it was the decision of the RSPCA to prosecute him for animal cruelty that alerted the police to his violence towards me, and probably saved my life.

'And then, when he wasn't there any more and we decided not to have another dog because we wanted to go

36

on more holidays further afield, we still kept up the walk. Ken's big on astronomy, of course. What he'll say when he hears I left his telescope behind goodness knows.'

'If he has any sense he'll thank God you got out safely and let the insurance worry about the rest. In any case, I should imagine Paula and Caffy have got the site secured very efficiently, and everything will be safe and sound till it can be rescued. Give me a minute and I'll come with you.'

We walked briskly, using torches. Most of the drives were occupied by cars, large and shiny under the intruder lights that clicked on as we passed. Some people had left their curtains open, living their lives for all to see.

Joy said, 'Letting all that heat out!'

'And showing passing strangers you've got a nice new shiny TV.'

She paused. 'I noticed you gave the curtains an extra twitch when you came in – but while it's a nice enough holiday let, and I know this makes me sound really ungrateful and I promise you I'm not, I'm just talking about your landlord, really, the furniture and equipment aren't really state of the art, are they? The place needs a refurb, if you ask me.'

Which probably explained why I got it at a discount, of course. 'To be honest with you, Joy, it's not Brian's knick-knacks that I'm worried about. It's more my violent ex.'

'Ah, of course. Someone in the village the other day was saying we must never tell any strangers where you live,' she said, patting my arm.

So, I was the subject of village gossip, was I? But perhaps instead of being enraged, I should accept that it was nice that people were looking out for me.

37

One of the houses seemed to have blackout curtains in its front bedroom, but someone hadn't drawn them very well: extraordinarily bright light spilt out. It didn't flicker as if it was coming from a TV or even an overvivid computer game. Despite myself I stared at it, dawdling to a standstill. What on earth needed that intensity?

Joy grabbed my elbow. 'Look, there's another of those white vans now. Just parking by that house.'

'But not staying very long!' Lights out, it pulled away sharply and headed away from us.

'Someone doesn't know it's a cul-de-sac,' Joy said with satisfaction, producing her mobile. 'You stay this side with your phone and I'll cross and snap him from there. Oh, it's just like something from an Angela Brazil book, isn't it?'

'Get out of sight!' I yelled, retreating behind a convenient Leylandii before I took a photo.

'That was all very cloak-and-dagger,' she said, as she dusted off her puffer jacket and rearranged her rather fetching fur hat.

'Someone who doesn't want to be seen doesn't want to be immortalised on camera,' I said. 'Just in case he comes for a second look, I don't want to go straight back down the road. There's that right of way to the main road down there, and one of the neighbours' security lights makes it nice and safe for pedestrians. This way. After that wonderful meal we need to add a few more yards and work off at least one more calorie,' I added, trying to sound less earnest.

'It would have been nice to check the number of the house that man was parking by, all the same. I can just nip back—'

'Or not. We can do it far less obviously. They're all in numerical order. This one's 29. One . . . two . . . three . . . four

– there we are: 33.' I laughed. 'If I accidentally poke a wasps' nest, Joy, I don't go back until I'm sure they've forgotten all about me. Kent might be a nice respectable place, but remember it's also close to London and the Continent: all sorts of undesirables rock up here and live lives of seeming respectability. People looking like bank managers get shot outside their des reses because they've been involved with criminal gangs.' And only after that improving spiel did I recall she'd lived in the area far longer than I had.

'You're right! I've seen footage on TV.' She didn't sound deterred.

'Did you notice the lighting in the bedroom, by the way? It must be costing in a night what the average householder would blench at if it was for a whole week.'

'Ken certainly would. He's forever switching lights off. Oh, Jane, d'you think we've seen a bit of gang warfare? How exciting! Actually, I remember Ken and me eating in a Chinese restaurant in Ashford and all the time a triad was holding a man prisoner in the cellar below. And once I was doing a big shop at Sainsbury's, and someone was shot in the car park. Not far from where Ken was parked waiting for me! Nowadays, we always assume it's one of those illegal immigrants.' She did not sound sympathetic.

'Quite – but don't forget someone in Libya or wherever is making a packet getting them out.' If not by drowning them. 'And, of course, there are gangs in this country completing what they started.' Then I buttoned my lip, lest I talked too vehemently about the people who ended Will's life without having the decency to kill him outright.

We walked in the prickly sort of silence that tells you you've jumped in too hard. But I couldn't end it.

She did. She touched my arm. 'I'm sorry, Jane. I'd forgotten all you went through. Didn't they say—' The touch became a grab. 'Oh, my God!'

A white van had pulled up right at the end of the right of way.

'About turn!' I said. 'Walk fast. No, don't run – it might attract attention, plus we can't risk tripping. Don't worry: we'll be home before he manages to turn round.'

We were. With the curtains tightly drawn, and the front door double-locked. Yes, the back door too. We were safe and sound. And to my huge relief the intruder light didn't come on for the next half-hour at least, when a glimpse through the peephole showed a fox strutting across the drive.

'Did your friend let the police know about the van incident?' I asked at last.

'No. She was on her way to the Marlowe Theatre,' she added, as if that explained something.

'Could you text her and ask her to let you have the number as soon as she can? I've got a police officer friend who may be able to help – though he's up to his ears in flu at the moment. I'll send him the photos I took tonight – the number's quite clear.' I showed her, forwarding them as I did so to Lloyd Davies. 'Now, I know it's rude of me, Joy, but I've got to do a bit of work before I head for bed – and I'm afraid I shall leave for work before you're up and about. I'm really sorry. But if your friend doesn't contact you, I'd be really grateful if you'd try her again tomorrow and if you'd text me the details. Just in case . . .'

40

'Just in case it's something to do with your ex,' she finished for me, inaccurately, as it happened, but I let it pass.

Pitch-dark. The deepest of sleeps. And a woman's scream. I was up and out of bed before I realised it, almost falling downstairs as I hurtled onto the landing.

Joy emerged too, ruffled but to my amazement laughing at me. 'I can tell you're not a country girl,' she said.

I stared. 'A woman was screaming!'

'Put your phone away, dear. It was a fox. Or a vixen. Unearthly noise, isn't it? Ghastly. But nothing to worry about. Probably calling for that fox we saw on your drive earlier. Come on, you need a hot chocolate . . .'

CHAPTER FOUR

Flu or not, Lloyd Davies responded first thing the next morning, just as I sat down at my Wrayford School desk: *Keep head down, eyes and ears open, mouth shut. Avoid this bug. Sneeze!!!*

So you do know something, I replied.

Enough to know info useful. See previous advice. Sneeze, sneeze. All of it. Cough, cough. Sad face.

Keep bug away from Jo. PLEASE. She can't teach maths from her sickbed!!! Smiley face.

'You've only got an invitation from His Nibs!' Melanie Pugh declared, tapping the door as she entered and waving a piece of paper under my nose. 'Actually, more of a summons, to be frank.'

It was always Melanie's self-imposed rule never to betray any knowledge of the content of any message she'd just taken. If I chose to comment on – say – a particularly feeble excuse for a child's absence, she'd join in the conversation, but she'd never initiate it. 'Should I stand to attention while you read it to me?' I asked.

'At least you should sit up straight. If you slump like that your back's going to kill you before you're much older. Pilates, that's what you need. If only you could create an extra hour in the day. Which reminds me, Mrs Taylor wants to talk to you about the twins. Now. Only I told her you were in a meeting, since you'd only just got here and hadn't really sat down. So now she wants an appointment at nine tomorrow. I told her you'd be taking assembly.'

'Will I? Oh. Of course, Tom's taking year five to that wildlife centre. And actually, it's Tom who should be seeing her, not me. Would he be clear when he comes in?' Today he'd be late as it was his turn to take his own kids to school.

'I suggested that. She said something about organ-grinders and monkeys I don't care to repeat.' Rolling her eyes, she turned to the door, pausing, however, before she left. 'I'll go and fend her off. And a Mrs Penkridge called – her friend is going to contact the police about the vans. Mr P should be with her by mid-afternoon, so if she's not there when you get home, please don't worry about her – they'll be checking into a hotel and hunting for a temporary home.'

Phew.

I settled down to open my emails and check the weather forecast as I always did in winter. The wind, which had dropped to a manageable twenty miles an hour, was going to veer from the north back to the west, bringing more storm force winds. Lovely. Or not.

* * *

43

Seeing Zunaid always brightened my time at Wray Episcopi, even when he was full of cold and all I was doing was finding a packet of tissues for him. His best friend, Georgy Popescu, had gone back to his home in Romania for the down season: his parents were seasonal workers at a nearby farm. The children exchanged carefully written letters, a joy to behold: Zunaid showed me his before he sent them off, in case he'd made any mistakes, and carefully pinned Georgy's replies to the school noticeboard. Neither child imparted very much of their daily doings but, in Georgy's case especially, showed a detailed knowledge of English Premier League teams. Zunaid was inclined to give news about the school, to which we all hoped Georgy would return in the summer.

This morning he had something to tell me: he was so full of excitement that he almost ran to me as I went through the front door. 'Georgy's come back, Ms Cowan! Already!'

'Why do you think that, Zunaid?' I asked carefully, not wanting to dash his hopes too quickly – but no one would expect fruit pickers at this time of year.

'I heard his mother's voice, Ms Cowan. When we walked through the village. Talking in Romanian. Just like Georgy's mum.'

'Slow down, Zunaid. Who was walking through which village?'

'Pam and me. Pam and I. Last night, they let me go home to hers for tea, then we walked for the bus.' That would be in Wray Episcopi, then. 'I heard Georgy's mum shouting then.' He frowned. 'But she sounded very cross. I hope she wasn't cross with Georgy.'

'I hope not too. Lesson bell, Zunaid!' Normally I'd have

exchanged a few more words, but I suspected he'd made a mistake. I'd check with Pam next time I saw her. I prayed that he was right: it would be good if life came up with bonuses, not bombs, for him.

Meanwhile there was a small but loud gaggle of girls dawdling in the loo, talking in mock-Yorkshire accents – mimicking Jess Rhodes, the new deputy head, no doubt. Jess was a breezy woman, with an amazing gift for conjuring art from kids who could barely draw a straight line, so used were they to creating pictures on their computers. Using the radar ear every head develops, I gathered Jess was kind to slow readers but stern if she thought kids were slacking. She'd been scathing of kids who pretended not to understand her flat vowels – though I noticed she'd moderated them slightly since she'd arrived.

Hearing these girls, I thought I'd offer Jess a bit of subliminal support, and peered into the loo, touching my watch and jerking my head slightly in the direction of the classrooms. They linked arms, giggling, as they headed towards me, for all the world as if they were Disney princesses. But they had another thing coming if they expected me to give way to them. It didn't take them long to unlink their arms, as I eye-contacted each in turn. Lulabelle Petrie who might have successfully sued her parents, I think, for blighting her life with such a name, needed a longer, harder stare, worthy of Paddington Bear, come to think of it, before she too dropped her eyes and mumbled something that might have been an apology. I cupped my ear. Perhaps she was too busy tossing her pretty curls to notice. Was that eye make-up she was wearing? It had better not be.

'Now sound as if you mean it,' I said. 'We've talked about

good manners often enough in assembly – about giving up your seat on a bus or train when an adult is standing; about holding doors open for other people; about giving way on pavements if you're in someone's way. And about sounding clear and sincere when you say sorry. I don't want to have to remind you again.'

If Cecily and Kayleigh had thought of sniggering they soon changed their minds, and gave good clear apologies. They were satisfactorily subdued as they walked away.

Job done.

'Hormones,' Donna, this school's secretary sighed when I joined her in the office. Like Melanie in Wrayford, she was the eyes and ears of the school, with probably a little mind-reading thrown in. 'They start their periods earlier each intake, don't they? I've already had to top up my collection of sanitary pads. I reckon we need those blue disposal bins for the girls' loo, to be honest – like in the staff loos. Or we'll be having all the older girls demanding to use our loos next.'

I nodded. 'Good idea. Would you have time to contact the service?'

'On to it now.' The phone was already in her hand.

Donna and Melanie were chalk and cheese, but they were both so efficient, working way beyond their brief, that I would have loved to find a way to upgrade them on their pay scales. Something to discuss with Brian, perhaps, this evening. Before that, however, I made sure I chanced to run into Lulabelle, absolutely casually, when she was behaving perfectly well, pinning, with mathematical precision, information about the nominees for class reps on the school council.

'I hope you're standing for election,' I said, truthfully. It would be good to channel some of her energy into constructive action.

I didn't really expect her to blush but was astonished when she went pale.

'No?'

'Oh, no, Ms Cowan. No, I'd never get in.'

'You certainly won't if you don't try,' I said softly.

Biting her lip, she shook her head. 'I – I can't explain.'

Now I really was worried. Somehow I needed to get at Lulabelle's backstory, didn't I? But not now, not as the bell rang for change of lesson. I didn't want to talk in front of others and I certainly didn't want to give the impression I was hauling her into my office for a talking to.

'Just think about it, Lulabelle. You'd make a very good rep. And if you want to talk about it – or anything else – you know where I am.'

I soon had something else to discuss. I picked up an anguished text from Joy soon after lunch, begging me to call her when I had a moment. I didn't have a moment, not even for that. Not till I'd stood in for Karenza Yeo, the reception teacher, who'd got pulsating toothache and who had a chance of a last-minute cancellation.

'Go on,' I urged her. 'You never know when you'll get an appointment otherwise. And – you know what? – I shall enjoy a spell in the classroom. Kids are more fun than meetings any day.'

Joy's news, when I had a chance to call her, was that Ken had been delayed. While he was stuck in Wales he'd stayed with a fellow Mason who'd invited him to some event this evening. He didn't think Joy would mind staying with me another night. 'It's not me I'm worried about, it's you,' Joy declared bitterly. 'He spoke as if it was just a matter of booking a night in a hotel – which I will do, I promise, if you'd rather. I'm so sorry.'

'I shall be glad of the company,' I assured her, thinking perhaps more of her cooking skills than her conversation and then realising what a marvellous excuse it would be to restrict my visit to Brian to a manageable length. 'I've got to go and see Brian Dawes, but I should be home by seven-thirty.'

'Oh, he's back from hospital, then?'

'I didn't know that he was still in hospital.'

'A heart attack. Major. That's what they're saying in the village, anyway,' she said doubtfully, in the tone of a woman used to conceding she was probably in the wrong. I knew it all too well.

'Well, I shall get it straight from the horse's mouth,' I said, dropping my voice as if I was entering a benign conspiracy with her. I couldn't, of course: if I was seeing Brian as chair of the governors, it would be grossly unprofessional to reveal anything of our encounter, and if I was there as a sort of friend, it would simply be a betrayal of trust. I just wished the thoughts didn't form themselves in my head in such headmistressy terms. I might have been preparing the homily for the next assembly.

Lighten up, Ms Jane.

For someone the villagers had at death's door, Brian was looking reassuringly fit and relaxed when he opened the front door to me. Dapper, too – a light-blue cashmere sweater and smart jeans. He took my jacket with aplomb, laughing as I tried to flatten my windswept hair and pointing to the cloakroom, which had a mirror.

When I emerged, I followed the sound of Classic FM music into the sitting room, where we'd had one or two governors' subcommittee meetings. Like my temporary home, it made no claim to be anything other than a place where people happened to live – the decor was as neutral and unobtrusive as a big hotel's. The paintings, in heavy gilt frames, were impenetrably dark: you couldn't tell what they depicted. Did they need a clean? Or did they just need to be properly lit? Having seen Joy's improvements, I realised that overall the lighting was a bit stark, glittering back off the oil but picking out the dust in the gilt frames.

Perhaps I'd been staring at them too long, because from behind me came an impatient cough. Brian was offering me sherry – 'Or would you prefer a G & T?' he asked, picking up on my hesitation.

'If it's no trouble, I would, please. My temporary house guest has reintroduced me to them. But very much more T than G, please – I'm driving.'

'Of course.' But he was frowning. 'This house guest – how long is she planning to stay?'

Mentioning her presence to him had been on my agenda for the visit, of course – a matter of courteously letting my landlord know. But this was a sharp question. A year's experience had taught me that Brian never asked questions idly – they usually had a hidden agenda. But why on earth could he be worrying about Joy's presence? Was there a subclause hidden deep in my tenancy contract that banned long-stay guests? My gut tightened in a knot of suspicion. Perhaps an airy smile would loosen it, as I waved a hand to stay the flow of gin. 'Only until her husband gets back from a Masonic jolly. She'll be off as soon as he arrives. Meanwhile, she's coddling me as if I was her daughter.'

He laughed. 'And there was I worrying she was imposing on you, when you've got more than enough to worry about. Cheers.'

'Your very good health,' I responded – it was a conventional enough toast, and pretty apposite, in the circumstances.

'And yours.' There was a long pause. We sat, me in an armchair, him on the sofa. At last he said, 'I was very grateful for the way you dealt with my . . . issue the other night. And no doubt kept it entirely confidential.' He spoke airily enough but clearly wanted reassurance.

'No one heard anything about it from me, I promise. But you should know that the word is in the village that you've been hospitalised with a major cardiac problem.' I hoped he'd find it amusing.

Perhaps he did. His frown was rueful. 'I do have a heart problem, but it's not that serious yet. But without intervention I could have had a stroke or any other problem associated with hypertension. Thanks to your – I can only call it bullying, Jane! – it's been diagnosed before too much damage has been done. I've had a lot of tests, though, and I've got to go back to discuss the next move. So thank you very much for your amazing response to what I thought was a simple question.'

I narrowed my eyes. 'Simple my foot. Come on,' I laughed, when he didn't. 'You knew you had a problem, Brian, and just wanted me to reassure you that you weren't making a fuss about nothing. So I did. That's what friends are for,' I added, prompted by the gin.

'And friends are for something else too,' he responded, with an ambiguous smile. 'No one knows better than you and I the state of the school's finances, and how they simply won't be able to match the demands put upon them. Thank goodness you got the capital expenditure on the buildings out of the way, while we had the chance. You and the cricket club, of course.'

'Symbiosis,' I said. 'They needed the showers and adult loos, and though the school could have managed without, life's much better with them.' I sighed. 'But the improvements here have left Wray Episcopi very much the Cinderella school.'

His short silence said as clearly as if he'd shouted it aloud that that was Wray Episcopi's problem. 'Well, we all need to tighten our belts – or get financial support above and beyond what we can imagine raising ourselves. Agreed?'

'Agreed. That's why we're having the meeting next week, isn't it, to come up with fundraising ideas? But you've already come up with a big idea, haven't you?' I smiled, but narrowed my eyes a little.

His shrug might have aimed at self-deprecating, but with shoulders that size and a neck that thick it would have been hard to achieve anything near. 'I may have done, as it happens. But I wanted to share it with you before I so much as float it in a full meeting. It wouldn't do to have a public falling-out, not at a time we should all be pulling together.'

'Of course not. But you're presupposing we shall fall out? Brian, you're not suggesting we turn the school into a nightclub? Actually,' I said, 'after our wonderful relationship with the cricket club, we could look at other groups wishing to use our facilities – the hall, for instance – couldn't we?

Zumba? Pilates? That sort of thing? It'd benefit the villagers too. Sorry. I interrupted.'

'But with good ideas.' He jotted on a pad he reached from a handy side table. 'Not at all controversial. As I implied, however, mine may be. Sponsorship, Jane – sponsorship. From a big name.'

I waited.

So, drat him, did he. He wanted me to question him, didn't he? To sound defensive?

The silence lengthened. The grandfather clock, a touch out of place in the undistinguished surroundings, chimed the half-hour.

Caving in, I said, pointing at the timepiece to show it was a joke, 'The clock's more than ticking, Brian: it's getting agitated.'

He tried not to look gratified at his silly victory. 'I was approached by a contact in a business meeting the other day – we had further talks yesterday, when I was supposed to be *hors de combat*. Which is why I wasn't upset by the rumours that I was ill. All very hush-hush. Even I don't know the name of the sponsors, Jane. But they want to come in with a lot of cash. And not just this school – Wray Episcopi too.'

Both? Why both? I feared the Greeks even when – especially when! – they came bearing gifts. 'Enough to enable them to change our policies? Our identities? To turn us, in effect, into academies?'

'Good God, I hope not. No, I've not been a governor all these years to want to hand the school over to other people. The idea is that they fund certain specific areas – the library, for instance, or maths and science. Or non-core subjects, like art and music.'

'And this would be out of the goodness of their hearts or would they want lots of favourable publicity?'

'You wouldn't expect something for nothing.' He sounded genuinely affronted.

'You do, Brian. You give hours of time to the school, but you get nothing back but a nice glow of satisfaction at having served your community,' I countered. 'You're a genuine philanthropist, like governors and volunteers everywhere. And I know – which no one else does, of course – how much more you give, mysteriously finding a little cache of money here and there when it's needed most.' Heavens, I could use another gin and tonic like this. By willpower alone I kept my hand over the glass when he raised his own in enquiry. 'What's your sense of this potential benefactor? Come on, Brian – you're a fine judge of character. I've seen you in action with both kids and staff.'

'I chose you to be head,' he observed, ambiguously.

I raised what I hoped was an equally ambiguous eyebrow.

'I might need your support to block it,' he said in a rush. 'This offer. I propose to go along with it till I find out more about who we're dealing with, but – to be honest, Jane, you've only been voicing my own questions. Will you trust me?' He reached for my hand.

Cue shimmering violins in the background. Or not. We exchanged a firm handshake, neither more nor less. Because, actually, I didn't trust him. Not an inch.

CHAPTER FIVE

'Georgy's mum? No, I've heard nothing in the village about the pickers being back. But they wouldn't, not this early, would they?' Pam croaked, first thing next morning at Wray Episcopi. Her eyes were runny and her voice gravelly with a cold.

'I wouldn't have thought so. Not unless they plant as well as pick. But Zunaid was adamant he heard a woman speaking – shouting – in Romanian.'

'And he's so bright you wouldn't doubt him. My ears – I wouldn't rely on them. They're not good at the best of times, but being all bunged up like this . . . But once I can, I'll keep them open, if you see what I mean. Georgy didn't mention coming over in any of those letters of his, did he? Not once.'

'He was more concerned about Tottenham's new midfield player, someone with a name like an eye chart. And he was worried about an Arsenal player's injury. A child with just a handful of someone else's dust as his birthright and he's worried about a man who earns a million or more a month. The question is, though, if he didn't hear Mrs Popescu shouting, who did he hear?'

'I'll talk to him on the way home. Always assuming I've got some voice to talk with.'

'Thanks. But you have to look after yourself, Pam – get that cousin of yours to take over here for a day or so if needs be. She's not you but she's OK. Zunaid needs his Pam to be well, you know.'

'I'll be fine.' She waved a face mask at me. 'And I'll be using this at the servery. Don't want every last kid to get this.'

Actually, I wasn't keen on getting it myself, but when I backed away it was with enough exaggeration to make her laugh.

There might be a pile of admin waiting for me in my office, but one of my jobs was to keep an eye on everything happening in the school – and also the playground, where today it was Karenza's turn to supervise the daily run round the circumference. Everyone else was running, staff and children alike. I joined in with the last little group; gratifyingly they speeded up. I didn't like what I'd heard, so I ensured they were too breathless to continue talking in a pretty fair imitation of Jess's Yorkshire vowels, and not in a kind way, either. On impulse I accelerated, catching up with her – not hard, since she was quite new to this daily exercise.

'Just a quick question, Jess – do you have a Twitter account?'

'No. Never felt the need. Why?'

'I'm always worried about online bullying.'

'Oh – the three princesses. Them and their blonde hair and blue eyes. Silly cows. They've tried it on in class. Or as they would say, *claaass*.' She had just enough breath to produce an exaggerated southern vowel sound. 'Don't worry. I'm on to it. No, they've said nothing racist yet. Too fly to risk anything quite so flagrant, I guess.'

'Let them just try!' I patted her arm.

'Actually,' she gasped, 'I know it's a truism, but bullies are often just responding to bullying in their own lives. Is there anything I should know?'

'Not yet. But you'll be the first to know if I do find anything. Meanwhile, your happiness is at least as important as theirs: I'm not having my deputy in any way taunted or undermined.'

'Except by this damned running! It's killing me, gaffer.'

I pointed at Karenza. 'Don't give up. She's signalling it's the last circuit.'

Parents worrying about their children getting wet; a long meeting in Canterbury about music initiatives needing money we hadn't got; a child with an asthma attack whose inhaler had run out. Average day, really. I was ready to go home and slob around for half an hour before addressing myself to all the work I missed during the day. Except Joy's presence precluded slobbing.

We didn't have room for a car park, so everyone had to park on the road. My car, splattered with passing mud, reproached me as I walked towards it. Since the local garage had closed, I'd not had it valeted. It had been cleaned just once – there'd been a village hall fundraiser in early January, when it had had a quick hose down. Now it was a disgrace, especially compared to Joy's car. Maybe, I told it, the Merc would no longer be there to put it to shame. Maybe Ken would have arrived and swept her off to a luxurious hotel until their insurance company found them a temporary home. Maybe.

The abandoned garage had become a pop-up car wash. I'd priggishly avoided it because it was part of the black economy and probably wasn't green in the way it disposed of all the detergent and water involved. But today almost of its own accord the car headed that way: yes, a team of men was waiting. They crowded round with desperate eagerness. For some reason I'd been expecting a crowd of disaffected kids: I got middle-aged men. Despite the cold that had me huddled into my fur-hooded puffer jacket, none wore more than a tatty fleece. Perhaps the energy put into cleaning and polishing kept them warm? Unlikely: there were more hanging round dispiritedly than working on the car. On impulse, I dug in my purse for coins, enough for them all to have a couple of pounds or so, plus the change from my twenty-pound note. My head told me off for helping people avoid tax; my heart said it knew hunger when it saw it.

Were they embarrassed by the pitifully small tips? None of them made any eye contact. No one spoke at all, except me, in what rapidly became overbright and overloud tones. Perhaps – surely, I was mistaken – they were more alarmed than embarrassed by my attempts at largesse. Next time, I'd take food. Yes, I knew there'd be a next time.

Meanwhile, I had a more immediate problem – though I assured Joy it wasn't a problem at all, I cursed to see the parking place on my drive occupied by an even bigger vehicle than Joy's, which I'd had to box in. Ken's. Not a Merc, but one of my least favourite vehicles, a 4X4 with a huge boot tacked on, in black with lots of chrome. Maybe if you needed to transport cows or sheep there was an excuse for it, but as far as I knew Ken's boats were no more than a metre long or high. Perhaps he'd upgraded and needed all the space. At least it was filthy dirty compared with my now gleaming vehicle.

Joy was on her own when I let myself in, to find her pressing a G & T into my hand. 'We should be looking for a hotel,' she began.

'Too late for that. You're both staying here,' I said, cursing the prospect of an evening's social chat when I really had a lot of stats to deal with. 'It'll be absolutely fine.'

'Even though Ken's got a really bad tummy bug?'

That almost stopped me in my tracks. 'Of course. Though actually, Joy – oh, dear, this is so embarrassing! – I must try not to catch it. You're not allowed in school until forty-eight hours after diarrhoea and vomiting have stopped. And that applies to me as much as to the tiniest reception child. So I'll have to ask him to stay in your bedroom and just use the en suite for the duration. I'm really sorry.'

She touched her nose. 'Between ourselves, I don't think he's as bad as he says he is. I think a water-only diet will soon effect a cure! Especially if we keep him in isolation. It's a pity there's a TV in there because he'll think being ill's a good idea . . . Meanwhile, I've got a moussaka ready to go in the oven: if we can't finish it, then we can pop the rest in your freezer . . .'

* * *

What's the etiquette when at two in the morning your overnight guest is being treated by paramedics, whose blue-flashing ambulance has been parked outside your front door for an hour or more? And then they go away and leave him? Let's say I got a lot of work done, and produced tea and coffee when I felt it was appropriate. Joy couldn't work out why they hadn't taken him straight to hospital, because he was clearly ill, occasionally groaning in pain. Clutching mugs of hot chocolate, we talked in whispers, although the kitchen was the furthest point from the guest room.

'They think it's a virus, but they said to phone again if there's no improvement,' she said, clearly torn between anxiety and exasperation. 'And here's you, one of the hardest-working people I've ever met, losing the sleep you need. Off you go – back to bed. This is my problem, isn't it? It would have been if we were in our own house, after all. Oh, that damned fox! We should call David Attenborough. Here, have a biscuit. No point in going to bed while you're still shaking like a leaf.'

I couldn't argue. But I did have some relaxation exercises on my iPod, even if I doubted I would actually drop off. I was deeply asleep, however, when the paramedics turned up again at six-thirty, their arrival coinciding nicely with my alarm. Poor Joy was trying to pack an emergency bag for him, picking a few clean clothes from the case he'd brought back from Wales and rooting through the stuff we'd managed to retrieve from her house. I made her drink tea and eat toast while she did it.

'Stop talking about finding a hotel, Joy! If they keep him in hospital, this house is your base. Don't even think about moving out. Understand? It's one thing you simply don't have to worry about. I insist. And I shall go into fierce head teacher mode if I hear a word of argument.' I raised an eyebrow and a threatening finger, extracting a tearful laugh.

Having heard nothing from her all day, I contacted her at about half past six, just as I was about to leave school. She called back immediately, happier to talk than to text.

Her distress oozed out of the phone. Ken had been admitted and would be staying in overnight. But he was frightened as well as in pain, and she was going to stay with him till later in the evening.

'Are you staying with him?'

'Oh, I'll get a taxi home. No problem.'

'Remind me, which hospital is he in?'

'William Harvey.'

I thought quickly, though I didn't tell the whole truth: I hadn't planned a visit to Will, but one wouldn't come amiss. 'In that case I'll be able to give you a lift. I'm visiting my sick friend tonight and it'd be nice to have some company on the way home.' That was absolutely true. There were some nights when I couldn't hold back the tears. 'I could text you ten minutes before I head for the car park so we can meet up.'

I suspected that I wasn't the only one of Will's friends to have given up regular visits. Most of us had persisted as long as there was any hope for him. But as I took my place beside the figure now propped up in a specialised chair, splints on hands and feet, his head lolling as far as the padding round his neck permitted, I saw one sign of activity. Alongside the Pooh Bear I'd given him – we'd once planned expositions together – was an Eeyore looking so inexpressibly depressed I wanted to wrap my arms round him and cry into his blue-grey plush coat. Someone had put something round his neck – not a gaudy bow matching a cerise one on his tail that might have perked him up a bit, but something metallic. I investigated. On the end of a fine chain was a small gilt medal, with a head engraved on it. St Jude, according to the legend on the back. The patron saint of lost causes, according to the scrap of information my memory suddenly and unexpectedly threw up.

Perhaps it wasn't something I should tell Will, as I sat beside him. But there was a lot I could. The idea was that the speech might stimulate his brain and that one day he might – just conceivably might – regain consciousness. No one ever spelt out what quality of consciousness it might or might not be. All this because vile associates of the picture-hunting Lady Preston had decided one evening to stop a concerned police officer from doing his job.

If I couldn't hold his hand as I talked, at least I could keep my hand on his arm, occasionally squeezing it lightly for emphasis. I gave him all the good news about Zunaid's school progress, adding that I wished I could magic his dad and auntie to the UK. Perhaps I touched the St Jude medal as I did. Then I regaled him with news of my new guest – how long she'd be with me I'd no idea, but presumably as long as it took to get a diagnosis and treatment for Ken. 'She's unexpectedly kind,' I continued. 'She cooks wonderfully. She's made the house a home. She even keeps her car clean. Which inspired me to take mine to a hand car wash – yes, mine, the one you said I could try growing carrots on.' So I told him about the activities on the estate that I'd seen on my walk with Joy, just as if he could hear and understand and bring his detective's brain to bear on the issues. Just as if he'd cock his head and tell me to get together some more evidence.

Almost as if.

But not quite. I couldn't feel the tension of the man who'd wanted to kiss me but couldn't because of my involvement with a case. Or the tension that had driven me almost crazy the night I'd almost called him back to my bed.

Martin, his regular nurse popped his head into the room. It was time I left, his kind smile said – not for Will's sake but for mine.

CHAPTER SIX

I can deal with kids on sugar rushes, but how should I treat an adult, a guest in my home, who'd rejected with dismay the very idea of a takeaway or fish and chips only to find she'd forgotten to make the pasta sauce she'd promised? And was now well down her second extremely stiff G & T and weepy with stress over her husband, who was struck down with diverticulitis, which I'd assumed was a chronic disease, not an acute one. Now she was staring with horror at the bowl of crisps I'd put in front of her as I silently replaced the gin glass with one full of water. Good crisps, too, the sort I rely on when I've not eaten all day and am too tired even to look in the freezer except to reach for some cheese to go with them.

Actually, getting food inside her must be the best option, and, yes, I had a lovely selection of frozen M & S and Waitrose meals. All I had to do was get her to make a choice.

* * *

What I had noticed, but she hadn't, was that even in the short space of time it took her to get out of the car and into the house, and me to pop the car into the garage, which was blessed with an automatic door I could operate with a zapper, three or four cars had hurtled over the estate rumble strips. They were probably going too fast to register the door rolling gently down a few inches from my bumper before I let myself in via the internal door opening straight into the kitchen. Even the most impatient late commuter tended to be more circumspect. So when we'd eaten I suggested a repeat of our constitutional.

'I'd no idea those meals could be so tasty – and have all those nutritional details on the packets, too,' she said, looking hopefully at the wine bottle, which I was putting back in the fridge.

'Absolutely. They're my lifeline. I don't think it's raining, and after all that time at the hospital we both need some fresh air. Just one circuit,' I urged her, as I passed her her jacket and her mobile. 'You know that Ken's safe and sound, and you'll need to be strong when he comes out,' I said, locking the door carefully behind us.

'He should never have had a flare-up like this!' Was that anguish or fury? 'Actually, he's never ever had one as bad as this. When I'm in charge of his food he's fine. But when he's with his old friends he thinks he can just be one of the lads and ignore his diet,' she said, ready, by the sound of it, to weep again. 'And now he'll be in hospital for the best part of a week while they rehydrate him and give him intravenous antibiotics. Just when I need him to be fit and well, too, to look for a house and everything.'

A week! 'You're fine here, as I told you,' I said, hoping

I sounded neither grudging nor too jolly. I'd needed refuge often enough, hadn't I, and been dependent on the institutional kindness of strangers – the least I could do was pay back a little of that. 'You said that Ken has a telescope: have you ever used it? It must be wonderful to be able to look up and identify what you're seeing on a night like this.'

'It's much better out by our house – and yours, of course. No lights to pollute the sky. Just us and space. All these wretched security lights!' she tutted, as our stroll lit them up in a chain reaction.

There was no sign of any foxes, or of the speeding vehicles. It was as if the latter had been swallowed in a sinkhole – or more likely, accommodated in one of the many double garages with swiftly moving up-and-over doors. From one of the little side roads, a white van emerged, properly lit and doing a sensible speed. It had no distinguishing marks at all.

'Are you going to join the village Speed Watch group? Wrayford and Wray Episcopi combined?' Joy asked. 'Oh, it'll all be official with police training and proper equipment. They're having a preliminary meeting about it tomorrow evening at the Cricketers. I meant to go but it all depends on Ken, of course. And Jane, I really could do with your advice. You've been in this position before. How do I make a decision about where to stay in the long term?'

'I had a lot of support from both the insurance company and the letting agency. I suppose it helped that I work pretty closely with Brian Dawes, who seems to own pretty much everything round here.'

'You couldn't ask him?'

'I think you should try official channels first,' I said

firmly, thinking of his possible health problems, not to mention my chronic reluctance to be beholden to him. 'Your insurers probably have an approved list.' I pointed to the house with the brightly lit room, which was still being used, though the cracks round the blackout blind were slightly smaller. 'Now, let's just check that house number before we go home . . .'

Friday. And though Zunaid meant very well indeed, and was right to be proud of his attainment, what he said made me feel sick. He'd bustled up to me in break.

'When I spoke about Georgy's mum the other day, I said she shouted. And I was going to tell you that she shouted again last night. But now I know the word is not shout, but what girls do when they're being silly. The word is scream. Ms Jane, why should Georgy's mum scream?'

Had he heard a fox too? 'I don't know, Zunaid. Was it a short silly scream?'

He shook his head solemnly. 'Not a playground scream. The sort of scream I hear in my country – heard in my country – when something bad had happened. Do you think they have bombs in Kent?'

'No, I don't. I know they don't. There are no bombs here. You're safe, Zunaid. But tell me where you heard this scream?'

'Last night at half past six. Oh, where, not when. Where we were before, walking back from Pam's to go back to my foster parents' house on the bus. I like Mary and David very much, Ms Jane, but I love Pam most in the world. Except my dad and Auntie Noor.'

This time I took his head between my hands and kissed

his hair. 'I know, Zunaid.' But I mustn't make any promises, they said, lest someone else had to break them. 'Did Pam hear the scream?'

'She says her ears are all bunged up.' He put his fingers in his ears and looked round comically. 'And she talks as if she's holding her nose.' He gave a huge grin. 'Like I do. Only my ears aren't bunged up.'

'So they can hear the lesson bell?'

He put his fingers back. 'Nothing, Ms Jane. Nothing at all.'

'Zunaid's sure it was a scream. I suppose I could have suggested it was just a vixen on heat but didn't want to confuse the issue . . . So you weren't aware of anything amiss, Pam?'

She put down her slotted spoon, wiping her hands on a towel she'd tucked into her apron pocket. 'Didn't hear a thing. But he tugged my hand in exactly the same place as he did last time, and I tell you straight, Jane, I'm worried. Either he's having flashbacks to Syria or he's hearing something real. Maybe a fox. OK, it probably was. Nasty stinking creatures – they should bring back hunting, that's what I say.'

That was one discussion I wasn't entering into. 'But it's in the same place as he heard this woman talking Romanian . . . I was thinking about telling the police, but I don't think Zunaid needs any sort of official cross-questioning, just when he seems to be settling in so well. Not without cause, anyway. So let's just find exactly where you were when he heard the shouts and screams. Just you and me, perhaps? This is one of the nights when he has to go straight back to his foster home, isn't it? So after school? We can drive past it and then I'll drop you off at yours.'

'But it'll be dark.'

'It was dark when he heard the women. It's not a matter of shoving our noses in anywhere dangerous, Pam – but I want to pinpoint the location exactly before I can talk to Lloyd Davies about it.'

She gave me a searching look. 'So, you've changed your mind about the police and Zunaid?'

I returned the look. 'Only if we see anything amiss.'

But once I'd screamed and maybe people thought it was just a fox.

With Pam in the car beside me, I did no more than stop and register the site. If I had to do any scrabbling round in the brambles not knowing who or what was the other side, I'd rather do it in daylight. And no, of course it wasn't my job: it was the police's. But with Lloyd still ill – genuinely ill, according to his wife Jo – there was no one else I could bother with simple hunches. Oh, I'd phoned 101 to have the information recorded, but the call handler was clearly unexcited. Still, if there was somewhere to poke a nose in, mine would be one of the first there. Which might explain why, with a pile of work to be done, and absolutely no time to make any commitment to a cause even as worthy as stopping petrolhead idiots systematically ignoring the village speed limits, I turned up with Joy at the initial Speed Watch gathering at the Jolly Cricketers.

Our local road safety police officer – I didn't even know that such a role existed – was one Eoin Connor, according to his name badge. He was a spring-loaded young man with not an Irish but a south London accent who bounced around the large room usually reserved for wedding receptions filling us all with zeal and commitment. He made it clear – and kept repeating the caveat – that we had no powers of arrest, and were there mainly as a deterrent. Then came a minimal amount of paperwork with our personal information. Then operational details – that sounded a remarkably technical term for speed guns, safety jackets, responsibilities, including the fact that we always worked in threes, safety precautions. Oh, and we'd get the chance to practise tomorrow afternoon. We couldn't fire the speed gun till we'd been trained. So I fell at the first hurdle – on Saturdays, despite the weather, I'd still be training our women's cricket squad.

'Can you come a little earlier? I'd hate you to miss out,' Eoin assured me, eyes as appealing as a red setter's. 'It only takes five minutes but it's the law and there you are. Go on – one-thirty?'

How could I resist that smile? And resist smiling back – not to mention hanging back at the end of the meeting and asking Eoin if he had other responsibilities besides hellhound motorists? After all, he'd been eye-contacting me all through his talk.

'I'll only be able to judge that if you sit down and tell me the problem over a drink,' he said. 'I'm parched after all this talking. And school's out tomorrow.'

'So it is. But I can't drink, Eoin – I've not eaten and—'

'Now there's a coincidence: neither have I. And I gather Diane does wonderful food.'

'She does. But I've got a friend staying with me . . .' How would Joy react to playing gooseberry to our sudden little flirtation? Or would she go off in a huff, since she'd pretty well dragged me along? 'And she's got far more information than I have about our problem,' I declared truthfully.

'In that case it would be a pleasure to invite her along too,' he said. His eyes said something else, however.

'Why shouldn't you enjoy a nice moment with a handsome young man?' Joy demanded later, as Eoin headed to the Gents' loo.

'Because only yesterday I was sitting holding another young man's hand?' Metaphorically, at least.

'Will's. Will who's in a persistent vegetative state. If he'd died outright, Jane, last autumn, would you be worried about flirting? Well, I suppose you might, but what you're worrying about is a whole lot of might-have-beens that might well not have been at all. Sorry. Too much gin. When we've walked him round the close I shall retire to bed with my earplugs in. Understand?' In an unaccustomed gesture she reached across and patted my hand.

How she felt about being treated as Eoin's aged grandmother as he helped her down kerbs and manoeuvred her round badly parked cars, I'd no doubt learn later. But he listened carefully to our joint narrative, occasionally interrupting to clarify points and muttering under his breath when he learnt, apparently for the first time, about calls to 101.

'If it's not something they can deal with online no one bothers,' he chuntered.

Then I pointed to the blackouts in the brightly lit room. 'They're like studio lights.'

'Now that's very interesting, isn't it?' His enthusiasm was probably genuine.

Joy agreed. 'I was talking about it earlier today to Ken, who says one of his friends has a studio in one of the bedrooms. And an old-fashioned darkroom too. No, not here – not this one.'

Suddenly Eoin said, 'I'm not so sure it's a good thing for you two to be seen walking round with a cop in uniform. Take yourselves off home, now, and I'll catch up with you in just five. Number fourteen – right?'

'But—'

'Let's do as he says, Joy, and I'll get the coffee brewing.'

Far from keeping her promise to head for bed, Joy insisted on making hot chocolate for us all, even producing the biscuits she'd made the other day. Was she being deeply ironic or simply assuming that sugar was better for us all than a massive ingestion of caffeine? Or perhaps she was simply responding to my anxieties – about myself as much as anything else. Whatever the reason, the chocolate was beyond good. So good she made us all a second mug.

Eoin was content, it seemed, to charm us both, with hardly any reference to what he might have seen.

Then Joy jumped in. 'Did you know Will Bowman? One of Jane's friends – a detective?'

What on earth was she doing?

Eoin's face turned from a mask of comedy to a mask of tragedy. 'I still do know him. Inasmuch as anyone can know him. If I could, I'd add, "God rest his soul" – but maybe it's too early. Who knows? How do you know him, Jane?'

Joy again. 'She goes to visit him quite regularly – such a strain.'

71

'A strain for all his friends, isn't it?' I asked Eoin directly. 'We became friends when he was dealing with a murder at the house I actually own – not this one.'

Before I knew it, Joy was off again, telling him how she'd alerted me to the problem.

'Actually,' I said, cutting across her, quite rudely, I suppose, 'there's another potential issue. Shouts and screams in woodland near Wray Episcopi. The shouts were in Romanian. And maybe there's an international language of screams.'

'You heard them when?' Eoin's smile faded. He was all attention.

'Not me. But someone whose word I'd trust absolutely.'

Joy leant forward. 'Aren't you going to take him to see where it was?'

Something random dawned in my head with creaking slowness: Joy wasn't sober.

Now I came belatedly to think about it, I wasn't either.

What about Eoin?

But she'd asked me a question. 'Not at this time of night. We need broad daylight. And I'm beginning to think – I do apologise, Eoin – that I might have had more to drink at the Cricketers than I realised. I'm so sorry. Long day. Long week. All rounded off by that wonderful soporific hot chocolate.'

'Oh, that'll be the Amarula,' Joy declared beatifically. 'I always put a really good slosh in hot chocolate – a trick I learnt on one of our trips to South Africa.'

Eoin's smile was back. But it was a little grimmer. 'How much of a slosh, Joy?'

She shrugged as if it was a ludicrous question.

Eoin was on his feet. 'I'd best call a cab, then, and leave the car here. Thank God it's unmarked. Jesus, you know the ABV of that lovely stuff?' He was already tapping his phone.

Poor Joy – far from freeing up our inhibitions, she'd inadvertently locked me in a chastity belt.

It didn't take long for a cab to appear, minutes Joy filled with artless gossip. As Eoin headed for the front door she kissed us both goodnight, though, and tottered off upstairs.

Eoin and I merely nodded to each other, embarrassed by our tipsiness.

A fox grinned at us from the end of the drive, apparently heading to cock his leg against a rear wheel, but shrugging when the car drew off.

CHAPTER SEVEN

Eoin's car disappeared from the drive early next morning before I was even up, a note on the doormat telling me he'd talk to me about my information when I turned up for my speed gun training. A short conversation was fine by me, backed up by a map I'd downloaded and marked with a time-honoured X. No. I deleted that.

All very efficient.

The speed gun training was easy: the speed of an approaching car was shown on a nice clear screen. Eoin drove towards me at a variety of speeds. After six or eight passes, he pulled up, getting out of the car. 'There you are – a fully accredited member of the team. Now, I can see you're all ready for your cricket – but in this weather, for God's sake?'

'In the school hall. Ball skills. Just to keep the muscle memory alive.'

'Of course. Anyway, one more question: who gave you the information about the screams and why didn't they come straight to us? OK, so that's two.'

'Which can share an answer. The person who told me was one of my pupils, a five- or six-year-old. No, don't look at me like that. He's got ears like radar scanners. And he knows a scream when he hears one. Somehow or other he escaped from Syria.'

'Poor little bugger.'

'Zunaid also heard shouts in Romanian.'

'You're sure it's Romanian?'

'I wouldn't be. But he is. His best friend's Romanian – the son of seasonal fruit-pickers – and Zunaid's got an amazing ear for languages. A real gift. And I trust him.'

'Even so, hardly someone we could ever use as a witness.'

I could feel his interest ebbing. 'You've got to find what made the woman scream before you'd need him to be that?'

He nodded. 'How long does this cricket business last?'

'An hour. No more.'

He checked his watch. 'That'd give us an hour of twilight: I'll pick you up at the school hall.'

'I'm surprised you keep visiting Will Bowman,' Eoin said, by way of a greeting, as I fastened my seat belt a hectic hour or so later.

'He was a good friend. That's what you do when a friend needs you.'

'Do you think he still needs anyone? It's a shame he was ever saved, if you ask me.'

'Not a day goes by without my wondering if I'd been

wiser not to do that mouth-to-mouth. But all I could do at the time was my best.'

'It was you? My God. Sorry if—you know.'

'I told you, with the gift of hindsight I dare say I'd have done better to hold his hand as he died. So having kept him alive . . .'

'You're doing your best to get him back to life. Sorry to sound brutal, but if there was a power cut at the hospital, I'd be thanking God. Let the poor bastard die.'

I didn't argue. Couldn't.

We pulled into the side of the road opposite the lay-by Pam had indicated. We got out and walked across, but Eoin gestured I wasn't to step on to it, even though it was tarmacked, like the road. 'Though countless people will have done, I suppose. And parked and dropped their rubbish and driven off. Christ, if you knew how I hate litter.'

I looked round thoughtfully. 'There's no sign of any here – isn't that weird in itself? Though we did have that high wind – perhaps it all got blown into someone's garden. There's nothing in the mouth of that bridleway either. Or the other one.' I pointed to the two paths running off the lay-by – the one directly in front of us wide enough for one man and his dog, the other, at a forty-five-degree angle, a metre or so wider.

In silence we walked five hundred metres or so up the narrower one, and then, returning with nothing except muddy boots for our trouble, we agreed to explore the other one. We set off very slowly.

We'd barely gone fifty metres when he said, 'You're quiet.' As if he wasn't.

'I have a terrible sense of déjà vu, that's why. It was

76

on a track like this I found what remained of Will.'

'Ah. I can't imagine we'll find anything like that, but with the light going like this I'd say there's no point in upsetting yourself by going any further. Another time, maybe. Do you think it's worth talking to the little lad again? Or to that woman Pat?' he added, heading back downhill.

'Pam. We could see if she's in, but I'd bet that if she's well enough – she's got a vile cold – she'll be in Canterbury with Zunaid's foster family. She'd love to adopt him if she can. But you know what officialdom's like.' Hearing a horse behind us, I stopped short, turning back up the path. 'Lulabelle!'

'Good afternoon, Ms Cowan.' She looked down at me from her pony, which seemed quite large for a child her age. The flowing locks were invisible under her hard hat, and the girliness had been replaced by jeans and a unisex top and a hi-vis waistcoat. She touched the peak of her hard hat in a neat salute.

As if she was an adult I introduced her to Eoin, whose title I used.

'Police?' she asked, suddenly lisping like a very little girl. 'Has someone done something wrong?'

'We don't know, Lulabelle,' Eoin said seriously. 'You've got a better vantage point than we have – have you ever seen anything unusual. Heard anything?'

She grimaced. 'Actually, I'm not supposed to be here – you won't tell, will you, Ms Cowan? Dad'd kill me.'

'Why do you suppose he'd want to do that?'

'Oh, he keeps on about not riding on my own in case Snowflake puts a foot in a rabbit hole and throws me. And stuff about never talking to strangers.' She looked with cool, amused eyes not at me but at Eoin. 'I'm sure you've heard the same from every dad.'

'And every dad – and every mum, for that matter – is absolutely right to tell their sons and daughters about the dangers of what they're doing,' he said, not amused at all.

'Snowflake's like totally sure-footed. And if anyone tried to talk to me I'd just gallop away.'

He stuck his hands on his hips. 'You might—'

I sensed that Eoin was about to argue – pointlessly – about the practicalities, so I interrupted him. 'Have you heard any strangers talking – not necessarily to you, but to anyone else round here?'

Before she could answer, a quad bike hurtled up the hill. Snowflake moved uneasily but Lulabelle quelled any attempt to bolt. The bareheaded driver yelled, 'And what the hell are you doing out on that bloody nag and talking to a pair of random rustics when I told you not to? Bloody get down now and walk him home. Understand? And I'll deal with you later. As for you two, you should be ashamed of yourselves.'

'Dad, they're—'

'Do as you're bloody told! Now!' he screamed, grabbing the bridle with one hand and her arm with the other. 'Off. Walk. Now!'

'But—'

'Best go, Lulabelle,' I said quietly, smiling with more kindness than I'd ever felt for her. I could hear the sniffed-back sobs as she obeyed. 'Mr Petrie, I'm Jane Cowan, Wray Episcopi's head teacher.' And we ought to have met before: how on earth had he slipped through the parents' evenings net? 'And this is PC Eoin Connor.'

Eoin flashed his card. Why Petrie had chosen to ignore his uniform I wasn't sure.

But he wasn't about to apologise. 'Well, you should know better than to encourage her, that's all I have to say to you. And stick to the footpaths; don't go trespassing on my land.' The bike disappeared in a smelly, muddy cloud.

'Wouldn't it be lovely if his brakes failed?'

'So long as he didn't go flying across the road and smash up my car.' He turned to follow him, more decorously, of course. 'Well? What are we waiting for?' He started walking.

I was actually wondering what it was that Petrie didn't want either his daughter or us to see. But the light was fading fast, and any attempt to turn back might he construed as an attempt to return to last night's brief flirtation, which was long dead.

He said nothing about my being involved any further, indeed said very little about anything on the way back to Wrayford, where he pulled up on my drive just long enough for me to get out. He was off before I got the key in the front door.

I just hoped that the second rental option that Joy's insurance company came up with was better than the first, which even I'd have found cramped. Predictably I'd been pressed into service as an adviser, a role to which I was probably suited, given my nomadic experience. But I could think of much better ways of spending a Sunday morning than driving round in drenching, unremitting rain. Actually, I could think of one worse one – showing Eoin round more miserable woodland paths, had he invited me to, that is.

By now Joy and I were on the fourth place, and I was beginning to think almost longingly of the preparation I should have been doing for the Monday evening meeting about fundraising. Even helping the police with their enquiries might have been more fun. Clearly none of the properties was in any way comparable with Joy's own home, but two were quite acceptable, in my eyes at least, given the fact that she needed a home to move Ken back into when he was discharged from hospital in a very few days' time. A home, yes, but not mine. At the very least they must have a lot of closer friends to turn to – fellow Masons, for instance. Dare I suggest it?

In fact, I didn't need to. She pressed me to join her for lunch, which turned out to be at their golf club. I don't think I'd ever been in a place so full of extraordinarily bright men's clothes before. Joy put down her menu and closed her eyes wearily. She opened them when a waiter appeared with our wine. Just half a bottle, at my puritan suggestion. 'Thank you: it's fine. This is absurd, Jane. I can't think how I came to involve you in all this. It must be bringing back all the wrong sort of memories for you. And when you offered me a bed for the night, trailing round the countryside with me looking at dire housing certainly wasn't part of the deal.' Before I could shake my head in a half-hearted attempt to deny the truth of what she was saying, she added, re-energised, 'And now I'm going to be terribly rude and leave you on your own for a moment: there's a man over there I know. Tony Carpenter. A member of Ken's Masonic Lodge. He owes Ken a big favour. I'm going to call it in.'

She toddled off to the table dominated by a tall man in his

sixties, well-dressed in non-golfing gear and good-looking in a beaky way. Soon she was returning with a big smile. 'Sorted, as you youngsters say. He does private lets. If the insurance company won't meet all the rental, that's between him and Ken. He and his wife – doesn't she look horribly like Mrs Trump? – will take me over, if you're happy to drive my car back to yours.'

I nodded, as if being offered the keys of a Mercedes was an everyday event. 'Will your insurance cover me?'

She slumped. 'Oh. Oh, I don't know. It's something Ken always deals with. Tell you what, we'll call a taxi. Unless – oh, Jane, this would be so much fun – you'd come with me!'

CHAPTER EIGHT

I'm used to dealing with grim stuff on my own. But when I want to share a laugh I miss not having close friends living nearby. Texting Jo and Lloyd wasn't quite the same as nipping round for a drink and a natter. And I did want to share Joy's news. She'd really fallen on her well-shod feet – a wing of a Victorian vicarage big enough to house in comfort the family of the most philoprogenitive clergyman, decorated and furnished as if it was first cousin to a stately home. Better still, Ken's affluent friends followed her back to my place, filling their Bentley with what she couldn't get in the Merc and they all drove off with a serene disregard of the speed limits she'd signed up to enforcing. Despite his generosity to Joy and his undoubted charm, I didn't take to Tony Carpenter, nor he, I suspect, to me. Too much of Brian Dawes' assumption that the world turned for his exclusive benefit, perhaps. Mrs Tony – Alexia – was very quiet throughout, to the point, I thought, of being watchful.

Joy and I exchanged warm hugs, with lots of promises to keep closely in touch, as if we weren't due to be neighbours once all the building work was complete; I really hoped we would manage to continue as friends, though I suspected it might be harder when Ken was on the scene. Meanwhile I'd certainly miss her cooking and her conviction that drinking is a team sport.

I must remember to tell Brian at the following evening's meeting that my lodger had departed. But a late-night check of emails told me that he had to send his apologies – something important had cropped up. Then a veritable rash of other apologies pinged into my inbox: there seemed to be a local outbreak of something sounding horribly like norovirus. I doubted if the meeting would be quorate, but everyone, to do them justice, had attached a list of suggestions.

A quick phone call to Hazel Roberts had the meeting postponed. There! I'd lost a lodger and gained an evening's freedom, though I did have a staff meeting to precede it.

The following morning, I found I'd lost half a school. Two half-schools, to be precise. That dreaded tummy bug. So, any follow-up work on Lulabelle would have to wait. As for the teachers, the protocol was for each one to draw up a schedule of work they meant to do each day, so if we had to bring in replacement staff, progress would be as seamless as possible. Our regular staff meetings would be simply exchanges of emails, to reduce cross-infection. As for cross-county initiatives, we would have to clear our attendance with the organisers first to see if they were prepared to take the risk. But viruses sneak up on even the best prepared, and on Thursday I had to quarantine myself at home for the last two days of the working week, a nuisance since there were plenty of ends to tie up before half-term. By Friday morning, I was actually fine. Bolstered by a call from Joy telling me that Ken was out of hospital and recovering well in his new surroundings, I decided to take to the increasingly spring-like lanes on my bike. Birds were beginning to sing; the sky was a clichéd but welcome blue; there was even some warmth in the sun. Of course, I wanted to feel guilty – but if we told the pupils to play outside and avoid other people, I was only doing a grown-up version of that.

A cycling incident last summer had made me paranoid, so I now sported a camera on my helmet. I'd still not graduated to proper Lycra gear, however. I probably never would, come to think of it. After a lovely tootle round, I knew what called me: home and that pile of work I'd felt too ill to tackle the previous day. But I might venture out for another hour the next morning, especially when the next crop of emails told me that the Speed Watch team had managed to put together their first trio of members and would set up not far from the school at nine on Saturday morning. It would be nice to reciprocate this gracious gesture with one of my own, so I cycled over with the last of Joy's biscuits and made them fresh coffee with the school machine.

They looked remarkably official: hi-vis jackets; someone with a clipboard and pen, ready to jot down the numbers of vehicles driven at least ten per cent over the speed limit; the speed gun held a bit more ostentatiously than Eoin had recommended; a camera – he'd insisted that this was only to be used to record the details of offending vehicles, which were then to be wiped immediately.

It was all very jolly; Joy's biscuits got a lot of compliments. But they snapped into immediate action each time a vehicle approached, and noted with gusto anyone doing more than thirty-three. Some topped forty, including a woman with two kids in the back, an unsecured dog and a mug of coffee on the dash – and a mobile in her hand. All the law-abiding drivers else got a cheery wave, often giving one back. It was a pity that some of those didn't involve all the fingers of the hand, just one or two – but perhaps when your bonnet was dipping sharply because you'd just noticed the speed limit you couldn't spare the rest of them.

There was more village activity in the evening – a fundraiser for the village hall, the hub of so many activities. Usually the committee asked for bring-and-share plates and made money from admission charges, a raffle (I'd donated a couple of bottles of bubbly) and a bar. This one, however, was being organised by another newcomer to the village, Xanthe Boot, who had decided that the late-lamented village shop was ripe for conversion to a tearoom. Everyone wanted to support her – even if the building work had to go to outsiders, the venture would eventually bring work for villagers. There was no sign of her when I arrived, but interesting smells emerging from the kitchen.

The first person I ran into was Brian, wrinkling his nose over a glass.

'It's all very well this stuff being complimentary, but I'd rather have paid for a decent wine, not this Greek stuff.' He interrupted his complaint to kiss me on the cheek in a belated greeting. 'You know she's paying for all the food herself? A bit of a taster for her new venture.'

'I wish her every success,' I toasted the air with my own free wine and sipped. Brian's judgement was spot on. 'Sun and sea and sand make your tastebuds a bit more forgiving, don't they?' I added as quietly as I could in the general hubbub.

'They do indeed. If only Diane could have catered for this event. I hope the tearoom won't damage her trade, incidentally.'

'She's never wanted to take on that end of the market, has she? Cupcakes are diabetes in a paper case, according to her.'

'I certainly prefer her savoury dishes any day of the week. What a shame so many people have been struck down by the norovirus – there are far fewer people here than I expected.'

'Plenty of time yet – I'm congenitally early.'

He smiled. 'I prefer the term "punctual", myself – since I'm afflicted with the same inability. I hear you had the virus – are you fully recovered?'

'You should have backed away hexing me before you even spoke to me,' I said with a laugh he didn't join in. 'I'm fine, thanks, and have been since Thursday afternoon – or I promise you I wouldn't be here.'

'Did your lodger prove a good nurse?'

'Joy? Oh, I lost her last weekend. And she's now ensconced with her husband in an amazing let, big enough for a family of six. They'll rattle round in it like peas in a colander. Cosy it is not. Nor convenient. And I should imagine their heating bills will be higher than their ceilings.'

'You don't sound impressed.' Brian didn't want to feel that I was criticising his properties – any of them.

'I'm impressed, but by no means envious. Do you know their landlord – Tony Carpenter?'

Brian always seemed to pride himself on being suavely unshockable, but he responded as if I'd trodden on his well-shod toe. 'Not personally. Though I gather he's a leading light in the Masons.'

'Do I gather you're not a fan of his?' Of course I did, or I wouldn't have asked the question.

There was a moment's hesitation before he asked, 'Impressed by the Croesus of Kent?'

'You don't sound as if you approve of him at all.'

He asked a question that really took me aback: 'How many really rich people have you met that you'd whole-heartedly admire?'

Clearly, he didn't number himself in the ranks, which surprised me.

'Oh dear: I don't seem to know any rich men. Simon's family was loaded, but never thought of themselves as rich, and as you know the words "admire" and "Simon" really don't fit into the same sentence. Lady Preston . . .' I tailed off quickly before I could insult his former friend, whom I deemed to be both bad and mad.

'Cassandra? I dare say she'd be rolling in cash if she ever found those mythical paintings of hers! Assuming they're masterpieces, as she seems to. I'd never have had her down as appreciating fine art, however, unless she happened to be looking at a Stubbs.' He snorted, then asked, 'Is she still making a nuisance of herself?'

'Her lawyer is, and seems intent on pinning the blame for losing them on me. Whatever they are; whoever they're by; how many of them there are – I've not a clue.'

'All this extra pressure when you should be giving all your attention to running – indeed saving – the school!'

But it was time to adjourn to the tables to which we'd been allocated and that ended any meaningful conversation that evening.

Sunday lunch brought the welcome return to my life of two friends: Lloyd Davies had recovered from his flu enough to fancy a roast, and Jo's appetite too had returned after her brush with the norovirus. If it had been an evening meal, having eaten and drunk my fill, I would spend the night in their spare room. This time, instead of too much wine, I took along organic chocolates and some single estate Cornish tea.

Lloyd, who probably knew as much about my past as anyone from his police colleagues, had instituted himself as my minder-in-chief, and I wasn't surprised when over an old-fashioned upside-down pudding he turned the conversation to any adventure that might have befallen me in the past week.

'Stomach bug apart? Well, I suppose the most exciting thing was becoming a fully signed-up member of the village Speed Watch team.'

'Heavens, Jane,' Jo chipped in, 'you do know how to live, don't you? When are we going to see a handsome young man waltz into your life?'

'Have you got a spare one in your ballroom dancing classes? Well, then. Oh, actually, I did have one in my life in the form of PC Eoin Connor, who positively exudes charm.'

'A man from Traffic? Jesus, you do pick them, Jane,' Lloyd sighed, gathering up the dishes. 'One-track minds, cops in Traffic.'

With an expressively raised eyebrow Jo took them from him and headed for the kitchen to make tea.

'He seemed quite interested in something I had to tell him. That stuff about unmarked vans zooming round Wrayford – remember, I texted you when you were ill? And some other oddities on the estate.' I told him about the blacked-out room with ill-fitting blinds. 'But then he seemed to lose interest – I dare say he's as busy as the rest of you. Didn't I hear there's another Operation Stack in progress?' This was the euphemism for apparently all the lorries in the UK having to be parked on the M20 whenever there was a problem with crossing the Channel. It must have been dire if you were travelling, but it wasn't much fun for locals either. 'But I would have liked to explore the woods a bit further. Two reasons: one of my pupils swears he heard screams from someone speaking Romanian. OK, this could be a kid's fantasy, but he's bright and reliable. Secondly, because the man who owned them was so keen we left without doing so. A man called Rufus Petrie, who happens to be the father of another of my pupils.'

Returning with a tray of mugs, Jo frowned. 'That name rings a bell, you know. Something – I'm sure he was in the news five or six years ago – maybe longer. Lloyd – any ideas?'

He scratched his head. 'Maybe longer. But this flu's fogged my brain: I'll Google him—' He half got up.

'You know the rules, Lloyd: no electronics till we've completely finished our meal. And that includes tea. I didn't know they grew it in Cornwall, Jane. It's delicious.'

'Green tea delicious? That's going a bit far! It always reminds me of compost heaps. Sorry, Jane.'

I waved away his apologies. 'It's supposed to mop up free radicals.'

'Always assuming the Home Secretary's left any out of detention,' he countered.

Jo made a winding gesture. 'Always makes that joke, doesn't he? And I've an idea he got it from you in the first place. This here Rufus Petrie, Jane, and his woods.'

'It turned out that he's the father of one of our Episcopi pupils. Weirdly, I'd not met him before, not even on parents' nights. Weird, that.'

'Lulabelle! What sort of parent lumbers their kid with a name like that?' Lloyd asked.

'It's coming back now,' Jo said. 'Petrie . . . Remember that woman who died under the influence of God knows how many drugs? One of some girl band? Left behind a baby daughter and a husband? Could he be the widower?'

'It might just be. Any ideas, Jane? Six or seven years ago? Maybe eight?'

I shook my head. 'That wasn't a good time for me. You know what it's like when . . . you lose sight of the larger world. Google's the answer,' I added more positively.

And, when Lloyd had stowed the last plate in the dishwasher, Google provided the answer. Lulabelle's mother had died in a freak accident involving enough ketamine to kill a horse. Ironically it was the horse that killed her. It stumbled, fell, and rolled on her – but it, unlike its rider, was not under the influence.

'So, I'd guess he was right to be frantic about his daughter hurtling round the countryside on horseback,' I said. 'And maybe losing her mother may explain her weird behaviour – half unpleasant princess and half child afraid to fail. Anyway, no more school talk, or Jo and I will bore your ears off with our budget problems.'

'I could recite them in my sleep,' Lloyd said. 'But then, she knows the police service shortages by heart too. So, how are you proposing to spend this coming week of indolence? You know we're off to Cornwall for a couple of days tomorrow?'

'So, I'd better not do any Miss Marpling?'

'I'll go further: I'd like to extract a promise that you won't.'

Jo chimed in: 'You really need to take it easy, like I do – that bug was nasty.'

I grinned. 'So just a bit of gentle cycling?'

'And end up in some hedge in the middle of nowhere like you did last summer? That's a really good idea – I don't think. Now, tell us all about this ex-lodger of yours and her new abode . . .'

I waxed lyrical – I might even have exaggerated the height of the rooms, the depth of the carpet, the breadth of the vistas. 'Why can't women be Masons too?' I ended. 'I'd love a middle-aged Prince Charming to turn up in his Bentley at the golf club and provide me with a palace.'

'A couple of snags there, Jane,' Lloyd observed. 'You don't play golf and you'd say you were rattling round the rooms – just as you did when you moved into your current place.'

'I'm glad you didn't cast Brian as my Prince Charming, at least.'

'Would I dare? Who's Joy's prince, anyway?'

'A sleek guy with a wife who could double for Melania Trump – all sharp cheekbones and sharper clothes. Tony Carpenter.'

Lloyd's eyes headed briskly for his hairline, but he mimed zipping his mouth.

'Tell you what,' he said, 'instead of a rich man, you'd be better off with a cat.'

CHAPTER NINE

It wasn't a cat but a dog that an embarrassed Lloyd wished on me first thing on Monday morning in an early phone call. His mother had torn a calf playing tennis (though no one would have dared add, 'At her age?', which must have been pushing seventy). It wasn't a serious injury, but bad enough to preclude her from taking her very active Schnoodle for the long walkies it enjoyed. Geoffrey—

'Geoffrey?'

'I know. Ma's a fan of Geoffrey Boycott. But Geoffrey doesn't favour long slow innings – he's a bit of a bouncer. If he could just come and stay with you full-time for a few days, or – and this might be even more of a pain, come to think of it – maybe you could tool over to Lenham twice a day and walk him there.'

I had the strongest suspicion that there was nothing wrong with Mrs Davies senior but a strong desire on the part of her son and daughter-in-law to keep me out of trouble. I had to eat my words when I went to collect him, though. Maggie Davies had her foot up and a pair of elbow crutches.

'Marooned for five days, according to the physio. Something to do with scar tissue healing the right way,' she said. 'And there I was planning on painting the lounge.'

'Which would have been fun in itself with Geoffrey trying to help,' I pointed out.

'But so much easier without Lloyd ditto,' she said.

Geoffrey, greyish-white and about knee-height, had a smile both charming and possibly untrustworthy. He and I got used to each other while we walked down to the village store to buy supplies for her – and of course him. The only problem was when I tied him up and went inside: his howls were heart-rending.

'Don't worry – Geoffrey always does that,' the woman beside me by the pet food section assured me.

On the other hand, he was clearly an experienced passenger, waiting with ill-disguised impatience for me to clip him into the car, which was stuffed with his bed, enough toys for a playgroup and food and treats for five days, by which time Maggie assured me her physiotherapist insisted she start walking again. Clearly, he was disconcerted, to put it mildly, when he found he wasn't returning to his person, but he had a good sniff round my house – my bears had retreated to the safety of the wardrobe, where they gazed down from the very top shelf – and seemed reassured.

Geoffrey was, of course, an open sesame to the neighbours: everyone stopped to exchange doggy stories, and to introduce their various companions to him. He also gave me nominal protection (penetrating barking, rather than penetrating teeth) if I wanted to walk in places I'd normally have avoided in the dark – our estate being one of them of course. Through Geoffrey's new acquaintances I learnt that the blinds and bright lights had gone from our neighbour's house, and that, according to a neighbour I immediately got into conversation with that evening, the road was much quieter generally.

'Day and night these cars came and went. Vans, too. I mean, it's just an ordinary holiday let. I suppose we should be grateful they didn't have a big party and smash the place up,' added the woman whom I only knew as Dolly's mummy – Dolly being a scrap of a dachshund that Geoffrey treated with casual disdain. 'Apparently there have been a couple of those up at the vicarage – you wouldn't expect that at the home of a man of the cloth, would you?'

When did I last hear that term in conversation?

'After the goings-on with the last man, you'd think they'd be more . . . more considerate, wouldn't you? It's the Church's reputation we're talking about, after all.' She sniffed disparagingly. But before I could say anything, however, she asked with no change of tone or pace, 'Now, how did you come to have this handsome young man, then?'

What crazy rumour was this? Was I supposed to be involved in some ecumenical orgy? It took me a second to grasp that she meant Geoffrey. 'I'm looking after him for a friend.'

'But you're obviously used to dogs.'

'I used to have one – but he died . . .' I still couldn't explain the circumstances to anyone but my therapist. Ironically it was the involvement of the RSPCA that brought him finally to justice.

'And you didn't get another?'

'You know how it is . . . and the hours I work, it wouldn't be fair, would it?'

'I'd always walk it for you. The more the merrier.'

Dolly and Geoffrey appeared to disagree.

I shook my head. 'Thanks. But it'd be like farming out a child.'

'A lot of people do that – as you must know from experience. Poor things – in my day mothers stayed at home to look after them properly. None of this nursery business.'

'But since then the economic climate has changed, of course.'

'And not for the better, either. All this fundraising you're having to do for the school – you shouldn't have to. It's the council's job! Now, Geoffrey dear, that's rather rude, you know.'

Geoffrey was no longer ignoring Dolly – he was doing his best to get very close to her indeed.

We went our separate ways.

Our evening walk was less sociable but more intriguing. It was true that there was no longer any activity at the original house with blackouts and bright lights. Further down the road, however, at number 39, tucked away in a little sub cul-de-sac, two or three cars were parked outside another house. The driver of one was banging hard on the front window with his keys, yelling in a way not likely to endear him to Dolly's mummy.

Eventually the front door opened a crack – it was held by a chain, I think – and a young woman told him to remove himself. I didn't speak a word of her language but the gist was clear. She repeated the suggestion with considerable vigour, and managed to close the door. I'm sure she spoke an East European language, but I'd have needed Zunaid to tell me if it was Romanian.

By now I'd photographed the car and gathered up Geoffrey's offering. I also clamped my free hand over his mouth to stop him drawing attention to us by barking: I was terrified the driver might take out his frustration in the way Simon used to do, by kicking an innocent animal. In fact, there was every chance he might use a human as a punchbag instead. Then another car arrived at the same address. It took only the shortest of sentences from the first man to make the second reverse sharply and go on his way.

Geoffrey and I followed suit – an indirect way home, via the useful alleyway I'd shown Joy. Then, having locked him up, I set out again, and, with my business card in my pocket, made my way back to number 39.

'Hi,' I meant to say, 'I'm Jane, one of your new neighbours. I was wondering if you wanted to come and have a coffee tomorrow morning.'

I got as far as 'Hi.' I couldn't understand a syllable of what she was saying – and no doubt she wouldn't have understood if I'd managed to issue my invitation. What I did understand was the violent gesture sending me on my way and the slammed door.

Even though the anger and violence weren't personal, they shook me – as a reminder, even a very dilute one, of Simon's behaviour. I edged away, shaking, nauseous. I wanted—and then I wondered, dimly, what the woman might want. Was there anyone lurking behind her telling her to get rid of the unwanted visitor – just as Simon had controlled my life? If only I'd had the forethought to bring a pencil so I could scribble a note. While the impulse was still strong, I hurried home and actually wrote one – but what if this brought not her but her putative assailant to my door? Torn between self-justification and shame I tore it up.

But I did have some school headed paper. And on my computer was a copy of the letter we sent to newcomers to the village inviting them to bring their children to the school. A general, non-specific note – with the bonus that of course it had my name on it. If she was as desperate as I'd once been she might just see the connection with the visitor she'd driven away.

Breathing deeply, I forced myself back up the drive, sliding it silently through the letter box.

The next afternoon Geoffrey and I ventured as far as the school, where he sat warming my feet until he became truly bored. So ten minutes' work accomplished. Ten! I gathered up some files, stowing them in my bag. Idly I wondered if I could simply ignore them and offer an excuse: 'Someone's dog ate my homework.' But it didn't work like that for grown-ups, did it?

Our route home was via the church and then the vicarage. This was an unremarkable building, nothing like the Rectory, a lovely Georgian house owned by one of the village millionaires. The last vicar had died, as a result of what my fellow dog-walker had called goings-on. There'd been a long interregnum before the appointment of a new vicar, due to be inducted into the parish very shortly. But the diocese hadn't let the place lie empty. It had been let out on the commercial market to benefit not parish but diocesan funds, according to Carol, one of our churchwardens, bitter at the lack of a parish priest for a year. I knew how hard she'd had to work to cover the services – somehow she

97

and Mike, a new recruit to the Parochial Church Council, or PCC, had sourced retired priests, trainee priests, two archdeacons and a variety of lay people. She wouldn't have minded all the hard work if only the parish had benefited financially from the lack of a full-time vicar.

The vicarage looked very sorry for itself. Geoffrey was keen to check for canine activity. We were greeted, perhaps cautiously, by a woman probably a dozen or so years older than me, though her wild greying hair, contrasting with almost perfect skin, made it hard to judge.

Geoffrey took her smile as an invitation to put his paws on her thighs.

'No, Geoffrey!' I snapped, pulling him off and making him sit, but she shrugged aside my apology saying, with more than a grain of truth, that it would be hard for her jeans to be any dirtier. 'And I hope you won't mind if I don't shake hands with you, just Geoffrey, but I'd need to scrub mine first. Oh, my husband's the new vicar, Graham West. I'm Izzie,' she added, trying in vain to persuade Geoffrey to shake paws.

It sounded like a name straight from Thomas Hardy. 'Jane Cowan,' I responded. 'The village school head. Surely you shouldn't be doing this?' I said, pointing at a half-full skip. 'The PCC were assured that it would be professionally cleaned.'

'Cleaned, yes, perhaps – but not cleaned out, which I find I've got to do first. Well, no one said, but it's obvious, isn't it? I've never seen so much stuff – it's as if people fly-tipped in it. The magazines and DVDs . . . I know there's much worse online, but they're vile enough. Recent stuff, too: I know that the police had to remove . . . material . . . after the last incumbent's death.'

I looked her in the eye: she knew, didn't she? Mark Stephens had, as people observed, done everyone a favour by topping himself. Not the train driver under whose wheels he fell, of course. There was a rumour that the poor man was still on sick leave.

'Who on earth was it let to?'

'A pair who had sold their place and were waiting to emigrate. For some reason they cut short their tenancy, and then there was a series of short lets. You ought to see what they've done.'

'I'd be very interested.' I tried to sound neutral. 'And maybe I can give you a hand.' Geoffrey was keen to lead the way.

She shut the door behind us. 'Even the smell!' she wailed. She looked close to tears.

'Quite.' Sex and unwashed bodies overlying fresh emulsion paint – prison yellow in the hall and purple in the rooms I could see. Had someone tried to freshen up the place or to cover something they wanted kept hidden? 'Goodness! How many mattresses does a house need, for goodness' sake?' There were four or five propped against the hall wall, with another visible in what was once the study. 'Is it like this upstairs?'

'Exactly. But more a smell of cheap scent. I don't know where to start, Jane,' she prompted me as I stood arms akimbo looking at the chaos.

'You want my advice? Then you don't start. Not till you've called first the police and then the diocese office.'

'Police? Why the police?'

I spread my hands theatrically. 'This isn't normal household rubbish, Izzie. Someone's been running a business here – and, last I heard, a brothel isn't a legal business.'

'Would they be interested? I thought they tended to turn a blind eye.'

'It rather depends on whether the sex workers are there of their own volition for safety's sake – and even then it's against the law – or if the women are what the media would probably call "sex slaves".'

She went pale – to my surprise, because I'd have thought being a vicar's wife you'd all too quickly understand the vile things one human could do to another. But what she said was far more banal. 'But if the police get involved it might mean we can't move in!'

'There's no reason to suspect anyone's been killed here, is there?' I asked jokily.

She dropped her voice. 'There is some blood. Was. In the bathroom. Someone's messy period, I thought. It was the first thing I did – to clean it up.'

Did I need to tell her that it was very unlikely that she'd managed to eradicate it completely?

'Should I dial 999?'

I scratched my ear. Trust Lloyd to be on holiday when I needed him. 'It's not as if there's still a body here – Izzie, there isn't, is there? But 101 takes for ever to get through, and then you don't seem to get much action. Tell you what: I once worked with a very nice officer, DI Elaine Carberry. I could text her?'

'I wouldn't want to waste anyone's time.'

'She'll soon tell me if she thinks you are.'

Elaine rang me within a minute. 'I'm just finishing a meeting and I'll come straight over after that. It'd be good to catch up outside a hospital room.' She was another of Will's regular visitors, though I'd not seen her for a couple of months. 'See you in about an hour.'

Not so good. It meant I was closeted with Izzie for the duration, with no more work at school and a much shorter walk than I'd intended. 'You look as if you could use a cup of tea,' I said mildly.

'From that kitchen! No thank you!'

'In that case we can go back to the school – I'll text Elaine and tell her.' As she locked up behind us I continued, 'When did you say you planned to move in, by the way?'

'This time next week.'

I frowned, and not just at a delighted, effervescent Geoffrey who clearly thought we had another adventure ahead of us. 'Do you have to get permission from the PCC to change locks, and so on?'

'What a strange question!'

'If people squatted in an empty house, there's always the chance they might do it again. And I gather squatters are the very devil to remove.'

'Surely . . . Actually, you mean it, don't you? Won't it be expensive to get a locksmith in?'

I was only going to offer to do it myself, wasn't I? Like when, Jane? 'The guy who's done the security for both my schools is very reasonable, and he'd probably give a discount if I leant on him. Ecclesiastical, if not educational. He's a good honest man and wouldn't overcharge anyway. In fact, since you have to live here, I do think the PCC or the diocese should pay. The churchwarden's a decent woman and would surely try to tap any budget she had if she saw this lot. You have shown her, haven't you? Oh, Izzie! This isn't just your problem, you know.'

CHAPTER TEN

I hardly recognised Elaine Carberry when we met her outside the vicarage. Wearing a very sharp suit and boots to die for, she'd lost weight and changed her haircut and colour.

'HRT time,' she said gleefully in response to my widened eyes. 'Plus Robin's got an incredibly high cholesterol count so we're on a joint diet.' Robin was in a branch of the National Crime Agency dealing with the sort of online images he wouldn't even talk about, preferring long conversations about cricket. Actually, I was glad that there was a physical reason – all too often I'd seen changes like that in women of my acquaintance when they were embarking on new relationships, and I liked both her and Robin too much to contemplate their hurt if the marriage wobbled.

'I really think Jane's overreacted,' Izzie said as they shook hands. 'Squatters, that's all it is. And now they've gone. All I need to do is clear up.'

'Well, I'm here now, getting a bit of country air, so there's no harm in my taking a look, is there?' Elaine spoke so kindly and reasonably that had I been Izzie I'd have taken immediate offence. She stood aside for Izzie to unlock the door.

Izzie gasped. 'I was sure I locked it. Sure. But maybe . . .'

'Golly, a kid with a bit of wire could have dealt with the lock in five seconds flat.' Elaine produced plastic overshoes from her elegant shoulder bag. 'Yes, put these on, will you – I know you've been in and out, but there may still be bits of stuff on the carpet and elsewhere that will bring a smile to the faces of our scenes of crime people.'

'But—'

In her own way Elaine was as steely as Paula; without being abrupt, let alone abrasive, she waited till we'd both followed her in donning the protective footwear. 'Excellent. Now, what have we here? What was it that worried you, Jane?'

Me. Not Izzie. 'Apart from all these mattresses and the smell? Well, jokingly I asked Izzie about blood, and I gather there was some in the bathroom.'

'Which I've already cleaned up,' Izzie said. 'Someone with a messy period, that's all.'

I wouldn't let myself exchange a glance with Elaine.

'Let's go and have a look. Could you just shove your hands in your pockets and try not to touch anything?'

'Would you rather we stayed down here or even in the garden? You can trust us, but I can't vouch for Geoffrey.'

Elaine's rare smile emerged. 'You know what, he looks to me as if he needs a tree. I might as well have those back.' She held out her hand for our unused overshoes. 'Then I shall actually need you, Izzie, to see it in case anything's been disturbed.'

I don't think Izzie realised what she was implying: that Izzie had indeed locked the door and that someone had been in – and with luck – out in the space of that empty hour.

'See you in a moment or two.' She closed the door behind us. 'Oh, some of my team should be along in a few minutes.' She looked at me meaningfully.

I nearly screamed in frustration, because I could have won gold for Team GB in the Nosiness Olympics, but I followed Geoffrey obediently as he snuffled his way round the garden. I also tried to make conversation with Izzie, but it was clear she was in what I would have called in one of my pupils a silly strop. Yes, I had gone too far, too fast. I'd barged in and taken over a situation that was absolutely nothing to do with me. I ought to apologise, but equally I knew I'd done the right thing. The speed with which Elaine, a woman as busy as me, had appeared, seemed to confirm that.

The silence between us deepened.

It was Geoffrey who broke it. Having left several messages, he turned his attention to the end of the garden separated from the lawn and flower beds by a sagging trellis. There was a collection of empty flowerpots, a greenish plastic compost bin and an incinerator surely far too small to deal with the amount of rubbish even a small garden like this would generate. Yes – someone had actually had a bonfire on what was surely a rhubarb patch.

Not everything had burnt, and it was the residue that attracted Geoffrey's attention.

Izzie grabbed my arm. 'Why should anyone burn new shoes?'

'Can you think of any good reason?' I asked grimly.

'I think we should tell Elaine,' she said in a barely

audible whisper. 'Or those policemen just arriving.'

Their arrival coincided with Elaine's reappearance – she was beckoning Izzie to check over the house. So it fell to me to show her colleagues what Geoffrey had found. For some reason one of them had dog treats to hand. She made a friend for life.

'So all this suspicious activity in your estate has been logged, Jane?' Elaine confirmed, as, leaving a couple of officers on guard, we returned to my office in the school, much to Geoffrey's confusion, though he welcomed the water I poured into a redundant flowerpot saucer. We had to drink our coffee black, but none of us complained.

'Except for one incident, which may or not have been significant.' I told her about the woman at number 39 sending me emphatically about my business. 'Apart from that, everything should be. But I gather you've had as much fun with the flu and norovirus as we have, so maybe not everything's where it should be.'

'You don't need to apologise for our failures, even assuming there are any. I admit nothing's come to my ears, not yet anyway, but that might mean that the reports seem random, with no sign of a pattern. And if you show me the house where you saw the ultra-bright lights and the one with the irate woman then I'll think about our next move. And as for young Zunaid, I'd like a trained officer to talk to him about what he heard. God knows how long it'll take to find one and fix an appointment, though. God, these cuts! The usual woman's just started maternity leave. I assume we'll get a replacement but don't hold your breath.' She seemed to notice Izzie for the first time. 'After all you've been through, I'm not surprised you look knackered. But going round your new place with me was a really brave thing to do, and helpful too. If someone did move stuff while you were over here, then it gives us a time frame for our enquiries.'

'Items were moved?' I squeaked.

'I think so,' Izzie said, 'but I can't be sure. I thought there were a couple more black sacks . . . But the place is in such a mess I can't swear . . .'

Not one for overt emotion, Elaine continued briskly, 'Obviously you need to upgrade your security immediately – what's that, Jane?' She took the printout I gave her with the locksmith's details. 'Yes, use the firm the school uses and bill your PCC. Oh, and tell them I want a copy of the key the moment they've finished. Jonah – that's the guy you deal with, isn't it, Jane? It's a good job you haven't moved out of your existing property. I'd advise you to stay put and hang the consequences.'

'We can't. It's needed for my husband's replacement. And we're here in an arrangement called house-for-duty: my husband and I live for free in the vicarage in exchange for him working in the benefice.'

'Christ, that sounds medieval! Sorry, God.'

It was hard to read Izzie's expression: maybe she was simply trying not to look offended or perhaps she had more serious concerns than a bit of casual blasphemy. She replied firmly, 'It is in a way, but it suits us because Graham has a good pension from his previous employer and we can let out our property in London. And he doesn't work quite full-time.'

'In theory, anyway,' I muttered. My experience of part-time workers in a variety of roles told me that employers usually got far more than value for money from them. 'I'd agree, Izzie, that this is a problem for the PCC and ultimately the diocese, since having a house is fundamental to your deal. They want Graham – they house Graham: that'd be my take on it.'

'Dealings with the Church of England aren't always as clear cut as that,' Izzie said darkly, getting to her feet.

Under my breath I repeated an urgent mantra: 'Not my problem. Not my problem. Absolutely not my problem.'

Elaine seemed to share my view. 'You have a roof over your head for a few days at least. I shall need your address. Meanwhile, we need to get you over to Ashford so you can make a short statement about what you saw and what you did. Do you know the area? Could you make your own way there? – it'll save an awful lot of to-ing and fro-ing if you could. Let me just make sure someone's there to meet you.' She turned away to speak into her phone.

'I'm so sorry, Izzie,' I began, standing too.

She tightened her lips. 'I suppose in a way I should be grateful. Imagine if you're right and it is a crime scene. My God, what if I really did wash away evidence?' She sat down hard.

'I think they'll have electronic equipment to detect any you left behind.'

'Oh, absolutely,' Elaine chipped in. 'And actually, Izzie, though you did quite a good job, you missed some. So our clever people will be able to test it. Menstrual blood's quite different in composition from the everyday stuff, by the way, so we should be able to eliminate it, in the old cliché, from our enquiries.' She fished a card from her bag and wrote on it in a lovely clear script. 'If you're sure you can make it to

Ashford, show this to whoever is on Reception. They'll sort out both a parking space and someone to take your statement immediately. Thank you so much for being so understanding.' With a technique I used myself, she swept us from the room.

We walked with her back to her car – I noticed Elaine didn't return the soon-to-be-redundant house key – and waved her off. 'I ought to have offered to go with her, oughtn't I?' I said.

'She's a grown woman. She could have asked if she wanted you to. I wonder what she does when she's not being Mrs Vicar.'

'Funny – I never thought to ask. I know I told her my job, but she never responded in kind.'

We exchanged a mildly puzzled shrug.

'And now to Little Orchard Close. Mind if we go in my car? Will the dog be OK? I know he should be anchored, but . . .'

'He won't tell if you don't,' I assured her.

Kicking her boots off in my kitchen, Elaine made calls while I made tea. The conversations obviously weren't private – in fact, she was probably ensuring I didn't have to ask for information she'd given to someone else. The gist was that she wanted the records of all the calls logged in connection with the immediate area so her team could start work. She also wanted access to number 33. A bit of attention to number 39 wouldn't come amiss.

There was a mutter from the far end.

She snarled, 'There can't be all that many letting agencies, for God's sake. At this stage I don't want the bother of a warrant – a friendly estate agent or whatever will understand that.' She ended the call. 'You must know all the letting agencies in Kent after your peregrinations!'

'Lovely word, Elaine – I've always got space for an extra literacy assistant, you know. Actually, I do know one agent reasonably well. He does a lot round here. James Ford. He's a decent guy and has been really kind to me. He'd also want to know if there's a problem like the one at the vicarage. Shall I call him now?'

'That might save a lot of bother. What nectar this green tea is – I've never come across anything like it before. Smells of roses! Hey, can I snitch that apple? All these kilos later, I still can't persuade my stomach not to rumble at tea-and-biscuit time.'

'The tenants,' James told us, as he unlocked the front door of number 33, 'were due to leave this coming weekend. I'd no idea they'd already departed and left the property empty. Not part of their agreement at all.' He stopped on the threshold. 'Wow!'

I expected a repeat of the vicarage chaos, and I'm sure Elaine did too. What James revealed, however, was a completely pristine interior, smelling strongly of fresh paint. I'd swear the carpets were new, too.

'I must have a fairy godmother!' he breathed.

'Or,' said Elaine, more prosaically, 'tenants who made such a mess they had to have a radical clean up.'

James's eyes rounded. 'You mean—'

She pulled the door shut, put out her hand for the key and said almost smugly, 'Let's just say that you can put a coat of paint over a mess, but you can't pull wool over our experts' eyes.'

* * *

Geoffrey was still asleep in his basket when we got back, but immediately marked down James as a soft-hearted man who would probably know where I'd stowed the dog treats.

Elaine, however, was more concerned with eliciting facts. 'Is your firm responsible for letting out number 39, too?'

One hand on Geoffrey's head, he fished out his phone and scrolled down. 'No, I'm afraid not. I've a dim idea that it's a private let. It isn't one of Brian's, is it, Jane?'

I shrugged – not a huge, outraged, 'how should I know?' shrug, but one that suggested perhaps Elaine's team should contact him. 'This is his number,' I said, jotting it down for her.

'That's the pompous git who chairs your governors and fancies you? OK, rhetorical question.'

'I told you – I could use literacy experts like you.'

Much to Geoffrey's dismay, James left almost immediately.

'Time I was off too,' Elaine declared. 'But before I go, there's just one question. Of all the officers in Kent, why should you contact me? I'm not your average general crime investigator, as you know. I specialise—'

'In migration and people trafficking. And I've got yet another set of people you might be interested in too: some guys at a pop-up car wash. All middle-aged. All dressed in rags. All emaciated. And not one of them speaking English.'

'My car's due a clean – point me to them.'

CHAPTER ELEVEN

Technically I'd not wasted a whole day, but it did feel as if I had. The bagful of work I should have completed now sat in my study, regarding me balefully. Why not delay supper even longer and make a start now? Geoffrey had had enough excitement for one day and could wait till later for his walk. Or I could open one of the bottles of wine Joy had left behind, put my feet up and indulge? There were even some of her meals in the freezer.

The phone.

'Brian, here, Jane. I wonder if I might trouble you for some more of your invaluable advice. Perhaps we might meet for supper at the Cricketers?'

Advice? Especially invaluable advice. I was intrigued: I associated Brian more with dishing it out than accepting it. The Cricketers was always a good choice. On the other hand Diane strongly discouraged dogs in the bar, a practice of which I'd hitherto approved whole-heartedly, and I wasn't sure I should leave him in a strange house, his battery of toys notwithstanding.

We would meet at eight-thirty. Geoffrey would have to take his chance tethered in the deep porch outside the bar, or maybe his pretty face and tiptoe walk would soften Diane's heart enough for her to make an exception. I pocketed a supply of treats and a couple of poo-bags. Yes, I'd need my torch. Geoffrey peered at me through his extraordinarily long eyelashes: clearly, he couldn't understand the logic of turning out in a dark and now rainy night. And he really did not like being left outside the bar, even though there was a kennel of sorts and a supply of water. Tough. He was a dog.

Again Brian looked old and tired, responding to my question about his health with a worried shake of the head. 'It seems I'm not quite as fine as I thought I was. Angina. I've got a spray and some more pills and been referred for a battery of tests. Quickly. I should avoid stress,' he added, sitting heavily. 'And stress seems to be following me around. God, Jane, I could use a drink.'

'It's OK with your medication?'

'In moderation and preferably red wine.'

At least moderation meant he'd be able to drive himself home. So we ordered Shiraz and a bowl of olives. Catching my eye, Diane raised an appreciative but amused eyebrow: were we really becoming an item? My answer would have been an emphatic negative: having seen more of his worse side than his good, I still didn't really trust Brian, and though I respected him in some situations, I hadn't found myself liking him in many.

'Have you heard from your guest since she left?' he

asked unexpectedly. Or perhaps not. He seemed to have been interested in Joy's presence as soon as she arrived.

'She says she's fallen on her feet. She loves their friend's apartment. Ken is getting better every day and is capable of dealing with the insurance. I gather he's tried to tell Paula—'

'That's your builder extraordinaire—'

'That sums her up nicely. He's tried to tell her how to do her job, which since her prompt actions stabilised the house long enough for the insurance company to decide whether to rebuild or repair – and opt for the latter, as it happens – is pretty foolish. He doesn't want her walking away now.'

'But that means your own project will be delayed even longer.'

'Apparently not. Paula and Caffy have recruited some more workers, and of course Paula can supervise both sites simply by standing outside one and yelling across the flattened fence at the workers on the other – as I have no doubt she would if she ever had to raise her voice. I shan't have to trouble you more than six weeks longer than we agreed,' I added.

'"Trouble" isn't a word I associate with your tenancy. But – and this is why I wanted to talk to you – I seem to be having problems with one of your temporary neighbours. Their next-door neighbour has complained and they're being very awkward about giving me access.'

Why on earth should he want to consult me? I wasn't a property millionaire. 'Not number 39, by any chance?'

'Number 4, as it happens. Why do you ask about 39?' His voice was decidedly sharp.

'Because the woman there's had a couple of importunate visitors – loud, violent-voiced men.'

To my amazement, he covered my hand with his. 'Poor Jane – it must have awakened very unpleasant memories. But that life's behind you now. You're part of a community that likes and respects you – cares for you.' He spoke as if the last verb was hard to frame.

'Thank you. I appreciate your saying that,' I said, rather formally, and then withdrew my hand, not so abruptly that he could take offence, but not too slowly either.

From outside came a banshee wail. It reduced everyone in the bar to silence. Another wail. It had to be – dear God, it had to be Geoffrey, didn't it? 'My responsibility,' I groaned as I made for the door.

He trotted in with a smile on his face. Diane didn't return it. 'Sorry, Jane. If you want I can put you and it in the function room while you eat, or I'll put whatever you order in foil as a takeaway if you care to wait outside. Up to you.'

Scarlet with embarrassment, I nodded. 'Fair enough.' I turned to Brian, but he was taking a phone call, which didn't seem to be going well. He was oblivious to Geoffrey's presence and its effects.

'I'm so sorry, Jane – I have to go. Something very inconvenient has popped up. Oh, who's this?'

'A dog I'm looking after. So, your going's not a problem. We've got to go too. Sorry, everyone.'

I should have spoken fiercely to Geoffrey. Indeed, I did talk pretty firmly. But perhaps I wasn't as emphatic as I should have been. He might have led me into one embarrassing situation, but he'd probably saved me from one even worse. However, despite all his blandishments, he wasn't going to sleep on my bed. He wasn't even going to come upstairs. Ok, so I ended up sitting with him in the kitchen till he fell asleep, but in the end I won.

Wednesday dawned dark and dull, with rain slashing audibly on the windows. Just the weather for dog walking. And, actually, for getting through a great deal of work. The question was, here or at school? If I walked to school, that would constitute a good walk for us both. In my rucksack I packed enough for Geoffrey's needs, including a thick towel, a supply of food for us both and a change of clothes, despite the waterproof everything that covered me from hair to toes. His complete disbelief at having to set out made me wonder how Maggie Davies had dealt with vile weather, though from what little I'd seen of her I'd have thought she'd be feisty enough to stride through blizzards.

I had just towelled Geoffrey down and stripped off my rainwear when someone rang the doorbell. The screen showed Brian waving rather self-consciously at the little camera. He had both the key and the security code at his disposal, but I liked his courtesy in letting me know I had a visitor. Geoffrey retired to his blanket with a couple of treats and his favourite toy, a distressingly realistic rubber hen, oven-ready but for the very vivid head.

'It's about Cassandra Preston,' he said, nodding as I pointed at the coffee machine and stowing his umbrella in the plastic bucket I'd used for mine. 'Yes, please. Black is fine. Thanks.'

Since I'd not yet set the heating to override I flicked the fan heater on and sat at Melanie's desk, pointing him to the visitor's chair, which was actually more comfortable than the equivalent in my office – a conscious tactic, as it happens, to deter protracted visits.

'I'm going to visit Cassandra tomorrow,' he said heavily. 'Would you believe it, it's the first time I've ever been to a prison? But I thought as a friend – as a former friend – I might be able to talk some sense into her about this obsession with finding what I still think are non-existent paintings in Wray Episcopi school. Thank goodness I'm not a governor there! I might bring some little influence to bear . . . I used to play bridge with her, for goodness' sake!'

'I suppose she thinks – assuming they do exist – that they might be valuable. But her solicitor's letters have never specified an artist or artists. "Please return our Monets" I could understand. It's very kind of you, Brian, but it could be stressful. Do you think you should wait till you've had the all-clear from your doctor?'

'That may be some time coming. I didn't have time to tell you last night, but he thinks I'm looking at bypass surgery – at the very least a stent or two. He's booked me in to see a consultant. I thought I'd try to sort this out . . . while I can.'

Even while I was expressing hope and saying everything positive, I couldn't shake from my mind what the villainous Edmund says in *King Lear*, about wanting to do some good before he dies. In the event, of course, Edmund was too late. And he did die. But I didn't think modern medicine regarded stent insertion as anything other than pretty routine, if serious, surgery. But it became an evil little earworm . . . Wanting to do some good before . . . Wanting to do some good before . . .

'Do you think,' I asked quickly, as if to stop the words bursting out, 'that her grandfather might have given them to someone else? Or asked someone to look after them?'

116

He looked as if Geoffrey had spoken. 'But she's adamant they were given to Wray Episcopi School.'

I nodded. 'But people – what did Hillary Clinton call it? Misremembering? That's it. People misremember. Tell her the school has been subjected to a police search. Tell her none of the staff ever recall ever seeing anything that could loosely be described as art, apart from the stuff the kids produce. And even the most delusional parent wouldn't confuse little Johnny's painting with a masterpiece in oils.'

'They would these days,' Brian said darkly. 'Think of the parents who praise appalling violin scrapings or pretend the child can hop when it needs two feet.'

We shared a laugh. Geoffrey got up, wagging his tail.

'That dog,' Brian asked. 'How did he arrive in your life?'

'He's not a permanent fixture, I'm afraid. His person has a leg injury – can't give him his daily walkies. Sorry, Geoffrey, I didn't mean we were going to have one now. Back to Squeaky Chicken. Good boy. So he's only here till the weekend. I shall miss him and be relieved in equal measure – after that fiasco last night! I hope it didn't embarrass you.'

'If it did, my instant departure would have embarrassed you. So I think we're quits, don't you?' He put down his mug. 'I can see you came to work, so I'll take my leave of you. But I'll report back, if I may?'

'I'd be more than grateful. Don't let the visit upset you. Prisons aren't nice places, though a women's jail might be less awful than the male equivalent, I suppose. But remember your health is worth more than any picture.'

CHAPTER TWELVE

'Yoo-hoo! Geoffrey!' It was Dolly's mummy, like me braving the drizzle that seemed to be almost as drenching as the proper rain earlier in the day.

I wasn't taking Geoffrey for his evening walk at seven-ten precisely for nothing. One reason might have been that he'd been housebound while I'd done a supermarket run and stocked up in a way that would have made Joy proud. However, more importantly, seven-ten was the time we'd met Dolly before. Would we meet them again? We were in luck.

Casually, I waited for them, keeping Geoffrey on a somewhat tighter leash. I didn't want any public displays of lust tonight, not when I wanted to pick Dolly's mummy's brain. She obviously knew far more about the estate than I did, and I was sure she would talk as we walked. I would be hiding in plain sight: what could be less threatening than two women swathed against the weather walking two small dogs? The first thing was to establish her name. Mrs Jennings. But I was to call her Enid. All girls together, then. As we walked gently round, far more slowly than was Geoffrey's wont, I asked her about each of the neighbours in turn – which had dogs, which hadn't. Of course, her answers weren't confined to canine ownerships. She gave me snippets about practically everyone. The downside of this was of course that she must gossip about me to everyone else: I must obviously keep my life as blameless as I could.

Number 2, I discovered, was owned, but rarely occupied, by a career criminal, who somehow managed to evade the new proceeds of crime legislation and keep his property. Number 5—

'Someone was saying something about the people at number 4,' I murmured.

'Oh, that! It's one of your friend's properties. At least people say he's your friend?' The tone of her voice invited me to deny him, in the manner of St Peter, so she could dish the dirt.

'Brian Dawes? Yes, he's my landlord, and he's the chair of the school governors – and very hard he works too.'

'You're not an item, then?' Amazingly she managed to imply disappointment that I might be lovelorn and satisfaction that she could speak freely. 'Some would say he's a very good catch.' As if I was a Jane Austen protagonist. She clearly didn't think much of him, however.

I'd have loved to ask why not, but couldn't manage to stoop so low. I gave a sort of sideways explanation of why there was no possibility we might be together, which had the benefit of being partly true. 'You may have heard I was friendly with a police officer. He was grievously injured last year – he's still in a deep coma.'

'Oh, of course – you poor girl. But that doesn't stop Brian Dawes sniffing after you. Well, that's men for you – and you an attractive young woman, still, of course. Now, the lady at number 5 is a professional woman – like yourself. She works in a hospital. Number 7 – that's the Staffie family – I don't have much to do with them, though, not until they muzzle that dog of theirs.'

We got all the way to the high 30s with no information worth talking about.

'There seemed to be a bit of trouble at number 39 the other night,' I said mildly.

'If you ask me, she's no better than she ought to be.' Where had she dredged up that expression from? 'All these men trying to see her and she's shouting the odds and slamming the door.'

'You don't get the idea they're harassing her?'

There was a puzzled silence. At last she conceded, 'It's hard to tell with these foreigners. Time they all went home.' When I didn't immediately concur, she added, 'It'd make your job a lot easier, all these migrants' children taking up your time.'

'We only have a couple – and they're actually refugees, escaping from a terrible war zone. You probably remember that lovely service we had at the village church for a refugee child who was killed here, and the archbishop came. One of my pupils planted a tree.' Was I being assertive enough? Probably not. I should be nailing my colours firmly to the mast. But perhaps softly, softly might in time change the mind of someone whose opinions I could never share.

120

We waited while first one dog, then the other left a few messages. Then I had to use the poo-bag.

'You know what some people have started doing? Bagging up their dog mess – as they should! – and then dumping the bag on people's walls. And one hung some on my friend's tree! Would you believe it!'

I could be properly, genuinely shocked. By now we'd circled round and were approaching number 14. I got my house key out. 'You were saying something about number 4 – Brian Dawes' place,' I prompted.

'Was I? Well, I think it's time he looked into it – there are a lot of flies around, even at this time of year. Mind you, it's well maintained – the post's gathered up every day, and the bins and sacks are put out and taken in on the right days. The garden's a bit of a mess, but then, it is February and maybe they haven't done their spring tidy-up yet. It must be in their contract to get it done, same as it is in yours.'

Now wasn't the time to confide that part of my deal with Brian was that I had a regular gardener – at his expense. Or maybe I paid for it in a higher rental. That wouldn't surprise me.

We came to a halt at the end of my drive. 'I really enjoyed our chat,' Enid said. 'I feel so much safer being with another person, not just Dolly. If there was a problem, I'd be defending her, not the other way round.'

'All I can say about Geoffrey's heroism is that he howls very well. Is this the time you two usually take a walk? Because I agree with you. One equals exercise with a poo-bag, two means a nice chat.' And spying on one's neighbours.

* * *

121

I didn't want to spy on Izzie West, just to contact her to ask how she was getting on after yesterday's difficulties – but I didn't have her number. Nor in all honesty could I ask Elaine Carberry for it. The best I could do was to ask Elaine to pass on my number in case Izzie should want to speak to me, so, while my supper was microwaving, I texted her to that effect.

Her reply came just as I was settling Geoffrey for the night.

Sorry. Major incident north of Thames – all hands on deck. But wd be gd to catch up tomorrow – have U got time for lunch over here in Ashford?
CU by the front entrance 12.30?
Better make it 1.00.

It was only as I finished my meal that it dawned on me that Elaine had never had time for lunch before. Neither had I for that matter. And despite an hour dealing with some really exciting statistics, a little niggle of anxiety remained. Did she know something about Will that I didn't?

On Thursday morning I decided to drive past Joy's house and mine en route to a session working at Wray Episcopi school.

I found Caffy in charge of the building site – while Paula was sometimes disconcertingly brusque, Caffy was often disconcertingly empathetic. 'I still don't see you moving in here,' she said, although it was quite clear that progress was being made. 'Too many associations with last summer's case – and in particular Will.'

Sometimes I couldn't stop myself wincing when someone mentioned his name. Caffy wrapped me in an immediate hug. 'I'm sorry. But I suspect you'll not stop worrying about the poor man until he's finally allowed to die,' she said, the kindness of her tone and the concern in her face belying the crudeness of the words. 'Have you had a chance to talk to one of his care team?'

'I've no official right to – and they have to observe patient confidentiality, of course. What I'm afraid of,' I added, because I could always say things to Caffy that I didn't even admit to myself I was thinking, 'is that they'll dredge up some distant relative who's not seen him for years who will raise all sorts of legal objections to whatever the courts decide. Caffy, there was stuff in the papers about new tests showing that even those in the deepest comas could be stimulated into brief periods of quasi-consciousness: what if they do that to Will?'

'It'd muddy all sorts of moral waters, wouldn't it? Why's your car shaking, Jane?'

'I suspect it's Geoffrey the dog telling me he's bored. Have you got time to come and meet him?'

'What sort is he? Because I can't get near long-haired ones. Or cats, for that matter. I wheeze. I sneeze. I weep.'

'He's a short-haired, hypoallergenic one – a schnoodle. I think you'd like him . . .'

'Maybe I'll just wave through the window . . .'

An apologetic text arrived from Elaine as I parked near Wray Episcopi school: she was going to be tied up much longer than she expected: would tomorrow work? Better still Saturday? Maybe with Robin?

Saturday fine, I texted back. *Nice pub near Lenham?*

Saturday was the day I was due to return Geoffrey to Maggie Davies, and I had an idea I was going to need cheering up afterwards. Meanwhile here at Wray Episcopi there would be a mountain of work. While Tom would soon be back at Wrayford to deal with any crises there, here I had no second-in-command: Jess had asked to take off the whole half-term break to fulfil a longstanding commitment. Donna, the secretary, was due in, however, and would no doubt already be working her way through the correspondence so she could brief me when I arrived.

'If the mist clears,' as I unclipped him, making sure his lead was firmly attached as I did so, 'we'll have a nice long walk.'

Possibly. But just in case I'd bought a towel as well as some toys.

Donna was already at her desk when we walked in, greeting Geoffrey with pleasure. We worked through quite happily till lunchtime on pleasurable admin: very well, I exaggerate. But a bit of concentrated efficient work always made me feel better afterwards. Only as we ate our lunches did I deal with what was in some ways a more important question: Lulabelle Petrie. Of course, I had access to her file, with all the pupil records and reports in it, but long and detailed as they were – and these days had to be – they were so full of the phrases Ofsted like to hear that in fact they said nothing, not about the child herself. Orwell must be rotating in his grave at the number of clichés educated and intelligent people are almost required to use these days. But I wasn't going to rant at an entirely innocent Donna over my taramasalata: I just wanted her take on Lulabelle, whom she probably saw around the village as well as in school. And where even the most irritating pupils generally moderated their behaviour when their head was on the prowl, the secretary might not have the same effect.

'I knew her mother,' Donna said. 'Not well,' she added in response to my slight gasp. 'She was a teenager when I was a little girl. She was what was called "hoity-toity" in those days.'

'Come on, Donna, you sound as if you were around when *Lark Rise to Candleford* was written!'

She looked at me with an unreadable expression. 'You're neither a Kentish woman nor a woman of Kent, Jane. You never will be. In many ways you're lucky. Metropolitan. Travelled. Well, north of the M25. But people like my gran – she never even went to London till Princess Diana's death when she wanted to lay some flowers – are horrified by all sorts of things you find normal, you know. Gay marriage. Bringing a black woman to teach in a white school. She wanted me to resign when she heard Jess was coming here. We had quite a to-do about it. I can say Jess is great, that we're mates and go clubbing together – of course we do! Didn't you know? – but Nan still has what she calls "reservations".'

There was a lot I wanted to ask, but there was one question more important than the rest. 'Do those kids try it on with Jess?'

'They did. My God they did! But they picked the wrong woman. And I gather you said something to them?'

'Not directly. I wouldn't undermine her like that.'

'Jess didn't think you would. But Lulabelle went back into class in tears one day. She wouldn't explain but the rumour went round she'd been seen talking to you in the corridor.'

'She probably had. I'd been suggesting that she stood as a school council rep, but she was adamant she couldn't, which surprised me because my take on her was that she was confident and articulate. Actually, I was very impressed by her poise when I came across her in public.'

Donna narrowed her eyes. 'But?'

Was I as transparent as that? I sidestepped. 'What do we know about her father? I gather her mother died.'

'He's like you, an incomer. Actually, he's an incomer in two senses, if you see what I mean: a very big income indeed.' She paused so I could wince at her pun. 'No one knows how he gets his money, but there's always speculation in a village. They had Zunaid down as your love-child at one time, by that black police protection officer who came and stayed a couple of times,' she added affably. 'The thing is, Jane, you live not just in a slightly larger, more commuter-based village, you live in that funny little estate—'

'It's more like the suburb of a town than part of the village, isn't it?' I agreed.

'But you join in. You're involved with the cricket. Diane at the pub rates you. Joining the Speed Watch team was a big plus. To quote my nan, "If she stays another twenty years she might become one of us."'

'Tell your nan thank you from me. I think.' It was the word 'might' that chilled me. 'Now, Lulabelle. And her rich dad – who doesn't seem to have put in too many appearances at parents' evenings, especially since I arrived. I actually had to introduce myself to him. So embarrassing!'

'Oh, that's probably because he's got a woman. Nan thinks she's a tart, to use her word. In other words, a live-in lover.'

Poor woman, damned for doing something that was quite normal, just outside Nan's ambit.

126

But Donna seemed to agree with her grandmother. 'She does look a bit . . . a bit obvious,' she continued. 'A bit too much leg and cleavage. And much too much make-up, especially for the country. And you should see her shoes! I know you wore high heels when you came down here, but you soon twigged they were daft on our roads. Not her, though. Heels this high – higher.' Her finger and thumb separated alarmingly, before she giggled. 'What finished her off in Nan's eyes was that they had little bows on the back! Whatever she is or does, she's not trying to fit in,' she concluded.

Our laughter disturbed Geoffrey's slumber: the purposeful way he stood and stretched said all too clearly he needed a walk.

'Any idea how Lulabelle gets on with her?' I asked, fastening Geoffrey's lead firmly.

'None at all. Now we've got no shop it's hard to pick up gossip, isn't it? Her dad's a bit weird, though.'

The phone rang; Geoffrey had the temerity to scratch at the door.

'It's for you. Someone from the council. Look, shall I take him? We could go for a quick circuit of the village.'

I handed her a couple of poo bags. 'Take your phone and make sure he stays on his lead, however much he pleads. Promise? I've never risked letting him off yet and he goes home this weekend.'

CHAPTER THIRTEEN

I was so absorbed first by the phone call and then finding the information that the caller needed instantly that I lost track of the time. It came like a slap on the face to realise Donna and Geoffrey had been gone an hour, and that heavy mist was now swathing the place in grey. Had she somehow lost him, but was determined not to come back without him? By the time the idea was fully formed, I was pulling on my boots with one hand and phoning her with the other. When I was sent straight to voicemail, I was ready to run.

Where to?

Towards the village, of course. Where else?

In my anxiety, I could almost hear him whining.

I could hear him whining. And scratching at the door. But when I flung it open expecting to see Donna's apologetic face, there was no one there – just a small wet dog so dirty it was scarcely recognisable as Geoffrey.

His lead was still attached.

Though he was overjoyed to see me, and wanted to be fussed over like a prodigal son, he refused to come in. Refused. Back legs braced. No amount of cajoling would bring him in. Not even his favourite treats.

Where was my brain? I had to go with him, didn't I? Yes, I had my phone. I grabbed the small first-aid kit I keep in the car and took firm hold of his lead. 'Find Donna!'

I'll swear I heard him say, 'At bloody last!' as he set off at a spanking pace.

The lay-by that Eoin and I had looked at. Yes, he was definitely heading there. Not the bloody woods! Not in this fog.

I tried Donna's phone again. Nothing.

Now he wanted to go up the narrower of the paths.

As before, I saw Will's broken body and battered face. Geoffrey was tugging the lead with all his might. But just as his legs had locked earlier, now mine did. I must have been crying because something dripped off my nose, my chin.

Geoffrey came back and put his paws on my legs. Then he backed off, growling. He'd registered what I must have heard but not responded to – the slam of a car door and rapid footsteps behind me.

I wheeled round to find myself facing a police officer in full kit, looking grim. He spoke first. 'What the hell's the matter? Hey, call that little bugger off me. My God – it's Jean, isn't it?'

And there I'd flattered myself I might have made a bit of an impression on him. 'Jane.'

Geoffrey was still baring his teeth. Mud or not, I gathered him up. 'It's OK. It's Eoin. He's one of the good guys.'

Mopping my tears just spread mud all over my face. Any moment now I'd get hysterical. 'Eoin, do you remember—' I began, but then stopped abruptly. Keep to the facts. 'I think the school secretary may be somewhere in there too injured to move. She took Geoffrey here for a walk and he came back without her. To find me. He brought me here. And wants to lead me to her, I think. But – it was in a similar situation I found Will, and—'

'Flashback? Happens. OK, will he lead me up, do you think?' It wasn't the leading that was the problem, but Eoin's safety, I rather thought, from Geoffrey's teeth.

'Do you?' I asked dryly. I must be getting better.

'Shall I come with you? He'll be all right, will he, if I do?'

Forcing myself every metre of the way, I set out, trying to keep Geoffrey close to my side. Eoin followed me at a distance, muttering into his radio or phone – I was too busy keeping my eyes on the path ahead and trying not to think about anything to check. 'Have you tried her phone? We might at least hear it, if that bloody animal would just shut the fuck up.'

I tried. Voicemail.

'We'll just have to trust him. He's not done so badly so far.'

By now he was frantic, pulling me off what was left of a track. And there she was. Flat on her face. 'Eoin!'

One moment he was behind me, the next pushing ahead and, his body between me and Donna, was calling her name.

'No trauma that I can see,' he said, over his shoulder. 'Not like Will at all. Understand? Not like Will at all. But we need to get her to hospital before she gets hyperthermia. I'm calling for help now.' He spoke to me as if I was a child. In a sense I certainly wasn't reacting like an adult. But soon

I was beside him, stripping off my coat and handing him my first-aid kit.

'I'd say she twisted her ankle and then fell and clunked her forehead,' he said, pointing. 'Come on, Donna, pull yourself together. We need to have a conversation here. Jane, you talk to her: she'll maybe recognise your voice. And that bloody animal's, of course.'

I waved Donna, protesting almost as loudly as Geoffrey had been, into the ambulance, thanking God that she had family and friends handy to meet her in A & E. At last, I turned to Eoin to apologise for making such a cake of myself. The question of how and indeed why he'd turned up when he did hung unspoken in the air.

'En route from A to B,' he said helpfully. 'I like to go via lanes and villages I don't know very well in case I ever need to go through them fast. So my A to B is often via G and H.' His radio crackled, and he opened his car door. 'And here's a call to Z. You'll be all right?' he asked as an afterthought.

'My car's parked just up the road.' But I would have welcomed a lift, even that far. Still, walking would maybe cure the shivers and shakes I was suffering.

So I trudged back to school to get Geoffrey's toys and most importantly his towel to put on the car seat before I clipped him in. Then it would be bath time for both of us. And a very stiff drink for me. But not till I'd got rid of Brian Dawes, whose car drew up behind mine just as I parked on my drive.

'My dear Jane!' It sounded far more like an expostulation than an endearment. 'What on earth!'

'Geoffrey and I had a bit of a moment on our walk,' I

said vaguely. 'I'm just going to hose him down a bit. And I'm not sure I'm going to enjoy it.'

Brian did something he rarely did. He laughed. 'I'm not sure he will, either.' His face remained amused. 'I was going to say I'd found a dog-friendly pub and ask you to join me for supper, but I suspect you may be going to have your work cut out this evening.' He smiled and got back into his car, waving as he pulled away. He headed not out of but into the estate. It was none of my business where he went, I told Geoffrey, but he was asleep in my arms. Not for much longer, however. I wasn't dry for much longer either.

'Dogs have won awards for less,' Donna told me when I visited her at home the next morning. 'Royal Humane Society or something. Aren't you a clever boy, then?' Neither of us argued. 'I must have let him go when I fell.'

Donna's nan arrived, bustling in still wearing her coat and producing shop biscuits and instant coffee. She declared he'd done all right for a silly toy dog. Then she said I wasn't to tire Donna out.

Thanks for the warm welcome. But I was determined to stay long enough to talk to Donna a bit more. First there was work, of course, worth a mention since, as I told her, she was the cornerstone of the place. 'But that doesn't mean you have to come back a second before the medics say you can,' I added. 'Our dear old friends Elf and Safety for a start.'

'Well, the good news is it isn't actually broken. The bad news is that a sprain like this might take just as long to heal. And there'll be physio, of course. But my boyfriend had an idea. Actually, he's not quite a boyfriend yet. I only started seeing him a few days ago. He's a geek. Ever so clever.'

'You don't sound that keen, Donna.'

'Well, as I said, we're not an item yet, not by any means. It's just—no . . . Anyway, he suggested I could always work from home for you, my computer talking to the school computer. Would that be OK?'

'Let's worry about that when you're feeling better,' I said, for Nan's benefit. That door wasn't left ajar for nothing. 'A bang on the head like that might trigger headaches, mightn't it?'

She touched her forehead. 'It is quite an egg, isn't it? Nan thinks I must have tripped over Geoffrey's lead or something.' She scratched her head idly, but winced. And then, with obvious care, went over the same spot. 'I seem to have another lump here. Can you see? Pretend you're the nit nurse Nan's told me about.'

'I wish they'd make a comeback. But the way the budget is now – hey, this is a whopper. Are you sure they didn't see this yesterday?'

'They probably did. But I was a bit out of it to be honest. Thank goodness for Geoffrey!'

Not that she'd have been there if she hadn't been out with him.

'It's funny to bang your head on the front and on the back,' I said. 'You fell on your face, didn't you?'

'Yes. All this yucky stuff in my nose and mouth . . . So how did I come to get a lump here? Jane, am I going crazy, or could someone have hit me? I mean, Geoffrey was getting a bit agitated. I thought he just wanted to come back to you. And I was going to turn round, but then I fell. All that wet stuff. Ugh. Bugs, too.'

I took her hand. 'It's OK, Donna. You're safe now.

That's the main thing. But I do wonder if you should talk to the police – at least that nice community support officer, Ian Cooper: do you remember he came to talk to the kids about rights and responsibilities? That wasn't the title, but it's what it was about.'

'Oh, he's lovely! But I don't want to waste his time.'

'Let me have a word with him – he's due to talk to Wrayford School about the same thing sometime, so I can mention it then.' I didn't want to alarm her. But if someone didn't want Eoin and me to walk up the paths into the woods, didn't want his own daughter to go riding there, then was it possible he'd taken steps to ensure poor Donna went no further? I toyed with the idea of summoning him to the school to talk about Lulabelle, and raising the subject of the woods then. Or not. And since Donna's face had lit up at the prospect of talking to Ian, one of the most delightful young men I'd met in a long time – with a degree in philosophy to boot – Ian it would be.

Nan's eye appeared at the crack between door and jamb. It was clearly time Geoffrey and I made a move. 'I'm afraid he has to go back home tomorrow,' I admitted, as Donna fussed and cuddled him. 'I shall miss him, you know. Shan't I, Geoffrey?' What was I doing, making an admission like that when I was used to being stoic?

'Me too. Jane – this is an awful cheek – but I suppose he couldn't stay with me just while you're working at school?'

'If it's OK by your nan,' I said, hoping it wasn't.

But it was.

CHAPTER FOURTEEN

Ian Cooper was already sitting with Donna when, soon after two, I went to collect Geoffrey. Apparently taking his cue from the humans, he was looking unwontedly sober. He was pleased to see me, and even more pleased when I sat down, letting him sit on my lap. My lap! What was I doing?

Only agreeing to take Ian up to see where Donna had fallen, that was all. There was nothing like confronting your demons, was there? Perhaps Geoffrey might help chase them away.

As we walked, I talked, prompted occasionally by intelligent questions. Ian must have been a delight to teach; I hoped some of my little flocks would develop as well as he had done – it's a joy for any teacher to see a pupil blossoming.

He shook his head regretfully when I pointed to where

Donna had fallen. 'Unless she's actually been murdered,' he said, 'I can't imagine there being enough in the budget for a forensic examination, can you? It's a shame the medics missed that second bruise on Donna's head – or maybe they didn't. I might just swing by the hospital on my way back to the office and check. And of course I'll talk to my guvnor. And to Eoin Connor. What an amazing coincidence he happened to be passing and able to help.'

Come to think of it, I couldn't have put it better myself. But I didn't say anything.

He looked at me sideways. 'Would you have managed to overcome your phobia and come up on your own, do you think?'

'I hope so. I really hope so. With Geoffrey urging me on I might,' I concluded with a smile.

'I never met Will myself,' he said, setting us back down the path again, but then stopping and sniffing as if he were a human Geoffrey. But he shook his head as if to clear it of fanciful thoughts, and continued, 'but I can imagine – no actually, I can't imagine, can I? – what you and his friends are put through every time you see him. Best not to go on your own, I'd imagine. Pity they don't allow dogs,' he added, nodding at Geoffrey who was bouncing along like Tigger. 'He'd cheer anyone up.'

Did I too catch a whiff of something sweet on the wind? Now it was I who stopped and sniffed. Geoffrey, too, not to be outdone.

'It's a bit early for bluebells, isn't it?' Ian said at last.

If there was anything within a hundred yards' radius of us, we couldn't find it. Not even Geoffrey's nose picked up anything more interesting than the remains of a hapless rabbit, supper to some predator, no doubt. All the same, Ian didn't look any more certain than I felt.

'You wouldn't think of letting Geoffrey off his leash and telling him to find, would you?'

'He's not my dog to tell,' I said. 'But I'll try going with him. Come on: find!'

He evinced no interest at all. Indeed, the dead bracken and other undergrowth were hard enough going for adult humans with long legs. He looked up with pleading eyes, for all the world like a child demanding a carry.

We headed back to the road where Ian had parked his car, waving as he got in. 'All the same, you know,' he said, before he closed the door, 'I might just be able to find a friendly handler with a trained sniffer dog, though they're like hens' teeth. Tell you what, that little chappie looks done in. I know I shouldn't ask, but would you like a lift back to school?'

Neither of us argued. About either suggestion.

'Poor Geoffrey, having to say goodbye to Dolly. But she'll miss you, sweetheart. And I'll miss our little walks, Jane,' Enid said, patting my arm as we embarked on our last walk round the close.

'So will I. In fact, I enjoy them so much I might bring an imaginary dog to walk with you when I'm free. Would that be OK?'

'Of course – that would be lovely. We always go out at the same time every night.'

'But maybe I should have your phone number and you mine in case I have to miss coming for a couple of days – unexpected after-work meetings and such,' I added.

Producing our mobiles, we exchanged details and then, encouraged by our companions, we set off. There was nothing untoward at all to see anywhere: it was as if a collective decision had been taken to draw curtains, pour a drink and switch on the TV.

'It's quiet enough now,' Enid said. 'But you should have seen it earlier. Police vans and such a lot of shouting. Number 4.'

'Goodness!' I prompted.

'And then nothing. We saw them talking to a couple of people, three or four officers went in, and then they came out again. That's all. Oh, apart from an ambulance half an hour later. And a depressed-looking woman in a tatty car – a social worker, I'd say.'

'Did anyone leave in the ambulance?' I should be asking Brian all this, not gossiping with an acquaintance.

'Not that I saw. But then, I didn't want to look as if I was spying on them, did I?'

'You were just keeping a neighbourly eye on things,' I murmured.

Did Brian really ask the police to raid his property? A man who liked to play his cards so close to his chest he could barely see them himself? Geoffrey, to whom I addressed the question aloud as I gave him a vigorous brushing, had no more clue than I did. Perhaps, however, it was he who planted the idea in my head: why not phone Brian in a matey sort of way and commiserate with him on having such a problematic tenant. The trouble was that Brian and I didn't do matey. He'd not, for instance, thought to get back to me about his prison visit, though he must have known how interested I'd be. Or perhaps his heart was being troublesome again. Hell, why was someone so confident at school such an inept idiot when it came to adult relationships?

The only person in the village with whom I was on really easy terms was Diane, but Geoffrey's presence put the Cricketers out of bounds for another night, at least. However, I was now thoroughly in the mood for some human conversation and it dawned on me what a bad friend I was being to Joy: I had hardly been in touch all week.

'Jane!' she seemed genuinely delighted to hear my voice. 'I've been dying to get in touch but I know how busy you are.'

I hung my head.

The news of Ken was good enough, so long as he took things gently and stuck absolutely to his diet. He'd started to take a few walks in the grounds of their apartment, but it was a bit remote for her, with no one to talk to. 'Look, Ken's well enough to be left on his own now: why don't we meet up for a girlie coffee? Better still lunch! Tomorrow?'

'Oh, dear – I'd really love to, but I'm seeing someone else.'

'Ooooh! A he someone or a she someone?'

'A she.'

'Oh, what a shame. Everyone in the close wants you to have a nice he someone. It'd be so lovely to have a wedding in the village. But then, I suppose you might move away if you got married. Unless it was Brian Dawes, of course?'

I'd better break off that skein of thought. 'It's lunch with a woman friend – sort of work, really, I suppose.' Hers, not mine, of course. 'How about afternoon tea instead?'

'Lovely – but not tomorrow. I'm going to be . . . Tell

you what, Jane, a few people are coming round for drinks tomorrow evening. LBD. We shan't be able to have a natter, not a proper one, but it would be lovely to see you. Six-thirty to eight – Ken's a wonder with a cocktail shaker, and before you ask, he's so good with non-alcoholic ones you can hardly tell the difference. Yes?'

'Thank you very much. That'd be lovely!' I hoped I sounded enthusiastic. I told myself sternly it would be educational, if nothing else.

'Now tell me, how's Little Orchard Close getting on without me?' she asked.

I told her about continuing our tradition of nightly strolls.

'Walkies with Enid and Dolly? How lovely. Any goings-on to report? Come on, Jane, it's not gossip, just keeping me abreast of things . . . Number 4! Well, I never. Now what was Marie saying about them? Or was it Tess?'

I willed her to remember. In vain.

'But don't you worry – I'll find out all about it before drinkies.'

I didn't doubt her for a minute.

Inspired by my success, I resolved to phone Brian. Was I disappointed or relieved to find his number engaged?

Or pleased and disconcerted when he rang me straight back?

'As I said on the phone, I had to drop something off round the corner, and wanted to know if it was all right for me to pop in and update you about Cassandra Preston.' He drank the red wine I offered with every sign of pleasure. 'This is very good – though I now understand the jury's now out about whether it's actually good for one.' He chirruped to Geoffrey, who wagged his tail politely but stayed firmly by my legs.

'I can't imagine a prison visit would do much for your health,' I said dryly.

'Neither can I. But in the event, the visit was cancelled – at Cassandra's behest. Not for the first time I could have wrung her neck. I'm so very sorry, Jane – you truly don't deserve to have this hanging over your head, however unlikely it is that Cassandra will achieve what she wants. Anyway, I wanted to tell you about the problems at number 4. I'm sure rumours are swirling round already. Indeed, I have to say the police overreacted. If I hadn't been there I suspect they'd have bludgeoned their way in. Two vans of officers, Jane, when one local plod would have done the job in the old days. The woman who lives in the house is pretty well away with the fairies. She has a carer – an illegal, I suspect who is paranoid about people seeing her. And between the two of them they decided to leave a dead fox they found at the bottom of their garden for nature to dispose of. Hence the flies. If I'd lived at 3 or 5, Jane, I'd have been furious. In fact, they've been very patient, which is why I wanted your advice. Would it be in order for me to give both households a bunch of flowers or a box of chocolates to thank them for their forbearance? Or even both?' he added hopefully.

'A nice gesture is always a good idea. And the longer the nuisance the bigger the sorry-present. As for what it is, it depends on the age and gender of their neighbours, I'd have thought.' I ought to have taken him up on his use of 'illegal' as a noun, not just an adjective. Whoever the carer was, she was a human being, and a frightened one too, by the sound of it. I was so angry with myself that even to my own ears my next questions sounded accusatory. 'Have the police taken any action, by the way? Or brought in Environmental Health or the Borders Agency?'

Unsurprisingly he looked taken aback.

'To deal with the fox, and to check the carer's status. That's all,' I said lightly. 'It sounds as if Social Services should be on to the old lady's case too.'

'You're right,' he said seriously. He grimaced. 'I'm beginning to see the advantages of using a letting agency, after all. I don't want to be put in the position of having to give notice to someone who clearly has problems' – *Not personally*, I interjected silently – 'but if she can't manage – and the place was in a pretty poor state, to be honest – what can I do? You know, you were right to ask about consulting other agencies. That way I'd be legally in the clear, if not entirely comfortable if I did have to end her tenancy. And I certainly don't want to do it the way a lot of my fellow landlords are going about it, by simply raising the rent to quite disproportionate levels.' Suddenly he looked at his watch. 'Have you eaten yet? I think the Cricketers' kitchen is still open till nine-thirty.'

I pointed at Geoffrey, now firmly asleep on my feet. 'I'm banned till he's gone home.'

'Tomorrow, then?' He sounded quite eager.

'I've already got an invitation, I'm afraid,' I said. 'Drinks with Joy and her husband, at their new apartment. I'm afraid it might be a bit golf-y for me,' I added honestly. Probably mistakenly. I still wanted this man at arm's length.

'They're still guests of Tony Carpenter? I shall be interested to hear what you make of him, Jane.'

'Assuming he's there, of course.'

'I can't imagine he won't be.' He got heavily to his feet. 'He's a man who enjoys power. Before you say I do – and you do too, or you wouldn't be in the job you are – in my humble opinion he enjoys it too much.'

Disconcerted by his insights, I rose too, upsetting Geoffrey, who yelped plaintively as I said, very seriously, 'You're saying he's dangerous, aren't you? In that case, Brian, I'll heed your warning. I'll be very careful.'

CHAPTER FIFTEEN

It was Geoffrey's last long walk round the village before I had to return him to Maggie Davies. He smiled at various other dogs, apart from a couple, which for some reason raised his ire and his hackles, but, tail going on maximum swipe, he was on his best behaviour as we headed towards the yellow-waistcoated villagers constituting today's neighbourhood Speed Watch team. Until he recognised Enid, without Dolly, as it happens, and set off ahead of me, yapping enthusiastically.

A white van heads straight for him. No. Not him. Not me. Enid and her friends. It must be doing fifty. I'm screaming. Everyone's screaming.

But the van stops.

The passenger leaps out, not to see if anyone's hurt – one person's fallen backwards – but to grab the speed gun.

Now everything's in slow motion. He takes the camera

too and places it under the front wheel. Speed gun – back wheel. Just as it seems he's getting back in the van he comes at the group again. He's after the clipboard and the log sheet. The old man clutching it tussles as long as he can. Geoffrey and I are upon the attacker. But the board is wheeling in an arc over the hedge and the assailant is already being driven away.

I get most of the number. Most, not all. Dictate it to my phone. Then start to help. Geoffrey's as hysterical as the humans, quivering with fear. Enid's on her feet but in tears: I put Geoffrey into her arms so they can cuddle each other better.

The clipboard guy's determined to retrieve the board: 'It's got the emergency number and code on it,' he snaps when I tell him I'll get it when I've attended to the man still on the ground.

I get it. I dial. An immediate response is promised. And en route, armed with the partial number, they'll look out for the van.

'Any idea of the make or model?' comes the cool question.

'They all look the same' wouldn't be the right answer. The words come from somewhere. 'I think it's a VW. And I think we might need an ambulance. There's a man in his sixties who may have been knocked down, and he can't get up.'

I get a string of first-aid tips to pass on to Enid and clipboard man.

So far, so calm, cool and collected. But then my memory melts. What did the men look like? Either of them? They might have been wearing hoods for all my head can visualise their faces.

I anchor Geoffrey very firmly to a convenient fence post and see what I can do for the second man, one I now place as Adam, the village cricket team scorer, a retired pharmacist, who probably knows exactly what we should be doing. As much to stop him drifting into unconsciousness as anything, I ask him, much to Enid's obvious horror. But it appeals to his grim humour, and blow me if he doesn't start cracking fielding position jokes about short square leg. He concedes, as he dithers either with shock or as a natural consequence of lying on frosty ground, that he could do with an extra cover. But when he tries to groan at his own bad pun, it turns into an altogether more worrying sound.

'My hip, I shouldn't wonder. But never mind, I've been on the waiting list for a replacement long enough and this should bump me up to the top. Bastards,' he concludes, less stoically. 'I'll never forget that driver's eyes as long as I live. Blue as ice.'

So they were. And his companion's a rather paler, rather more intimidating shade.

Is it legal for witnesses to refresh each other's memories? Probably not. But it's one way of passing the time while you wait for the blues and twos.

And then, after all the interviews and statements, it was, as Adam would probably have said, down to earth with a bump. Geoffrey had to go back home to Maggie Davies; I had to meet Elaine for lunch and acquire an LBD and still have enough time to come home and titivate before the drinkies. Fashionably late would probably have to enter the equation somewhere. Elaine wasn't unhappy with putting lunch back half an hour, and was quick to recommend a dress shop within five minutes' walk of the Ashford pub where she suggested we eat.

Late and apologising profusely, she took three texts before she even registered my presence. Then she peered at me, as if seeing me for the first time. 'Lost a contact lens? Or are you starting a cold?' She backed sharply away.

'Neither. I had to take a dog I've been looking after back to his owner, and he just bounded over to her and let me leave without a backward look,' I sobbed.

'A dog! You're like this because of a dog! I don't believe it! Oh, sod the bloody thing,' she added, switching off her phone and stowing it in her bag.

'Neither do I, to be honest. Hell, I'm embarrassing myself, let alone you,' I added as she gathered a wodge of paper napkins and thrust them at me. 'Thank you. There. Or it might be something far more respectable – delayed shock.' I made the white van incident as violent as I could, earning a lot of sympathetic tutting. It was time to make an effort: 'How's things with you, apart from frantic?'

'I take it you mean how's things with Izzie and in Wrayford generally?'

'I actually meant how are you and Robin? And your amazing diet?'

'Oh. Sorry. We're fine. Yes, Robin's being dead spartan and his cholesterol's improving, but he's beginning to feel very depressed like I was when I had to go fat-free with my gall bladder. So he's considering statins. We shall see. He sends his love, but someone gave him a ticket for Twickenham. So that's us. Izzie's fine too, which makes a full house, I suppose. But she's fairly fizzing with fury. Hey, that's alliteration, isn't it? I don't think it's any longer directed at you, though, but at us for taking our time examining what I also happen to think is a crime scene – so well done you. Chips! You're having chips! Mind you, you're so thin I sometimes wonder if you're anorexic. You're not, are you?'

'Just busy. And I was barred from the Cricketers, all because of Geoffrey.'

'That dog.'

'Diane doesn't permit dogs in public spaces, and ninety-nine point nine per cent of the time I absolutely agree with her. I'd chain up children outside too,' I added, with partial truth. 'Actually, when Joy lived with me and made sure I took lunch and ate in the evenings – not to mention pouring booze down my far from unwilling throat – I put on a kilo or so. So yes to chips, and probably to dessert too. Sorry.'

She pulled a superior face: 'Nothing tastes as good as thin, didn't someone say?'

'Tell you what – if I order chips and you order salad, we could share both, couldn't we? Excellent.' I nipped off to place our order. 'So poor Izzie can't move in yet?' I prompted her as I sat down again.

She put her elbows on the table, shoving her fingers through her hair. 'Human blood. Hair. Some credible signs of a struggle. But no victim. No signs of a victim. And weird, considering the vicarage is actually part of your village, no witnesses at all, except for you and your suspicious eyes.'

'You can add a suspicious nose to that too. There's a funny smell in Wray Episcopi woods, but neither our PCSO Ian Cooper nor I could see any cause for it except a decidedly deceased bunny.'

'Ian? What's he got to do with the price of coal?'

More explanations.

'That's going a bit above and beyond for a PCSO,' she observed.

'Well, I think he fancies Donna and turned himself into a knight in shining armour. Anyway, when we picked up the smell he hoped he'd be able to get hold of a dog handler. The terrain was simply too rough for Geoffrey.'

'Oh God – don't start again!' She rolled her eyes. 'So Ian was going to get on to A & E to see if anyone had noted a whopping great egg on the back of the poor woman's head. The implication is that she didn't just trip, but that measures were taken by someone unknown to stop her going any deeper into the woods. And this is after this guy Rufus Petrie got in a strop with his daughter – and with you and Eoin Connor – for being in the same woods. Oh, and that kid of yours heard screams. I'm still on to that.'

Possibly.

'Hm. I'll just text Ian before the food arrives.'

Unsurprisingly – Elaine was the sort of woman to whose messages one would tend to respond to immediately – one pinged back immediately. 'Ah! Yes, a large lump was noted, but no, nothing at all showed up when she had a scan. And no, no one thought to mention it to her or ask where she'd got it because an M20 RTA with multiple victims happened to be arriving and broken bodies need faster attention than just bumped ones. So there we are. Oh, there's more: he thought he might go and have another talk with Donna to see if she remembers anything else.'

'I told you – real Round Table material. Meanwhile, how did you get on at the car wash?'

'Damn! I knew I had to do something. I dare say you know all about this, Jane – sixteen-hour days take it out of you, and when you're menopausal there's not always a lot to top it up with. Even with HRT. Car's still dirty, though. Do you think they'll be working on a Saturday?'

'I'm sure they'll be slaving away,' I said dryly, before clamping my hand over my accidentally punning mouth. 'Sorry!'

'Sounds like our police black humour,' she said. 'Bloody hell, that's some portion of salad!'

'And all those chips . . .'

We divided them up.

'Do you know anything,' I began, wondering if I was being disloyal, 'about a raid in Little Orchard Close yesterday? Number 4,' I added, when she seemed to hesitate.

'That's not on my radar,' she said firmly. Her face hardened. 'Are you telling me some idiot went in—you are. Shit!' She checked her phone. 'Some eager beaver's only gone crashing in on an area I wanted maximum tact. Softly, bloody softly, for God's sake! Only while they might nail a terrified carer, I'm . . . I'm not allowed to tell you exactly what I want,' she said in a rush, with an apologetic grin. 'Hey,' she continued with an ultra-bright smile, 'what excellent salsa this is!'

I pointed to her burger, which she'd ordered without a bun, though it still came with all the usual toppings. 'You are usually after the Big Cheese,' I said, enjoying her wince, 'aren't you? And I have a horrible feeling that that involves one of the residents of the close.'

'How's your social life these days?' she asked, with an audible crash of gears. 'Still seeing that pompous git?'

'The pompous git who happens to own number 4? Actually, I never have *seen* him, except in the most literal sense, as well you know. Anyway, tonight my social life is going to blossom: I've been invited for drinkies at Joy and Ken Penkridge's. After this I've got to find a suitable dress.'

'Your height, your weight, it should be a doddle. I'll come with you, just to motivate myself. Meanwhile, a big question – who are you going with? Not Brian?'

'He's afraid he'll run into someone he doesn't get on with. Actually, he's warned me off him. Tony Carpenter. He owns the apartment Joy's moved into while Paula and Caffy rescue both our houses.'

'Does he indeed. You know what, I really think you need an escort – someone who'd look good in a suit – it's not actually black tie, is it? Go on, phone Joy and find out.'

CHAPTER SIXTEEN

Despite Elaine's insistence that I needed looking after, I managed to shake off her suggestions for possible escorts, who varied from her rookie constable to Ian Cooper. Joy was a friend, after all, and wouldn't wish to expose me to any harm. She greeted me with a warm hug, repeated, in a purely social way, by Ken, who thanked me effusively for looking after her while he couldn't. There was something very public about this paean: was it meant to act as an explanation for my presence as an outsider in what seemed a very tight-knit group? However much I might object to the notion that Joy (and by extension other women?) needed to be looked after by a man, I simply smiled and turned the conversation to his health and that of his home. When he criticised Caffy and Paula, I said, 'When you know them as well as I do, you'll realise how skilled and professional they are. After all, they saved both our houses.'

Emboldened perhaps by my effort, or perhaps by her second drink, Joy added, 'They pretty well saved my life, darling.' She rather spoilt it by adding, 'I dare say I'd have stupidly gone dashing in to try to rescue things, only to have the whole lot crashing on my head. And you were pretty firm, too, Jane.'

'And you made my house a home, Joy.' I squeezed her hand in thanks. It was icy cold, despite the room's overpowering heat.

It was time to mingle, which I did, armed with a non-alcoholic cocktail, which was indeed really excellent. Would it be the dive into a tankful of piranhas that Elaine had predicted?

Not immediately, at least. I actually recognised and had quite interesting conversations with some of the men because of my cricket connections: George (it turned out he was actually Sir George, with a Ladyship wife) was a fellow umpire, and Nicholas and Toby, presidents of some of the clubs that had hosted Wrayford CC. Sadly their wives didn't share our passion for cricket, but occupied themselves with silently appraising my outfit, which I suspect they found wanting. Or perhaps it was my unvarnished fingernails. My attempts to turn the conversation to topics they might find more interesting ground to a halt when they told me how well their children were doing at private schools, to which they had to go because village schools were such rubbish.

To misquote Hamlet, a woman may smile and smile and think villainous thoughts. I could, anyway.

I mingled some more, ready to go home but for one thing – it would be horribly quiet. In any case, I'd not finished my circuit of the lovely room.

Eventually Tony Carpenter and his wife – Alexia – appeared, and though they recognised me from my part in Joy's removal here, were reluctant to acknowledge me until Joy bore down on them, dragging me with her. Alexia maintained a distant politeness I attributed to a recent acquaintance with Botox, so immobile were her features. The resemblance to Mrs Trump was more pronounced than ever.

Actually, the young women serving drinks and canapes resembled her too – all razor-sharp cheekbones and huge eyes. Somehow, however, their black uniforms combined with very heavy matte make-up made them look more like funeral mourners than waiters – a fact I decided not mention to Joy when the circulation round the room brought us together again. I did praise their discreet efficiency, however.

'Tony Carpenter found them for me. They're excellent, aren't they? So nice for Ken and me to be able to talk to our friends without worrying about who's got a full glass and who hasn't.' She looked round, dropping her voice so that it was only just audible through all the cocktail-fuelled yapping. 'So cheap, too. In fact, I don't think we're paying them enough. But Tony insisted we were.'

'Isn't there something called the national living wage?' I asked, knowing full well there was.

She shrugged. 'I've never employed anyone, so I wouldn't know. How much do you think it would be?'

I pretended to guess, but in fact gave a pretty accurate figure.

'But we're only paying half that! And it could be less, because they're supposed to pay for breakages. Oh, Jane – you know about these things: what should I do?'

'Were you supposed to be paying them direct – or Tony?'

'Tony.' Her face slipped from cheerful to appalled. 'Do you think I should pay them myself? And add a bit extra? Actually, it should be a lot more, shouldn't it?' She clapped her hand over her mouth. 'I don't think I've got that much cash. And Ken'll say I shouldn't interfere, so I can't ask him.'

'I've probably got some. You can borrow it, if you want.'

'Let's pop into my bedroom – I don't want people to know, obviously.'

I had fifty-five in cash, which wouldn't really be enough. 'I could go and find a cash machine—'

'I wouldn't hear of it. Ken will have enough to pay Tony what he asked, and I've got some . . . That should give them £10 or £15 extra. Oh, Jane, I never thought.'

'But you have now and you've done something about it. No one could do any more, could they?' I gave her a quick hug and was ready to follow her back to what I could only think of as the salon.

Instead she sat on the bed, saying, so quietly I could hardly hear: 'There's always more, isn't there?' Before I could even prompt her, she was on her feet again, saying ultra-brightly, as she steered us back into the melee, 'Time for one more drinkie. Such a shame you're driving, Jane: that blackberry gin cocktail is to die for.'

It took only a glance at her face to know that I should talk about the problems of driving. 'If I'd had the sense I was born with,' I agreed brightly, 'I should have come by cab. Thanks for that safety pin. What do celebs call it – "a wardrobe malfunction"?'

* * *

155

Lavender and Nosey cautiously descended from their high shelf to demand a return to the status quo, a satisfactorily dog-free environment, and watch me eat a cheese sandwich and sink a glass of Shiraz. They endured a series of rhetorical questions: why had Elaine been so keen for me to take Ian Cooper, of all people, to the party? He was young enough to be the son, if not the grandson, of some of my fellow guests. And though we might like each other, I would wager that he and Donna would become an item before too long. What had I missed, that he or, more to the point, the anonymous CID officer she'd mentioned in passing would have spotted? I'd certainly picked up on Joy's anxieties about the women waiting staff. Anxieties in general. Had anything been obviously wrong? Long sleeves. High necks. Trousers not skirts. Waiters' uniform, really. But very concealing. I'd somehow have expected Tony to make them wear something altogether skimpier. As I sluiced away my night's warpaint, I thought about theirs: could that flawless make-up conceal more than the odd blemish?

'There's always more, isn't there?' What had she meant by that? Joy didn't strike me as the sort of woman who would want to ponder universal truths: she had an eye for specific details. There was only one thing to do, I told the bears: I had to make room in my diary for a private conversation – one where Joy would feel safe to open up.

Izzie West most certainly did not to want to open up to me, though she came and sat next to me for the next morning's service, which I had cycled to like a Barbara Pym heroine. It was a very low-key affair, morning prayers from the Book of Common Prayer because, as the new priest, Graham needed to be properly launched – there was a proper term, but my 9.30 brain couldn't recall it – and still awaited the special service where this would take place. Not to mention, of course, the house, which would constitute his payment for his work in the parish. He gave a short, workmanlike sermon delivered in a voice so clear even the old ladies at the back could distinguish every syllable. I said everything proper, both to Izzie and to Graham, as he shook hands with everyone after the service.

'When our life is more settled I'd like to take our school assemblies. You're not officially a Church school, of course, but—'

I had to demur. After his predecessor's activities I would be surprised if many parents would want a priest to come anywhere near their children, but I could hardly say that. After all, I was sure there were rotten apples in every profession, even mine. And the C of E required priests to have every background check going. But this wasn't the place to mention such a large elephant. 'Let's talk about this at a more appropriate time. Here's my card: just call me when you've a moment.'

Taking it automatically he turned to the next member of the congregation without responding.

The last thing I expected as I cycled past the school on my way home was to see a woman running away from it. A child, yes – having committed some petty act of vandalism. But a woman? She wasn't making very good progress, either – tight skirts and high heels don't make good running gear. I bowled past her – and then slowed to a halt, turning with a smile and a flap of the hand. She froze, ready, I thought, to bolt back up the hill. 'Hi,' I began, trying to project, not shout. 'I'm Jane – I think we're neighbours.' Hands open, slightly raised – was I trying to prove I wasn't armed, or something equally unlikely? – I turned the bike back towards to her, my best head-teacherly smile of reassurance on my face.

'You live at number 39, don't you?' I said very clearly, 'I live at number 14. I'm the head teacher at the school.' Getting no response, I soldiered on: 'Would you like to come in for a coffee? It's nice to meet one's neighbours.'

She got the gist of what I was saying – I was sure of that. But possibly not all. I tried the technique I'd used to Zunaid, another smile.

She shook her head, touching her lips, and walked straight towards me, so I had to hug her or dodge out of her way. Hearing a car coming up behind me, I dodged and cycled back towards the school as if no interaction had taken place. When I turned, there was no sight of her, or of the car, which must have done a neat three-point turn to return whence it had come. Was she in it – by choice or by coercion? Striding down to number 39 and demanding to see her wasn't an option. I consoled myself with the belief that she possibly had enough English to understand numerals – and since she appeared to have been running from the school, she might well understand that word too. There was also a rather etiolated shoot of hope, too – had she been able to read that school-related flyer I'd put through her door? Had she sought refuge there? Or had she been checking it out as a possible place of safety? Much though I'd like to know, would it put her in jeopardy if I forced the issue?

I walked on into the village itself, to the pub. Because

the Wrayford has no shop, Diane arranged with the shop in the nearest village to deliver pre-ordered newspapers. You paid in advance. There weren't many *Observer* readers in the area, so usually my chosen read stood out like a liberal beacon. Today it was dimmed. Extinct. Or more precisely, taken by someone else. Without paying. Logically I knew I could turn to the online version, but I felt – yes, robbed, stomping off home as if hurting my feet would make the rest of me feel better.

It didn't.

CHAPTER SEVENTEEN

If I'd had Geoffrey handy I'd have gone for a good long walk on what had become a lovely early spring day: sun, birdsong, some greening on both ground and branches. A solitary stroll really didn't appeal, however – but a proper bike ride, as opposed to nipping from A to B, just might. But I didn't really have time for a pointless jaunt. Maybe I could go to Wray Episcopi to see how Donna did, maybe catch sight of Pam and Zunaid, and come the long way home. Why not?

The warmth had brought out other cyclists too, like an unnervingly unpredictable rash. Everyone has to learn to ride; everyone needs places to practise. My own preference was for dedicated cycle areas before I moved up to very quiet lanes. Very well, I once had a spectacular accident on just such a lane, but it wasn't my fault I ended base over apex in a very prickly hedge. The idea may be funny, but the reality isn't great, believe me. Hence my new best friend, the helmet camera.

Other people were taking learning very seriously, but very dangerously. What possessed that family of five to string themselves like wobbly fairy lights across both sides of a road? And, coming towards me, the parents, rightly proud of their twins' cycling efforts as they pedalled so desperately behind their parents that they kept veering into the middle of the road? Not even the most foolhardy driver was risking overtaking.

And what a good job too.

A horse shot from nowhere across the road. White. Riderless. The car that had been hoping to overtake me screamed to a halt, the driver leaving the door open as he leapt out. I abandoned my bike and ran helpfully forward – to do what, for goodness' sake? I knew nothing of horses, just that they were big with teeth in their mouths and iron on their feet. Even so I could see that this one was scared – terrified. It kept rearing up, rolling its eyes.

'Go to its head and grab the bridle. Not like that, you'll spook it and likely get yourself killed.'

'Over to you. It's called Snowflake. I'll look for the rider,' I yelled, running up the path that had so terrified me the other day. I knew that horse. I knew the rider. Lulabelle Petrie. Small child. Big horse. Worried father. Right to worry if she could be thrown like that. Lose a wife to a horse. Lose a child to a horse. My God.

Somewhere I found breath to call her name. Again and again. But when I stopped to catch my breath, all I could hear was my breath and the pounding of blood in my ears.

More running. More calling. And then I heard a shrill

keening – not a shout, not a yell – as if an animal were in pain. But human, surely.

'Lulabelle. I'm here! Where are you? Just call me. Just call, "I'm here".' If she had to frame words, maybe it would somehow calm her down. 'It's Ms Cowan, Lulabelle – come to help you.'

'Please, miss, please, miss – I'm here. I mean Ms Cowan.'

'"Miss" will do. I can't see you. Can you wave?'

Movement in the bracken. Lulabelle was struggling to her feet. I ran again.

'No. Don't come. It's so horrible. Oh, please!'

She fell into my arms.

The book said I should lay her down in the recovery position and wait for professional help. My head, my heart – even my legs – told me otherwise. First, I was sick. Very sick. As sick as she had been.

A child shouldn't have seen what she saw. No one should have seen what she saw. And yet its horror was hypnotic. Tearing my eyes from it, I gathered her up and ran.

'Don't you know anything about first aid? Bloody hell, you could have killed the pair of you slipping and sliding down that path.' The man who knew about horses was either furious or genuinely alarmed. 'Here, take the horse: I'll carry her.'

She clung more tightly than ever.

'We need the police. 999. Now.' I said.

He was the sort to argue. 'Ambulance, I'd have thought. Vomit means concussion.'

'I said police. Now. And they can organise a paramedic when they're on their way. Just do it.' It's hard to sound fierce and cradle someone protectively. 'I'm just going to set you down gently, Lulabelle. No, I'm not letting you go. I shall stay here. Anyone got any water?'

Someone emerged from a red BMW, arms akimbo. 'Will someone tell me when you can move that bloody car, not to mention that damned horse?'

'It's called Snowflake,' I told Horse Man. 'Bring it over here, please – it'll help Lulabelle if she can see it's all right. And some water. Anyone?'

As if by magic a child's water bottle appeared, and some baby-wipes. I tackled Lulabelle's face and hands. My own too. There was still some vomit on her riding gear. I mopped hopefully. Presumably Snowflake didn't mind the smell, or perhaps he was reassured by Lulabelle's arms and face against his neck.

'She's Lulabelle Petrie – lives about a mile from here,' I said, my voice little more than a croak. 'She'll need her dad, Rufus Petrie.'

The onlookers murmured in response to the name but didn't say anything helpful.

'Lulabelle, have you got your phone, sweetheart? We'll call your dad.'

'No. No! He'll be so cross. He'll take Snowflake away and I couldn't bear it.' At least if you pieced all the disjointed words, picked out from between the sobs and half-muffled screams, that was the gist.

I had to play the head teacher, didn't I? If I had the energy, that is. 'I'll tell him that it was Snowflake who helped us find you,' I said, with a vague approximation of the truth. 'Let me phone him.' I grasped at the crisp tone I used in school, though it sounded to me little more than a feeble plea.

Something worked. She dug in her jacket and passed it over.

I willed myself out of her immediate earshot. I had to think through every word I used to Rufus Petrie. I tried rehearsing them in my head. Useless. Perhaps they'd come when I actually spoke to him.

'Mr Petrie? Jane Cowan.' Yes, autopilot was working. Just. I'd have to override any interruptions if I was to deliver all the message. 'Lulabelle's OK – do you understand that? She's hurt, but not badly. But she needs you: she's witnessed a most horrible crime.' At last I had his silent attention. If I thought about it, I'd throw up again. 'We're here by the lay-by where we met before. The police are on the way. And the paramedics. The only thing she can turn to at the moment is the horse,' I added, overriding what I was sure would be threats against it. 'It saved her life, effectively.' I cut the call.

The man who knew about horses broke off his argument with the BMW driver to ask me what the hell I was saying.

'Look at them. They need each other. She understands horses even if I don't,' I added. 'And I take it you do?' I wanted to sound dryly ironic. In fact, I was trembling uncontrollably, my voice cracking if I gave it half a chance. I dreaded anyone trying to be kind and understanding.

'I suppose so,' he said. 'Look, you ought to sit before you fall.'

I managed to reach a ditch to be sick in. Just. I tried to push up from my hands and knees but couldn't. Couldn't even raise one hand to wipe the bile from my chin.

The green lights swimming before my eyes were replaced

by blue flashing ones. Real ones. And noise which stopped abruptly, though the lights continued.

Police? Time for another effort. Another failure.

Time for a mental bollocking. The sort I'd give myself when I'd thought I could no longer endure life. I was a grown woman. A child needed me. Even her horse needed me. I'd get to them even if I had to crawl.

I suppose I got about halfway before anyone noticed me. Red car driver. He yanked me upright and put something to my lips, snatching it away before I'd had more than a sip. 'Didn't someone have some wet wipes? Here.' He shoved a bunch roughly into my hand and backed away.

More twos, and more blues.

'This is the woman who brought her down. I told her she shouldn't have moved her – God knows what damage she's done. Just picked her up and carried her.'

'Her?' a male voice said. 'She's only a slip of wind.' A hand touched my shoulder. 'What's your name, miss? Does anyone know her name?'

'It's Ms Cowan from school.' Lulabelle's voice.

'OK, miss—'

'It's "Ms", I told you. She's very particular. She came to find me.' She started to sob again. Somehow she ended in my arms.

Until we were torn apart. 'What the hell are you doing, woman? I told you to keep away from here!' a man yelled. Rufus Petrie. Then he let go, but as if someone made him.

Soon there was a grotesque melee in progress, the police more interested in keeping apart the antagonists than finding out the cause. I didn't have the strength to step forward and yell at them. But it turned out it was no one else's job. Whatever I said seemed to establish a shamefaced truce, finally established by the arrival of what looked like another police car but turned out to be an ambulance. I surrendered Lulabelle to their care and turned at last to the police. No, actually, if the paramedics had proper wipes, I'd cadge a few for myself.

Handing some over, the male paramedic took me on one side. 'Why on earth did you bring her down here? It's the first rule of first aid: avoid moving the patient.'

'I know: her collarbone may be broken, and a few ribs. But the vomiting – that's because of something else. I can't explain . . . I absolutely need to talk to the police first.'

'I told you you shouldn't have,' Horse Man put in helpfully.

'I need to talk to the police first,' I insisted. 'They need to know. Now. Before anyone else does.' But when a harassed officer came towards me, all I could do was point up the path.

I couldn't frame the words.

There was a lot of discussion going on above my head. It seemed I'd passed out. In the middle of an argument about giving me brandy, someone was joking about my cycle helmet, saying it was a good job I'd kept it on. Helpfully someone responded by removing it. Some part of my head knew I had to keep it, beside me if not on my head. But I didn't want to remember why.

And then, horribly, I did. Hands tried to push me down as I struggled to sit up. 'There's footage on the helmet cam,' I said. 'They need to see it before they go up. And no one else must. No one else can see it or go up,' I added, furious

I couldn't say things clearly, even think things clearly, because of that one thing I couldn't get out of my head.

I was in a quiet room, not unlike a dentist's waiting room. Anonymous but comfortable. Or do I mean comfortable but anonymous? Caffy was holding my hand. Apparently when the police had asked if I wanted anyone with me while I waited to give a formal statement, I'd asked for her. Had I remembered that her partner, Tom Arkwright, was a senior policeman? I doubt it. Actually, I didn't remember asking for her. Perhaps Superintendent Arkwright was something to do with the case – though when I'd last met him he'd been leading an armed response team – and he'd suggested Caffy.

'You're going to need a lot of therapy, Jane,' Caffy was saying.

'Not as much as poor Lulabelle.'

'I disagree. I think you've got two things fighting in your head. The memory of finding poor Will and what has happened since. Then you've got the more immediate memory of what you found this time.'

'Which has gone, completely. All I remember is this horse dashing across the road.'

'Let's leave it there. Now, because Tom's involved, much as I want you to stay with us you can't. But I can come to your place.'

I shook my head. 'He'll need you, will Tom. Once he's seen – not just the footage on the helmet cam but the actual scene of the . . . Caffy, it's a dead woman, isn't it?'

She looked me in the eye. 'Yes. So where will you stay tonight?'

'Home.'

'Not on your own.'

If only I still had Geoffrey.

'I'll be fine. I hate it,' I told her, 'when stuff happens and I can't control it. Take being down on the lay-by. Throwing up. All these people milling round all chafing the fat—'

She laughed. 'I've never heard anyone but Tom use that expression. "Chafing" means "chewing" – right? So all these people were holding forth—'

'And none of them was saying or doing anything to the purpose. And I couldn't find the words to explain why they shouldn't be – or why they shouldn't go up that track. Because they'd find a woman—'

CHAPTER EIGHTEEN

At least I'd been checked over by a doctor straight from Trollope, who'd insisted on giving me two sleeping pills for later despite my equally firm refusal. I'd also got my statement out of the way. They'd offered to let me do it later, but I insisted. Once it was out of my mouth and on paper, I didn't need to remember it again. That didn't mean it wouldn't be stuck in my memory for ever, but it did mean I could start using the techniques for forgetting vile things my therapists had all worked at over the years. Caffy had offered to stay with me, still literally holding my hand, but I refused. She'd been through very bad times herself, and didn't need any of her latent memories nudged into activity. Let her remain the serene and fey woman she was, under all her practicality. It was good to have her waiting for me when it was all over: the chocolate she pressed into my wildly shaking hands – yes, it was organic and Fair Trade, of course, Caffy being Caffy – was as excellent as it was welcome. Comfort food to savour.

As mysteriously as Caffy had appeared, Jo and Lloyd arrived to take over, frogmarching me from the police station to their car. Who had told them where I was – Lloyd was clearly off-duty, in gardening clothes, by the look of it – and that I needed help? Caffy didn't know them: I had to make introductions. But need them I did. So any protests I made weren't very coherent and not at all forceful. Except for one demand: I wanted my cycle back. And the helmet.

Cycle? What cycle?

It took a long time for Lloyd's colleagues to discover that though the helmet was safe at the police station, no one had a clue where the cycle might be. Top marks for someone, then. Since it was fairly new and not the cheapest model, chuntering under his breath Lloyd phoned the evidence officer at the site.

'No, I'm not bringing her over to ID it,' he said tetchily. 'She's been through more than enough. And that's one place she doesn't need to see. If she ever does again,' he added. 'Yes. Straightaway.'

We'd barely got as far as the car when his mobile rang. 'You've got to be fucking joking! What sort of sick bastard does that? Rescue what's left of it. Fucking idiots!' He put a brotherly arm round me. 'In the past, Jane, we've agreed that a quick burst of anger can be really quite good for you. So, prepare to have one – and polish up a few choice swear words. OK, have some of mine.' He grinned shamefacedly at Jo. 'Right under the noses of my mates, some thieving shit's removed your saddle. He was just having a go at the

170

lights when he was interrupted. Scarpered. Into the sodding woods. Steal their granny's mobility scooter, some folks.'

'One consolation,' observed Jo, 'is that they won't be riding far on a saddle-less bike, will they?'

'Not if it's in the back of Seb Nelson's car, they won't. Which is where it should bloody well have been in the first place.'

'I know what you'll say, Jo, but I want to go and pick it up now, please. No, listen: I got the statement out of the way because my therapists have always said it's best to confront demons sooner rather than later. That's why I need to go. Not to the murder site,' I said carefully, 'but the lay-by. I'm going to have to see it every day anyway. And I'd rather do it now.' I hadn't convinced them. 'You know the advice they give about having a fall and getting straight back on your bike – except, of course . . . Oh, dear. Sorry.' At least I was giggling this time, not howling hysterically.

'Elaine!' I greeted the officer clearly making other people dance to her tune, 'I didn't know you were SIO.' I was quite proud of myself for remembering the title in such circumstances. 'Does this mean—?'

'Never you mind what it means, because actually I'm not. I'm just passing through. It's DCI Boyd over there: the one that looks as if he's just left your school,' she said. She gave me a brief hug but then pushed me away, her eyes searching my face. 'What in Hades are you doing here? You should be—'

'Collecting my bike. And actually, all your lot milling round with your striped tape and hi-vis jackets somehow sanitises everything – makes it like something on TV. Something I can switch off, I suppose.'

I'd never noticed how shrewd yet compassionate she could look. 'If that's how you feel, who am I to argue? Apparently that kid Lulu or whatever is having tantrums saying she wants to be in school tomorrow. I don't suppose,' she asked, trying hard to make it an idle enquiry, 'that you're intending to go too?'

'If Lulabelle's going, I have to be there to support her. Normality. Stability.'

'Which you need as much as she does,' she said accurately.

There was a tiny pause. 'Do you remember Jo and Lloyd? I think you met at that rather dramatic cricket match last summer.'

'Yes, of course – one of us, aren't you, Lloyd? And aren't you a maths teacher, Jo?'

'They've said they'll keep an eye on me tonight.' The two officers exchanged what I'd call a professional glance, somehow excluding me though it was clearly about me. 'Look, Elaine, I know you're short-staffed, but with all the goings-on in the close, and now this – what if someone recognised me? There were a lot of folk around . . . earlier. I'm a bit worried about my house – Brian Dawes' house, that is. What if—?'

'I'll do something more subtle than mount a guard on it, which we couldn't begin to afford to do anyway, even if it was much more than a case of "what if?". I'll yank a techie from his Sunday evening telly and get some monitoring stuff in place.' She could probably have explained what each individual component was called and what it did, but she always feigned a technophobe's ignorance. 'Just don't want him spotted going in and arousing suspicion, that's all.'

'I've got to pick up an overnight bag. I suppose he couldn't just go into the house with me and leave with me, as if we were off for a romantic dinner.'

'I'd best get hold of Toby Weston, then – he's the only techie I could face snogging. Not that you would, of course – snog him, that is.'

'Only very publicly.' The effort to sound perky – actually, to sound anything like myself – was exhausting me.

She put a hand on my arm. 'Go and sit in Jo and Lloyd's car – I'll get Toby to pick you up here.'

I was just doing what I was told when I had another idea: 'The school! The schools, actually, but in this case it's Wrayford, not the one up the road.' I jerked my thumb.

'What about it? No, hang on – Toby: have you had your Sunday roast yet? OK, change into something that looks as if you might be taking an attractive woman out for supper, bring some miniaturised surveillance kit and meet us in fifteen just outside Wray Episcopi. You can't miss us. Yes: that job. But yours is a nice clean inside one with a bit of acting thrown in. No, not the damned Gondoliers. Amateur singer!' she added in parentheses to me. 'Now, school? You want Toby to do something there too? Christ, my budget . . .'

Attractive! I was still wearing my cycling gear and when I'd caught sight of myself in a loo mirror I'd been appalled by the sight of this haggard, sick middle-aged woman. For a start I put my shoulders back. 'Actually, the school security system's pretty good – CCTV everywhere, a lock and a keypad.'

'And lots of kids surging in and out. A system's only as good as its weakest point, Jane.'

'I know, I know. I'll get on to the security firm now – they have an emergency number. Where the hell did I put my phone?'

Ostentatiously she walked round me. Then she turned to Lloyd and Jo. 'Is there an off button somewhere? God, you're a control freak, Jane. Just leave it to these people, will you?'

I was ready to snarl or scream – but there'd been enough screaming. I held out my hand for the phone and texted. A promise of immediate action pinged back. And now – now perhaps I did have an off button. 'Do you allow yourself chocolate, Elaine?' I asked, producing some of Caffy's from my pocket. All by itself, my hand embarked on a curious dance. I told myself it was natural to be cold: waiting for Toby was getting tedious. 'Will your colleague be long?' I asked through chattering teeth.

'Only from Bridge. Just be grateful he's not one of the team based in Essex.'

Jo and Lloyd were certainly happy with chocolate, even though they had to hold my hand still so they could break pieces off; eventually it transpired that Elaine was able to square the need for a bit of extra energy with what seemed a very flexible conscience.

Toby, the techie who admitted to having driven like a bat out of hell, liked it too. He was a chunky young man, pretty well my height, with a strangely rectangular body, the sort I associated with old-fashioned Welsh operatic tenors who'd not heard of the new vogue for singers to diet and use the gym. But he gave a charming smile, handing me solicitously into his car as if I were his granny. Elaine told us to meet up with Jo and Lloyd by the Cricketers, but changed her mind: we might just as well eat there. She'd deal with Diane, she added, before I could say anything.

Whatever she might have said to Elaine, and whatever she might want to say to us, Diane had kept the kitchen open for us – I hadn't realised just how late it was by the time I'd showered and changed and packed an overnight bag. Yes, and applied some slap. That was better. Diane asked us to stick to the specials board, not the longer menu. So the four of us sat down, Toby included, for all the world as if it was a normal Sunday that had been full of normal Sunday events. Only the fact that from time to time I couldn't stop my cutlery clattering on the plate reminded everyone that it wasn't. Toby spotted that I was distressed by Jo's solicitousness, and embarked on a self-deprecating account of his life on the amateur stage. At least laughing might disguise the fact I found I couldn't eat. Suddenly one of those sleeping pills seemed a very attractive prospect.

To my distinct surprise, as we went our separate ways Toby kissed me, continental fashion, on both cheeks. Not an air-kiss, either. He'd also insisted on putting his number into my phone in case any of his clever little gizmos seemed to be playing up.

'Was he flirting with you or not!' Jo laughed, as she checked I'd got everything I needed in the guestroom they always offer me.

'It'd show pretty poor taste, all things considered,' I said. She obviously wanted me to talk to reassure herself I was all right. 'In any case,' I added, 'he thinks of himself as a Thespian – and aren't all Thesps a bit lovey-dovey?'

'Or gay . . . Even so.'

'Sorry, Jo,' I heard my mouth say. 'He's not my type. Why all that business with the phone when he'd already told me all his little gizmos would operate and could be adjusted remotely? I still need that mythical ballroom dancer of yours to sweep me off my feet.'

I needed sleep even more. It almost hurt my head to talk. I didn't want even Jo's solicitude. I wanted sleep. I wanted Nosey and Lavender to hand. I wanted the day to end.

It wouldn't. Silly bits of conversation. The sweating horse. Some idiot trying to tell me about first aid. Another one trying to flirt. Flirt, for God's sake! When a woman had—

I reached for a sleeping pill . . .

CHAPTER NINETEEN

'It's fucking clothing, isn't it? Just clothes! You don't wear a fucking uniform! The teachers don't wear a fucking uniform! Why should my little princess? I ask you – pretty little things like her wearing grey and bottle-green. Trousers, too. And saying the boys can wear skirts. That's not right.'

Starting the Wray Episcopi school week with a huge row was actually very therapeutic. This doesn't imply that I swung off the rafters and yelled. Indeed, the louder my opponent, the quieter and more polite my responses. So when I got this huge guy leaning over my desk and haranguing me about his daughter's uniform choices (she favoured baby-pink in everything including sparkly slip-on shoes she was somehow supposed to run in) his face so close I got his spittle in my eyes, I was very quiet indeed. Very still. Not obviously watchful, but not taking my eyes from his face.

Don't think I didn't want to get up and yell back. The uniform colours had been the same since the Second World War, according to the records, white replacing yellow after a particularly bad attack of thunderbugs, which last summer had settled like black snow on t-shirts and blouses and made outdoor play impossible. Trousers – as long as kids sat cross-legged on the floor, there was much to be said for them, a fact that spread almost by osmosis as the girls grew older. Skirts for boys? Only as far as National Book Day and the dressing-up box were concerned, but I sensed increasing enthusiasm, which I didn't happen to share, for having a free-for-all about what was worn below the waist.

I could, therefore, have engaged in a logical argument, but that was to assume he'd be responsive to logic. And it felt perilously like going on the defensive. For the same reason I wouldn't reach for the panic button under the desk – thanks to Elaine's urgent intervention, both schools now had these, in the head teacher's room and in the reception area.

By now he'd got on to human rights and the length of our holidays and how we needed to do a proper day's work for our excessive wages.

I let him get on with it.

At last, like an Atlantic gale, he blew himself out. He might even have been looking a bit sheepish. Still silent I tapped the keyboard, printing off four documents:

Uniform policy – boys, girls, transgender
Dressing-up days policy – ditto
Bullying policy
Visitors to the school – code of practice

'If you want to arrange another meeting, Mr Crouch, I suggest you read those first. All four. And now I understand that for on another matter entirely the police will be here any moment: if you want to stay here and repeat what you've just said to me, that might be interesting. But I'd rather we had a quiet, constructive talk another day. Donna will arrange a time for you.' I got to my feet. 'Florence's reading is coming on very well, isn't it?' I added, as I held the door for him. 'It's lovely when hard work pays off.' I didn't specify whose.

I smiled him on his way, watching Donna, who'd insisted on coming in just for a couple of hours, arrange an appointment for him. Don't think I wasn't shaking inside: raised male voices with raised male fists take me straight back to Simon's time. If I saw a child like this, I'd kneel and gather them up for a hug. For a crazy moment I wished I could be scooped up in a comforting embrace.

Not Rufus Petrie's, however. Not that he showed any signs of wanting to touch me, once we'd shaken hands. Sitting down at my request, he was extremely polite, as icy as I'd been to Florence's father – but surely to disguise the fact that he was near to tears.

I responded with warmth. 'You're worried about Lulabelle being in school today, Mr Petrie? I am myself, to be honest. Could you use a coffee? I know I could.'

He smiled. 'Actually, yes. Yes please.'

I buzzed through to Donna.

'How do you keep your cool with a yob like that?' he continued. 'Yes, we could hear everything back there. Another minute and I'd have come through and decked him.'

'It's a good job you didn't – it's against school rules,

or I might have tried myself.' We shared a cautious laugh. 'Thanks, Donna. Now, the first sign of a headache and you go straight home: right? Promise? I don't want your gran on my back, do I?' I waited till she'd closed the door behind her before I said, 'Donna had a fall in the woods – those woods – last week. I didn't think she would come in, didn't think she should, as it happens, but stoicism seems part of her job.'

'Just as it's part of yours. Ms Cowan, I don't approve of your positively encouraging Lules to ride – that's what she says, anyway, but you may tell me different. And then yesterday you tell me she needs her bloody horse. Needs! I could have wrung your interfering neck. But actually, you may have a point. Do you know where she slept last night? Not in a hospital bed. Well, no one would want that, I suppose. But not in her own bed either. I found her curled up in the loose box. With the horse. Is it normal? That's what I want to know.'

'Let's just say I think it's something that her therapist should be aware of – you know she'll be offered specialist support?'

'Oh, I shan't bother with the police people. I shall get her someone from Harley Street. Now what have I said wrong?'

'Nothing. Your daughter. Your money. All I know is that for the immediate care after an event like that the people who the police use are excellent. Long term, if she still needs support, they'll be able to advise on the best person for her to talk to.' I felt I was justified in stressing the personal pronouns a little.

He raised a cynical eyebrow. 'What about you? Will you be going to the same one?'

I could feel another argument coming on. Being hectored on a totally private matter was not my favourite thing. But I managed to say, 'She would be seeing an expert in children's therapy. And although there are times I don't feel very grown-up, I'll be allocated adult support.'

He looked at me narrowly. 'They say you're seeing a shrink just to cope with this job.'

I was even more furious than I had been with Crouch, and my voice started to slip from my control. 'I don't think we should discuss rumours, do you? But if anyone suggests that to your face, you might respond that people have all sorts of reasons to need support.' I took a deep but not entirely calming breath. 'Now, Mr Petrie, do you have any particular concerns that need immediate attention?' I half rose, but sat as he pulled a comic face, and raised a pacifying hand.

'We've not finished our coffee, yet! Jesus, Ms Cowan – what should I do? That's what I came to ask. Not to be a bastard.' He spread his hands in a mixture of despair and frustration.

'Let her hug the horse. You could hug them both at the same time, maybe.' I smiled. 'She really wants to please you, you know: I wanted her to stand for the school council, but she's afraid you'd be cross if she didn't get in.'

He went white. 'In other words, you're saying she's afraid of me?' At first he sounded angry, even outraged – but then disbelief segued into something like horror.

'Do you think she might be?' I asked gently. Suddenly I wanted to be anywhere else. The effort of saying the things my training had taught me suddenly seemed enormous. Maybe the sleeping pill had left me hungover; maybe I was being unrealistic about my efforts to overcome yesterday's shock. I'd always prided myself on my ability to bury my problems in work: now I wanted to disappear under a duvet with Lavender and Nosey.

'We've not had an easy time since my wife died. You'd have thought it would have made us closer, but—' He drew himself up short. 'Your secretary said she could only allocate me a ten-minute appointment, because someone else wanted to see you. And I've an idea this conversation should take a lot longer. I've never done this bleeding-heart stuff, Jane.'

I didn't pull him up over the use of my first name. 'It's not an easy option. Yes, I do know from experience, as rumour told you. My ex-husband is currently doing time in Durham Jail for what he did to me. Hence my therapy. But after yesterday, Rufus, I'm not strong enough to talk about it, to be honest.'

'Of course – you saw what Lules saw. My God, I'm so . . . How on earth did you manage to carry her?'

This conversation was getting weirder by the minute.

'My head told me she was injured and what I was doing broke the first-aid rules. My heart told me no one should have to see . . . that . . . for a second longer than they had to. So—'

I couldn't manage this.

Donna buzzed.

'That means your next appointment is here, I gather. OK.' He got up. 'Thank you. And thank you for everything you did yesterday. I tell you – I'd rather she loved a cat, not that bloody horse. You probably heard about my wife.'

'Yes. I'm sorry. How does Lulabelle get on with your new . . . companion?'

'Irana? She's not a companion, Jane, or anything like that. She works for me, but not in the bedroom. But I bet the villagers have her down as my whore, don't they?'

'The same people who say I need a shrink. Let's say they wonder if she's a possible stepmother for Lulabelle.'

'And there I didn't have you down as a tactful woman . . .'

On what I think was a compliment, we shook hands, and I did my ushering out routine. Elaine was indeed waiting, with ill-disguised impatience. I did the obvious thing: I made the introductions, giving Elaine her full title.

'I'm not in charge of the investigation. But I am working on one aspect of it,' Elaine said, as they shook hands. 'How is your daughter, Mr Petrie?' I suspected she refused to use her absurd name. Perhaps she'd find 'Lules' easier.

'In school. She insisted. Same as Ms Cowan insisted. But I gather . . .' He gestured from her to me.

'Yes. Rather urgent business.' As if I'd prompted her, she added, 'Our officers are very good at supporting people in situations like this, Mr Petrie. They'll both be in safe hands.' She nodded his dismissal. What a professional.

The moment he was out of the door, she turned to Donna, asking, without preamble, 'Up in the woods the other day – did you fall or were you pushed? Or were you, indeed, whacked on the head?'

As if by reflex, Donna rubbed the spot. 'I don't know. I didn't even know I'd got a lump till Jane had a look at it. I believe PCSO Ian Cooper made enquiries at A & E and found it was logged.' Her face was on fire as she used his name.

Elaine's laugh was startlingly loud. 'Jane was right! And there I was trying to get her to take young Ian along on a hot date.'

'I don't class drinkies with a shoal of pensioners as a hot date,' I protested. 'And however lovely it would have been to have him as arm candy, even assuming he'd agreed to your plan, he'd have stuck out like a sore thumb. As it was, I managed to have a woman-to-woman conversation I meant to tell you about – only stuff happened,' I added.

'Maybe you could tell me about it now. Donna, if I tell you I'm sorry I tried to mess with your shiny new relationship, could you make me a coffee?'

'Of course.' Donna looked both embarrassed and irritated. 'Another for you, Jane? Or had you better move on to green tea?'

School secretaries!

Elaine sank back in my visitor's chair but soon realised this wasn't a chair for slumping. 'So, this Joy of yours is worried about something? Would it involve us?'

'I don't know. I'd rather it involved me first. A nice chat over coffee. But when the hell do I have time for a nice chat over coffee? With her or with Izzie?'

'She doesn't have time to scratch her head,' Donna said, coming in without knocking and not quite plonking the coffee in front of Elaine. She was much gentler with my mug of green tea. 'My nan made a cherry cake for me: I don't suppose either of you would like a slice?'

'Your nan? If she finds out you're sharing it with incomers, she'll kill you or me – I don't know which!'

'I'm not an incomer!' Elaine squeaked. 'I was born in Lyminge!'

'I'll take that as a yes,' Donna said, returning with two slices, one decidedly larger than the other. She closed the door behind her with a slight emphasis.

'Made an enemy there, didn't I?' Elaine observed. 'It's a good job you didn't take Ian or you'd never have got any work out of her again.'

We ended up sharing the larger slice, Elaine guiltily patting her stomach.

'Have you any news for me?' I asked.

'Some news but none I can share with you. Well, I can tell you the vicarage is almost ready to be handed over to professional cleaners: I absolutely don't think the new incumbent – is that the word? – should have to deal with it. We've taken some stuff, actually, but not everything. Skip time, I'd say. Actually, funny as this may sound, I just wanted to see how you were. And to tell you that for whatever reason, you'll have to find another place to have your car cleaned. The place you told me about is empty. Everyone's gone. Vamoosed. All their kit's gone too. What hasn't been taken has been cleaned to within an inch of its life. Well, all those power hoses . . . How long are you going to stay with Jo and Lloyd?'

'They've got lives of their own.'

'In other words, you plan to return to Little Orchard Close. I wonder what happened to the big orchard,' she mused.

'I'm an incomer, so don't ask me! You've no idea how much I want my own place, to settle in, to put down roots,' I said, surprising myself.

'Here? You want to stay here? Bloody hell, in your position I'd be scouring the Internet for new jobs.'

'Too early, career-wise. I need to prove I can make a go of these schools before taking on something bigger.'

'Who said anything about bigger? Except I see you in a bigger village – a town, or a city, that's more you. And I'd

185

like you to know I'm not happy about your being in that house alone.'

'Despite all Toby's gizmos?'

'It's just your being on your own – nothing to divert you. You could do with another dog. A huge Alsatian maybe. Better than Geoffrey.' She laughed at my grimace. 'You'd win a village fete gurning competition with that. What about just pulling a sickie and doing a bunk to a nice quiet spa for a few days. That would be good, wouldn't it? No? Anyway, I'd best be on my way. If I could just use your loo first . . .'

CHAPTER TWENTY

I hadn't exactly forgotten about the after-school fundraising meeting at Wrayford School, but it certainly hadn't been at the forefront of my mind. Printing off the paperwork I'd need was very much a last-minute flurry, not helped by the photocopier's insistence on jamming. I was actually on my knees sorting it out when my deputy, Tom, discovered me.

'Sorry, Jane, I've been meaning to get that fixed all day.'

'That's not your bag, Tom: it's Melanie's. Decidedly admin and secretarial.'

'Ah – you've not heard. Her dad's had a stroke. She's had to take a couple of days' compassionate leave. At least a couple, I'd say. Is that OK?'

'Of course: she works far more hours than she's paid for, doesn't she, and does far more tasks, too. Always the first with the first-aid box or the sick-bucket. Are you able to come to the meeting tonight? I know you don't have to, but if you weep and fall on your knees you might get a governor volunteering to help while Melanie's away.'

He held out a hand to help me to my feet. Heavens, I was only a couple of years older than he was. But it would have been ungracious to wave it away. 'Actually, I assumed I'd have to deputise for you – I never dreamt you'd be here. Are you sure you should be? Even if the rumours are only half-correct, no one would blame you for going to earth.'

'Is that a kind way of saying I look like death warmed up? I'd better put some fresh lippie on.'

To my further shame, I'd forgotten that as the new vicar, Graham West would automatically be a governor, and I hadn't done enough copies of the paperwork. While, somewhat to our surprise, Graham opened the proceedings with a prayer, Tom came to my rescue, slipping out, crossing his fingers as he went, and returning triumphantly before Brian Dawes, as Chair, began his opening remarks. The meeting was primarily concerned with the suggestions the subcommittee had put together – and in one or two cases acted on. The village cricket team would sponsor all the kids' sports kit, whatever game they were playing. A Canterbury sports shop had promised to provide at cost all our balls whatever the size or shape. A couple of stifled sniggers suggested that it could have been expressed more felicitously.

At this point a parent governor interrupted. If we were prepared to mount an exhibition of his work in the Wrayford School hall, larger than the one at Wray Episcopi, a local artist would take over responsibility for the scenery for our school plays and nativity, and even do some regular volunteer teaching. Since he'd already had the required background checks, this was enthusiastically welcomed until someone suggested it might be worth seeing some of his paintings first. If they turned out to be erotic nudes, then we might risk a lot of unwelcome publicity. Did I notice a hurried glance being exchanged between some of the members?

And so it went on. For each really promising proposal, there were two or three duds, which were nonetheless hard to turn down as we wanted the donors' goodwill.

At this point, Brian narrowed his eyes: 'I was under the impression that our subcommittee was authorised to make suggestions, nothing more. Am I right in thinking you've actually approached the donors – even closed the deal with them?'

'Only a couple. The balls and the kit. Though the artist's pretty committed. He's even come up with some designs. It might be hard to unpick.'

I let the bickering roll on around me. In any case, they were merely scratching the surface. I could see redundancies ahead. Or even a shorter school week . . .

Eventually Hazel Roberts, the Wray Episcopi chair, raised her hand and her voice. 'All this is generating more heat than light. Clearly, we have to ask Mr Turner – is that really his name? I wonder what his initials are! – if he thinks his work is suitable for family viewing. We may, tactfully, have to ask to see it. Brian and I will have to take on that responsibility, though it will be hard to do it without appearing to be censoring his one-man show. I'd like to confirm what Brian said: that the subcommittee members do not have authority to make firm commitments. They must consult us even if only by email – and the rest of us must undertake to check our in-boxes daily and respond to any suggestions within twenty-four hours. Now, let's quickly review their remaining suggestions and vote. Three minutes maximum per suggestion.'

Graham West gave a cough that was clearly meaningful: 'For something as important as this, it's surely wrong to impose a time constraint. The future of two schools and two communities is in our hands. I know how keen Jane is on meticulous preparation.' It did not sound like a compliment.

What was going on?

Hazel and Brian exchanged glances. An incomer having the temerity to sound critical of a more established inhabitant! Hazel said quietly, 'We all know by now that Jane has had a most appalling experience; that she insisted on coming into work and now to this meeting is immensely to her credit. Jane, we want you home and in bed by eight-thirty. Very well? First suggestion, please.'

Probably astonished by this takeover bid, Brian rattled through them.

I actually might have been following Hazel's kind orders about bedtime but for an unexpected visitor. Joy Penkridge appeared on my drive even as I was closing the garage door. I froze it in mid roll. She ducked in and sidled past the car.

'Such a good idea, this, being able to get straight into the house . . . Now, Marie and Tess phoned. Tess, actually. She told me all about . . . that business in the woods. And so I've come to take you back to mine. No, don't argue. The spare bed's aired. There's a meal in the oven. I've booked a taxi to get you back here tomorrow so you won't be late to school.' As I opened my mouth – possibly to say I was fine, she continued, 'Tony's persuaded Ken that he's well enough to go on one of their model boat trips, so you'll be doing me a favour, look at it this way, saving me from rattling round that great apartment like a pea in a colander. Just pack an overnight bag and we'll be on our way. No arguments, I said. You looked after me; I'm going to look after you. Oh, you poor girl – let's get you home.'

Her kindness had done what nothing else had done: reduced me to tears. I sat helplessly by while she packed a bag, including Nosey and Lavender without a word.

She had a glass of gin in my hand and a bath running the moment I was in her apartment, telling me it would take a good half-hour to organise food and I wasn't to hurry with my pampering, which included organic scented candles and a lot of bubbles.

'Actually, this was Ken's idea,' she said, pressing more casserole on me. 'When I said I thought you could do with some company and said I'd come to yours for the night he suggested a change of scene might help you. In fact, he suggested you might want to stay for a couple of days. Which you can, of course, and welcome, but I know you and work, don't I? Hence the taxi. Another baked potato? I know how you love them. No? Well, don't think I'm offering you coffee tonight, dear, or even suggesting a walk. It's drinking chocolate for you with just a dash of Amarula and then bed with those teddies of yours. And I'll call you at 7 a.m. prompt tomorrow so you can have a bite of breakfast before the cab arrives.'

'Tell Ken I think he's a genius,' I said. 'And you're my guardian angel.'

* * *

Next morning my taxi delivered me to my front door just as Dolly's mummy, Enid, was walking past. Perhaps not entirely to my surprise, she came and hugged me, lifting up Dolly to hug me too – or at least lick my face, something I'd never been keen on, even when Geoffrey did it.

I was happy to let her chatter away, all too aware that she didn't want to upset me by raising the topic she'd most like to hear. Much of it simply washed over me, because I was busy trying to remember my day's commitments. But I did hear one of her suggestions '. . . for our evening walk with us. Dolly loves your company, you know. And they say there's a warm front coming in and this evening will be like spring.'

I must move.

I agreed to see her at seven-fifteen.

On impulse I popped into Wrayford School, not because I needed to with Tom so efficiently in control, but because a natter about the previous night's meeting might be therapeutic. It was – if not quite as heart-warming as an Open the Book group performance. I could never entirely follow the order of the stories, which seemed to move at random from the Old to the New Testament and back again, but there was never any doubt about the sincerity of the actors. Today Jesus was healing lepers – or, as the actors said, people with leprosy. As the children trooped out in silent ranks, Tamsin Powell, the OTB leader, strolled over to me. Despite her years she looked like a latter-day Lizzie Siddal, even though her red hair was now greying. Today it was tamed into a plait.

'We've still not enough recruits to run sessions with you

at Wray Episcopi, though we are working on it. I tried to book an appointment with the new vicar – did you know we had to do that? – to discuss it, but apparently he's too busy to see us till early in March. Not a priority, apparently!'

'He and his wife have their work cut out until the vicarage is cleaned and decorated, I should imagine.'

'Were you any less work-orientated when your housing arrangements were in chaos?'

'No. But I was being paid, and he isn't. Tell you what, why don't you have a word with Pam Lunn, one of our dinner ladies – she's got her fingers on the village pulse. Or with Donna's nan.'

'Not that terrifying old bat? But you're right – a personal approach might work best. Have a good, quiet day, my dear – you're always in here.' She touched her heart.

Back in Wray Episcopi School, Cecily and Kayleigh might have been expected to be kind and supportive to their best friend, whose hands they insisted on holding wherever they went. Perhaps they thought they were when, having escorted her to the loos, they hung around in the corridor outside and devoted themselves to being so cheeky to Jess I almost gasped. Jess, however, had their measure, and promptly put them on playground litter duty for a week, with tidying stock cupboards as a wet-day alternative. She also put them on report, which meant their parents would be hauled in if they so much as squeaked for the rest of the term. Technically that was my job, but she was my deputy and I was happy to let her take over any role she fancied today. I knew I was no use to man or beast, ghost-walking about the place, and was tempted to retreat to my office and put my head down for ten minutes' sleep. On the way to do just that, however, I heard footsteps in an illegal run behind me.

I was just about to snarl when I realised it was Zunaid. Heavens, I still hadn't chased Elaine about getting a proper interviewer for him. But I couldn't think about that now, as he tucked his hand into mine. 'Ms Jane, when I was sad back home my dad would take me to the mosque to talk to Allah. There isn't a mosque here, and I know you call Allah God, but do you think we could talk to Him?'

'Do you think He'd hear in my office?'

'I think He hears us everywhere, but it's more polite, my dad said, to talk to him in a quiet place.' He led me purposefully, closing the office door behind us. If he prayed with his hands open and me with mine closed, I was sure neither Allah nor God would object.

At last I did what I'd never done before. I knelt down and hugged a child, kissing him on the forehead. 'Your dad was right, wasn't he?'

'He was always right. Except when my mother told him he was wrong.'

For whatever reason, I felt better after that. I even felt well enough, when I encountered Lulabelle on her own in the corridor, to gesture her to one side, asking her quietly to drop into my office, with her dad if necessary, at the end of the day. Or she could come alone any time.

She came alone, during the lunch break, full of apologies and asking if she should be gathering litter too.

'Would you feel happier with your friends? Because though you did nothing wrong you can join them if you want. So long as you pick up rubbish too.'

She shook her head silently.

'Would you like just to sit down and be quiet for a moment?' I thought about offering her Zunaid's prayer option, but this wasn't a faith school and I'd known colleagues threatened with disciplinary action for such a move.

'Ms Cowan – could you – just hold my hand a moment?'

I knelt beside her. 'I could offer you a hug if you'd like it? Not as good as Snowflake's shoulder, but it's there if you'd like it.'

Another shake of the head. 'I just want to be still, but if I'm quiet I just see—'

'I know what you see. Have you started your therapy yet?'

'She wants me to talk. I just want to be with Snowdrop and be quiet.'

'I'd like to be with Geoffrey, the dog I only borrowed for a week. There's something about animals.'

With a faded wisp of a smile she nodded, but turned away.

I might not be allowed to pray with her, but with Zunaid's example I could pray for her.

Enid had been right about the weather: if I'd been a countrywoman I'd have sworn I smelt spring when we started our walk. I wasn't lying when I assured her that spending the day with the kids had helped me a lot. Taking her cue from me, perhaps, she told me all about her grandchildren – she had five or six, all with trendy names, even more old-fashioned than their grandma's. Of course there was a Henry, but a Doris crept in, alongside an Elsie. Perversely I was waiting for the day when Gladys might make it into fashionable circles. Meanwhile, attempting to keep up with who was hoping to be a fighter pilot (Ianthe) and who a ballet dancer (Reggie) and making sure I said something appropriate about each one took my mind off . . . off stuff. It was like leaving a radio on low late at night – the burbling was almost hypnotic.

Until she changed the subject. Holding up her hand like an old-fashioned traffic policeman, she said, 'Listen to that. Just listen.'

I did as I was told. All I could hear was Enid's deep sigh – which sounded as if it was one of satisfaction.

'Isn't it lovely?' she prompted me. 'The silence. Not like last night. Goodness me, the foxes scared me out of my wits! Their screams. They're so human, aren't they? And they just went on and on. The vixen must have been on heat or something. I tell you, if I'd seen her I'd have gone after her with the garden hose. Actually, they make such a racket when they're really . . . you know, mating . . . that I might have cooled two lots of passion. But you never do see them, do you? Except once when I lived in Birmingham (oh, didn't I tell you? I know you're from round there), not all that far from the city centre; I was sunbathing in the garden – we used to do that before they discovered it made your skin age – and I fell asleep and dreamt someone was on the phone heavy breathing.' She demonstrated. 'And I didn't like that sort of dream at all, so I woke up and there was this fox just about six inches from my ear! Imagine! I don't like to think of what he might have done if I hadn't woken – they say some actually go into houses and attack babies, don't they? But they won't have my Dolly, will they, my precious? Mummy wouldn't let them.'

Dolly's entire rear end wagged agreement as she was gathered up in Enid's arms.

'I've only heard them once since I was here,' I said. 'When Joy was staying. Thank goodness she was – I was about to dial 999 and yell "murder"!'

'I'm not surprised. Actually, the foxes seemed to have alarmed a lot of people last night. We heard shouting and doors slamming, didn't we, precious? Up the road from here. But I couldn't see anything, though I had my hosepipe handy. Now, Jane, if you're nervous – and who'd blame you – my spare bed is always aired. What have I said?' She stared at me in horror as I sobbed.

'It's since Sunday . . . If people are kind I do this! Sorry, Dolly, I don't mean to alarm you. There. That's better.' I blew my nose emphatically.

She patted my arm. 'I was like that when my husband died. But I had Molly, Dolly's mother, for company. You need to borrow Geoffrey again.'

CHAPTER TWENTY-ONE

I needed Geoffrey even more after a Wednesday so full of meetings I was ready to scream. As it happened, the last one was held at a school not far from William Harvey Hospital, so I did what I still felt I needed to do whenever I was near – I went to visit Will.

As always, I spoke to him as if he could hear. Perhaps he could. I even paused so he could respond – but of course he never did. And often I told him things I wouldn't have dreamt of admitting to anyone else. Clutching Eeyore, I talked about the weather, about a few political skirmishes I'd heard about on the car radio. And finally, as if I'd talked myself in, like a cricketer taking time to settle in at the crease, I confessed, 'You've seen me when the job got on top of me. It's like that now. Only it's life. Seeing what I saw. Knowing what a child has seen. I'm supposed to be tough. Resilient. Do you remember, my nickname was Avo, because I was so tough on the outside? Well, I've got the soft buttery inside of a perfectly ripe avocado now. And I feel as if I'm being mashed up to make guacamole.'

'I'm not surprised.'

No. Not Will. Elaine. If she was embarrassed to find me lying alongside Will on his bed, she hardly showed it. She extended a hand to pull me upright.

'Will, I've come to take Jane to supper. Girlie night out. Robin's away on some course and she looks as if she needs a good square meal, doesn't she?' Ever tactful, my friend Elaine. 'But before we go, Will, I'll just update you a bit about the goings-on down the nick. First up – you remember the rumour that that crazy woman Fi Simmons was having an affair with Burke, that ego on legs from forensics? Well, seems it's more than a rumour: Burke by name, burk by nature. She's carrying a baby, and she told someone – in absolute confidence, of course – that he's the dad. Oh, and guess who fetched up just down the corridor from you: old Dave Blake. Smuggled all sorts of crap? Always carried a blade? Anyway, our friend Thompson – yes, Al Thompson – came off worse. We'd like him kept alive to face trial, of course. On the other hand, I wouldn't want him to get a single cc of a donor's blood that could go to someone more deserving.' She talked a bit more shop before concluding with a suppressed sigh, 'All right, Jane? Off we go.'

As always I kissed his cheek as I left.

There never had been a response and there wasn't now.

I was too tired to risk even a so-called small glass of wine, though Elaine reckoned the meat-laden Turkish meal would probably have absorbed enough to keep me legal.

Eventually we shared one, much to the extremely handsome waiter's amusement.

'I ran into your friend Caffy the other day by the cheese counter in Sainsbury's,' Elaine told me, neatly intercepting the questions I had intended to ask and which she no doubt was unwilling or even unable to answer. 'Isn't she strange? Immensely practical and competent, according to the friends of ours whose cottage she more or less took apart and put back together, but in other ways – no, I don't get her. Too fey for me. I like her fiancé, though – Tom Arkwright. A good old-fashioned cop. Honest. Decent. Gets results.'

'Yes, he's lovely, isn't he? I like him very much.'

'Have you met the other man in her life? Well, man and his wife, actually. Todd and Jan? Their surname's Dawes.'

'Wasn't there a pop singer called that back in the day? Made a mint, just dropped off the radar.'

'That's the one. He and his wife set up a charitable trust – not as big as the Gates', but big, with lots of donations from their mates. They don't just raise money, though – they get their hands dirty. Todd Dawes . . . Dawes . . . I wonder if he's related to your Brian? No – I doubt it. Chalk and cheese. They more or less adopted Caffy when she was really up against it – she'd managed to annoy some dead nasty people.'

I knew that already from Caffy herself. She'd been forced into prostitution at one time, before she came down to Kent, and got involved with drugs. Goodness knows how she'd ended up so serene. 'No, I've not met them yet. I fell in love with their house, though.'

'Who wouldn't?'

'You're not subtle, are you, Elaine? You want to tell me

what Caffy and Tom think about my continued visits to Will, don't you? Well, I know she wants me to let go. And I'd love to. I wish I'd never saved his life. But there's some proverb, Chinese probably, that says if you save someone's life they're your responsibility for ever. That's rather how I feel. Except, of course, I didn't save his life. I just saved his existence. I wish someone – but not me – would switch off the life support. There. Now I've said it.' I sank all my half of the wine in one go.

'Actually, someone wants to. There's an ex-girlfriend or two in the mix now. And a distant relative. In fact, the hospital are applying through the courts to let the poor bastard go, but one of the women intends to keep him alive whatever the prognosis and whatever the other women say. I've told the hospital's team that you should be consulted too, and the transplant team. No, actually, they can't be – supposed to be completely neutral, aren't they, so they can't be seen to recommend anything anyone could construe as brokering body bits. Oh. More alliteration.'

'I know what you're doing, Elaine. You're doing everything in your power not to give away any information at all about the . . . the dead woman. Not to mention the vicarage mess and the stuff going on in our close. You're gabbling away like a Christmas turkey about Will—'

'I think you'll find it's called briefing you. Stuff you really do need to know. Because in all honesty I cannot – dare not – say anything about the stuff in Wrayford and Wray Episcopi. If you don't know anything you can't say the wrong thing.'

'I bet I can,' I admitted ruefully.

'I'd much rather you didn't. Seriously. People's lives are

at risk, Jane, and I'd rather yours wasn't one of them. God, look at that baklava. No. I mustn't even think about it or I'll gain a kilo. You go ahead, though.'

'I'm too full already. But I shan't have a coffee either – I want to sleep tonight.'

I had never spoken a truer word. The trouble was, where some people slept more when they were tired, I simply lost my grasp on the whole process. I had all sorts of audio stuff on my iPod to settle me, plus my trusty bears, of course, but when I was desperate sleep became as elusive as a mirage. I'd finished the emergency sleeping tablets I'd been given, so tonight I would lay out lots of bait to capture it. So on the way home I stopped off at Sainsbury's to pick up, among other things, some drinking chocolate, Amarula and full-fat milk, plus a packet of camomile tea bags. What I couldn't find was a wand to magic away my fear of returning to the empty house.

Tough. I'd better just get on with it.

It was a fine night, but I still picked my way back to Wrayford more slowly than usual: twitchy and not concentrating properly, I could be a total menace if I wasn't extra careful.

I was rewarded by the sight of things I usually whizzed past. An owl, swooping so low over a hedgerow and so close to the road, it made me afraid his days were numbered. My lights picked out a badger that hadn't waited for culling but had taken the Dignitas option. There were a couple of purposeful foxes, going in opposite directions. Would they make the night hideous with those calls that sounded so like a mortally terrified human being? I was glad I'd not heard any since that night when Joy had had to reassure me. Clearly even a countrywoman like Enid had been distressed by what she heard when, this time, I was staying with Joy. With hindsight, I might have been tempted to dismiss Zunaid's claim that he'd heard human screams – but then, when I thought again, I wasn't. I tasted bile. No, if I stopped to vomit I'd be . . . Well, I wasn't going to throw up so I wouldn't need to stop. In fact, I pressed on rather more quickly.

The light was on in Enid's front room: it took a huge effort to forget her kind offer of a spare bed to go into my own place and do all the routine tasks that ought to reassure me but only left me more on edge. Should I have some music on to shut out unwanted sounds? Or would I really rather stay alert? No. I needed sleep more than I needed anything. Hot bath with lots of essential oils. The hot chocolate. One of the escapist books meant for holiday rental guests. Lavender and Nosey. There!

Until the screaming started again. The vixen, I told myself. I couldn't see her anywhere, but hoped, when a sudden, blessed silence fell, that Enid had been accurate with her hosepipe.

CHAPTER TWENTY-TWO

Jess was less assured in her position as my deputy than Tom, but since she'd been in the Wrayford Episcopi school for such a very short time, I was sure she'd grow in confidence soon enough – and what better way to find what you can do than to be dropped into the deep end? Not that she'd be there very long – but whereas she could have contacted me while I was in those endless meetings, my phone would be out of bounds while I was seeing the specialist support officer I'd been allocated.

The education department hadn't been over the moon to learn I was having what the irritating woman at the end of the phone referred to as mental health issues, but I assured her that the governors of both schools had promised to be supportive in any way necessary.

I wasn't a stranger to the therapy process, of course, which I always found a bit like root canal work for the psyche – not nice but very necessary. I left feeling wrung out but knowing I could deal with what had happened.

What about Lules? How would she deal with it all? I just hoped her father wouldn't turn the process into being about him and his money rather than the expertise of whoever was treating her. I also hoped her friends wouldn't lure her into joining them in some of the stupid behaviour they'd indulged in a couple of days ago. But whatever they were up to wasn't my problem for the next hour or so.

It was dusk when I set out for Little Orchard Close, which I did with startlingly little enthusiasm. As always I slowed down when I headed into the village, with or without the promptings of the Speed Watch team. Had those attacked by the van yobs the other day recovered? Once again I metaphorically hung my head in shame: an email to them wouldn't have cost much effort.

It might cost some effort to stop and speak to Izzie, who was standing at the gate of the vicarage looking hopefully up and down the road. But I did.

'You look frozen.'

'I am, I am. And goodness knows where Graham's got to. I came to see how things were going. At least it's empty now, quite empty. The cleaners will start work soon, and they say we can move at the end of next week, maybe. And the police have finished with the garden – one of the team says she knows a man who'll dig the rest of it to match and lay a lawn and stuff. And I dare say everything will be fine when our furniture and bits and pieces are in.'

'I'm glad you're feeling so positive.'

'You've no idea how hard it is.'

'It is hard. Very hard. As I know all too well.'

'Yes, but it was a tree that damaged yours.'

'There was a police investigation there too,' I said gently. 'Now, why not phone or text Graham and come and wait in the warm in my temporary base? It's only five minutes down the road.'

Her lips thinned. 'I said I'd wait for him here so here I must be.'

I was just getting back into my car when a text came through from Jess. Could I drop by if I had a moment?

Sighing, I replied that I was on my way. At least I didn't have to go back to that empty house for a bit longer.

Jess was sitting in my office with Cecily and Kayleigh when I arrived. Jess personified calm, implacable authority. The girls, ostensibly demure and penitent, actually exuded the opposite, with latent smirks on their faces. Jess stood immediately, offering me her seat. The girls, against all the school rules, didn't.

Jess challenged them with a silent eyebrow. They stood.

'Good afternoon, Ms Rhodes. Good afternoon, girls. Cecily, will you move that chair to this side of the table, please, so Ms Rhodes can sit down. Thank you.'

'That only leaves one chair between us,' Kayleigh protested.

'So it does. But it won't be a problem, will it, because you can both stand while you tell Ms Cowan what you've been doing wrong.'

'But—' A nudge from her friend silenced Kayleigh.

Very well, divide and rule time.

Jess had the same idea. 'So, Cecily, let's start with you. What have you done and why?'

Tears started to well up. Big, convincing tears – but some girls could produce them as a party trick.

'Would you like me to invite your parents in now – they're waiting in my classroom, Ms Cowan, with Hazel Roberts and another governor – or would you prefer to explain in private?' Jess managed to combine steely with sympathetic.

'I'm very sorry, Ms Cowan.'

'Thank you, Cecily. Could you tell me what you're sorry for?'

To my amazement Jess gripped my hand under the desk. But it was good to have someone beside me. This was bad news for everyone, not least the perpetrators.

'Getting my sister to tweet, Ms Cowan. About you. But Ms Rhodes made me tell her to take it down. So I did. Then she took away my phone.'

Which she wasn't supposed to bring to school anyway.

'What about me?'

'About you being mad. Like Lules.'

'Lules is mad?' I asked quietly.

'Must be, if she's seeing a shrink. And you're seeing the same one.'

I folded my hands on the desk. 'Tell me, Cecily, if Lulabelle had a sore throat and been taken to a doctor, would you have tweeted about that? If I'd twisted my ankle on our morning run, would you have tweeted about that? Would you, Kayleigh? Why not?'

Kayleigh broke first. 'Cos that's boring stuff, miss – Ms Cowan,' she said, with insulting emphasis. 'Not like being mad, is it?'

'Your best friend has had an experience no one, child or

adult, should have to endure, and is now being supported by specialist police officers. And you think you should tell the world she's mad?'

Cecily put in, 'Not Lules, miss. She's our friend. You. Only you're not really crazy, are you? I suppose.'

'You'd have to ask the police officer whom I spoke to this afternoon. I think the term for what both of us are experiencing is post-traumatic stress. Meanwhile I think we should talk to your families. There's not enough room here so we'll adjourn to the classroom where they're waiting. After you, Ms Rhodes.'

'It was a joke, wasn't it?' Kayleigh's mother said, her middle-class vowels and smart outfit clearly used to winning each battle. 'And in any case, I can't see why you've got a problem with my daughter because it was Cecily that did it.'

'I'm not sure the police will see it that way,' Hazel Roberts said, who had taken the teacher's chair. I was happy for her to take the lead. The whole business had rocked me, because I could see all sorts of repercussions for the children. And, let's face it, for me. So I sat on like the others on undersized chairs around a bank of child-sized tables hastily gathered into the middle of a room bright with charts and children's artwork, all far too happy and normal for the current scene.

'Police? Why the fucking police?' Cecily's father demanded.

Me too, silently. Police? Overkill, surely!

'Because both Ms Cowan and Lulabelle were affected by seeing the result of a most terrible crime, the perpetrators of which will one day come to court, we hope. And having' – Hazel spread her hand as if physically grasping for the right word – 'having this appalling tripe put into the public domain may affect the way the trial proceeds.' Hazel might look like an archetypal sweet old lady, but her delivery was steely.

'No, we can keep the cops out of it!' he insisted.

Hazel shook her head, calmly and quietly ignoring sundry interjections as she spoke. 'I have to notify them, though technically I believe any charges would be against Cecily's sister, whom I should imagine will hear from Ms Cowan's lawyers too. Meanwhile, it goes without saying that both girls are suspended till we discover the extent of the damage they've done. They must not speak about this in public or even to their friends – is that clear? And especially not on social media or to the press or TV. The education department legal team may well be involved too, on Ms Cowan's behalf.'

I nodded: yes, I understood all too well that my employers might seek to cut me off to protect themselves. But all they would learn from my face was that I was coldly infuriated.

Hazel hadn't finished. 'There will also be bills for repair to the school fabric, which has already been defaced with disgusting graffiti. This is more serious than you can possibly imagine, I'm afraid. I think that that is all we can achieve today.' She rose slowly, but as if she meant to, not because she was waiting for a second hip transplant. I knew she was in pain, but not so much as a flicker of a grimace crossed her face. 'I was mistaken: girls, I don't believe we've heard your apologies yet.'

* * *

Back in my office, Hazel and I sipped green tea: Donna had forbidden either of us caffeine. Jess, on the other hand, drank coffee that smelt like nectar.

I found myself pacing. 'There's something else, isn't there? The girls might have had their primmest faces on when they were with their parents, but there's something else. Something they know and we don't. Any ideas, Jess?'

'Now you mention it, I'm sure you're right. They were just too innocent, weren't they? Got to be faked, hasn't it?'

Hazel looked from Jess to me, clearly aghast. 'Isn't what they've done bad enough?'

'It's bad. But Jane – Ms Cowan's – been a teacher long enough to smell a rat.' She nodded as I flapped a hand: I was happy to be Jane. 'Now she mentions it, they were just too good. No sign of them backing up their parents' objections. But equally no sign of them looking truly penitent. What the hell are they planning?'

'What would you do?' I asked. 'If you were a ten-year-old with hormones,' I added with a sad grin at both women.

'Something like planting a computer virus with long-term consequences?' Hazel said. 'Except I should imagine your computers and the schools have every anti-viral program going.'

'Absolutely,' Jess and I said together.

'But,' Jess mused, 'I think you're right. Something like that. Something that might emerge when they're suspended – they weren't at all surprised by that, were they? – so they can't be blamed.'

'You're already had a rat invasion at Wrayford School, haven't you?' Hazel said. 'So something like that?'

'Cockroaches? Ugh!' Jess shuddered.

210

'How would they get hold of them? No, you don't just pop into a shop and ask for enough to infest a school kitchen . . . Except they might have done something to the kitchen, mightn't they? I'll ask the long-suffering cleaners to be even more thorough.'

'The coffers are bare, but I'll pay for a deep clean myself if necessary,' Hazel said. 'Anything, so long as we don't have to close the school. We need to keep parents on our side. And the best way to alienate them is to rob them of childcare.'

I sat down on one of the vicious visitor chairs, wincing. 'Is there a way we can question them? Now they're off-site?'

'Talk to the lawyers,' Hazel said. 'Have they sent you the statement they want you to read to the media yet?'

'Excuse me.' I checked my phone. There was certainly an email from them, plus a text from Joy, imploring me to stay the night with her since Ken was away. 'Let's print it off and see what they advise.' As for Joy, I was very tempted to accept her invitation. If, as was likely, the media had decamped to my house, then it would be nice to avoid them. On the other hand, I had a spine that ought to be stiffened: scared out of my own (if temporary) territory as a result of the actions of silly children? No. I'd text her back later.

'If only there were a back door we could spirit you out of,' Hazel said, hugging me as the printer drooled out a stream of paper. 'There'll be a media embargo on photos of the miscreants since they're so young, but sadly they can use anything they take of you – preferably one of you looking dishevelled and deranged.' She looked at me meaningfully: *I was to spruce myself up before I left the building, wasn't I?*

I nodded. 'Then all I've got to do is stick to reading them this text.'

'Of course, you mustn't go home. There must be someone you could stay with – Jo and her husband, perhaps? She's told me she's expecting you. Oh, and she says I'm to tell you her techie kids are already on to the tweet and dealing with it, whatever that involves.'

'Thanks. They're brilliant at things like that. But I'll be turning down her invitation, Hazel. And one from another friend. It's not my permanent home, I know, but the house in the close is my base, and I'm damned if I should be forced out of it. I'll print off enough copies of this to give to anyone who turns up, not just the guys outside here.'

Hazel shook her head. 'Half of me applauds your guts, Jane – but the other half wants to wring your neck for your stubbornness.'

Jess grinned. 'That's my gaffer for you. Jane, do you want us all to walk out together? Shoulder to shoulder?'

'Once I've combed my hair and applied some slap, I'd love that – hang on. I've got a text from Brian Dawes I'd better respond to.'

'We'll wait,' Hazel said. 'But I think we'll sit on the chairs in the office, Jess, don't you?'

CHAPTER TWENTY-THREE

'I insist,' Brian declared, an hour later. 'If necessary you can leave your car here and take a taxi home.'

We were in his brightly lit, anonymous living room, dominated by those gloomy oil paintings. The stiff G & T Brian was waving in front of me was very tempting. I took it, with one flailing grasp at common sense. 'If my car sits on your drive all night it'll be all over the village.'

'With every torrid conclusion in the book being drawn. Jane, my dear, the car can go in my garage. Sit and drink. You've been through tough times in your life, and I've put you through some of them myself.'

This sounded so like an apology I opened my mouth to protest.

But he was shaking his head. 'There are times when one needs to clean one's slate, and this evening is one of them. Any day now I take my overnight bag and head for the cardiac unit. Triple-bypass time. No, it's not that I'm at death's door; it's that I've decided to go private. I want to get it over with. You see, I have to confess, Jane, I'm mortally afraid.' He looked me in the eye. 'Statistically the operation is very safe, with transformative results. But one always has a lingering fear. No, I wouldn't mind dying under anaesthetic. It's—'

'It's worrying you'll end up like Will?'

He managed to look both guilty and frightened. 'I'm afraid – yes, you're right. I thought of talking to Graham West about it, but he . . . he's not terribly user-friendly, is he?'

'It must be hard for him, knowing what happened to his predecessor. I just hope he'll grow into his role here. And his wife, too. Izzie.'

'That woman who looks like a witch? Or a gorgon, with barbed wire instead of snakes for hair! I'm sorry, it's not very PC of me to use such terms.'

But that didn't stop him, did it? Supinely I said, 'We're just having a good gossip, Brian: it's not going to leave these four walls, is it?'

'And nor will anything you say, Jane – I hope you know that.' He stared into his glass, and drank deeply.

Before either of us could embark on anything like a personal revelation, however, he turned the talk to school. Both schools. The tweets, of course.

I talked him through everything Jess, Hazel and I had done. I showed him the press release.

Only then did he say what I really needed to hear: 'The governors – all those I've spoken to thus far – will support you to the hilt.' Suddenly he produced a most unBrian-like grin. 'Though I've not yet forced myself to have the pleasure of consulting West. He's not the person, incidentally, I've asked to deputise for me while I'm *hors de combat*: I've asked one of the parent governors – the one who's taken over the cricket club. His name escapes me just now – do you know, I can only think of one thing?'

Very soon, however, he had to drag his mind to something else. A call from a business associate came through, obviously urgent and important or both. Brian seemed flustered, promising to phone back later. It was clear his interlocutor wasn't keen on any delay.

Despite Brian's protestations I slipped off, abandoning the gin just in time to stop myself kissing him farewell. Waving goodbye, I made him promise to tell me when he had the call to the hospital, where I'd visit him as soon as he was allowed company. Probably I shouldn't have driven, but I did, arriving in the close without incident.

Fortunately, the night was cold enough to keep the waiting press in their cars, so I was able to pop the car into the garage, rolling down the automatic door before they realised what was happening. Then it was time to take a risk. I took a tray of hot chocolate out to them, along with a sheaf of press releases. I pointed to these, miming a zip across my mouth, as I beat a retreat. Mercifully they took the hint, the only sign of them ten minutes later being a row of empty mugs on the front step. I could make some supper, drink some more, have a hot bath and retire to sleep in my own bed – or what passed for it these days.

Until the screams started, that is. Bloody incontinent foxes. I'd give them screaming when I needed peace and quiet. If only I had a hosepipe handy. Or even a bucket of water would do.

So there I was, bucket in hand, standing on my front-door step. The randy vermin would regret this.

Except I couldn't see any of them, and I was more sure than ever that what I'd heard was a terrified woman.

999 time.

The call handler took my plea for help very seriously, but even as I asked for help I realised I had a problem. I wasn't sure where the scream had come from. All the same, she promised to despatch a rapid response vehicle 'to cruise around a bit', as she put it. Could I possibly stay alert and let her know immediately if I heard the sound again? I could. I had plenty of missed work to catch up on, after all.

Even as I turned the central heating on to override, I asked myself the question I didn't want to answer: why wasn't I getting dressed and walking round the estate in case I was needed?

I didn't have Geoffrey for company, that was why.

I had trainers and a dark tracksuit. I had a torch on a head strap. I had my mobile.

The bathetic part was that despite all this, I had an entirely peaceful walk round the close and was just about to let myself back into my house when a car turned into the road. It looked very much like an unmarked police vehicle, the sort that suddenly produce blue flashing lights when you're whizzing along the overtaking lane on a motorway. I flagged it down.

'Oh. Hi, Eoin!'

He looked quite blank, but then screwed up his face. 'My God, it's you, Jane, isn't it? What are you doing?'

'I made the 999 call about the woman's screams, and thought I ought—'

'Bloody hell, did you now! Well, get yourself into your place, lock the door and brew some of that hot chocolate for me. But no Amarula, mind! Be with you in five.'

He was. The conversation, such as it was, felt very stilted, perhaps because I had poured a healthy shot of Amarula into mine – or unhealthy, according to your view – and I really wanted to go back to bed and sleep, despite the heap of files on my table. Fortunately, the moment he'd sunk the last of his chocolate and then irritatingly checked the back garden for signs of foxes, he left.

Odd, I mused to Nosey and Lavender, that considering we'd once spent at least half an hour fancying the pants off each other we seemed to have settled into an awkward semi-hostility.

'Men!' one of them said not entirely clearly, and we fell asleep.

It was never going to be as easy as that next day, nor was it. Though I arrived at Wrayford School very early to brief the staff as I would later brief their Wray Episcopi colleagues, the media were already circling like buzzards – or the foxes I'd not seen yesterday.

I pinned a copy of the prepared statement on the door and left them to it. The staff would come in via the kitchen, not best Elf and Safety practice, but one I'd suggested to them all via texts. Meanwhile, I needed a strong coffee to wake me up. And some toast. Thence to the comfort of my – our – office.

As I came off autopilot, I tried to give more thought to – whatever needed thought. Which was a lot. But the more I tried to focus on budgets and staff development and one or two playground issues and . . . and . . . and . . . No, there was one thing bugging me from last night. I heard the screams. I dialled 999. I prowled round the estate. The police arrived in the form of Eoin. But Eoin was in Traffic, with particular responsibility for Kent's motorways, whether they were being used as roads or car parks. Because, I suppose, when staff were short, everyone had to do as my colleagues and I did – multitask, fill in for each other, cover when someone was off somewhere else. But – and this was what had dimly troubled me at the time – he'd made no reference to responding to an emergency call. And why, when the very first time we'd met we'd have been at it like a pair of those bloody foxes one moment, were we less than studiously polite the next? Though that might have been after Joy's efforts with the Amarula. Or was it after his walk round the close, when he'd shunted us back into my house because it wouldn't do for us to be seen with a cop in uniform?

But my musings had to be put on hold. The school had its first asthma attack of the day, promptly followed by our student teacher's dash to the loo to vomit. A late outbreak of the norovirus? I had to assume it was and sent her home. So I had to get someone in to cover the classes she should have taught, because the regular class teacher was on a day's training.

And then there was a text from Rufus Petrie to think about. Could he and Lules have a few minutes of my time sometime today? Sooner rather than later. And it might have to be at their place, not the school.

Hell. Twice hell. But why should he bring Lules into the discussion if he was going to bollock me to bits over her friends' indiscretions?

218

When I didn't respond immediately, another arrived. *Or at Wray School if it would help?*

It would. I had a few minutes while Tom was taking assembly. *If you could manage be at Wray School by 9.05? CU then.*

Melanie looked at me with disapproval when I asked her to bring coffee through when the Petries arrived. 'A visitor? With you looking like that? Did you actually brush your hair this morning?'

'Yes. But I've been tearing it out.'

She produced a can of Elnett, gesturing to the new cloakroom before she handed it to me. 'A spot of lippie wouldn't come amiss. And mop your mascara. Left eye.' She looked me up and down. 'Mud on your trousers, too.' The hairspray was followed by a clothes brush.

'That's more like it,' she said, as I returned her property. 'If only I could get you to stand up straight before your shoulders are fixed like that for ever.'

I'm not sure what sort of greeting I was expecting from Petrie. Controlled fury, probably. What I got was Lules hurling herself into my arms and him smiling apologetically over her head. 'She insisted on telling you herself and apologising.' He closed the door quietly as Melanie, having silently delivered coffee and a glass of milk, withdrew.

'It's all my fault,' the poor child was saying. 'I told them I was having help and they said it was childish and silly and I said if it was good enough for you – oh, I can't believe I said it!'

I'd been hugging her tightly, but pushed her away so

I could hold her gaze. 'I'm going to tell you something someone once told me: just because you leave a key in your front door doesn't mean anyone has to burgle it! They were your trusted friends and they betrayed your confidence. That's not your fault. Don't worry. Come on, President Trump will fire off a new tweet tomorrow or the day after and the Twittersphere will be far more interested in that. How's Snowflake enjoying all the extra fuss with your being at home? Didn't you promise me some photos?'

'So when I assure you I said not a word to anyone, you'll believe me?' Petrie asked quietly.

'Of course.' My hand, apparently of its own volition, reached out to shake his. Weird.

'Daddy – there's something else I've got to say.' The words almost exploded out of her. 'I've got to. I promised I wouldn't. But . . . You said in assembly last week it was OK to break a promise if you shouldn't have been asked to make it in the first place, didn't you, Ms Cowan?'

'Absolutely. We were talking about online grooming, Mr Petrie,' I explained.

He nodded. 'So what do you need to tell me, Lules?'

'It's Ms Cowan I need to tell, not you, Daddy. Ms Cowan, they've put something bad where no one will find it. So the school will have to close until they do. I'm sorry.'

I took her face between my hands, holding her gaze. 'It's not your fault, Lules. Even if you joined in then, you're doing the right thing now. Do you understand?' As she nodded doubtfully I asked, 'Could you recall what it was and where they might have put it?'

She shook her head, imploring me to believe her.

'It's OK. At least we know there's a problem and can start dealing with it.'

Petrie got down to Lules' level, pulling her to his shoulder. 'Any clues at all, darling? Anything that would help Ms Cowan?'

'An idea they got from the Internet,' was her muffled reply.

It was clear she didn't know any more. I could imagine them holding the information just out of reach to tantalise and torment her. But whatever they were planning – whatever they had done – I needed to know.

And I hadn't a clue how to find out.

CHAPTER TWENTY-FOUR

It was one thing to search the Wray Episcopi buildings as best I could without disturbing classes, which I had done, slowly but not at all surely; it was quite another to give it the sort of forensic examination it might well need. I could either ring the fire bell and get all the kids into the playground, where they'd be soaked to the skin in five minutes or—but at this point Hazel walked into my office.

'I've just been hearing your Zunaid read,' she said with a smile. 'Such a lovely child in every way, isn't he? Jane, what's the matter?'

I explained, pointing to my hand on the phone. 'I have to call the police, don't I?'

'Because of the empty threats of two silly girls? Surely not!'

'Even with the tiniest risk we have a duty of care.'

'You could go and talk to them.'

'In their own homes, assuming, of course I found them there? Legally I can't. Mustn't. And do you suppose they'd tell me anything if I was rash enough to try?'

She waved aside my objections, but came up with one of her own. 'Ah, you're afraid they'd trace the information back to Lulabelle and bully her even more.'

'In addition to everything else I am. But—'

'What if I go down instead?'

I really think she was prepared to. 'You'd expose yourself to more insolence. No, Hazel. I'm sorry to go against your advice, but this has to involve the police.'

'We don't want flashing lights and sirens! Not at this point.'

'Of course we don't. But we don't want a big bang and all the kids being blown to kingdom come.'

'What about talking to that nice lad Ian – the PCSO?'

I suppressed a sigh. 'Of course, we could. But he's not—' It was best to save my breath to cool my porridge. Hazel and I had always been allies. She'd been more than loyal to me: she'd been kind. The least I could do was treat her with respect.

'Donna will have his number.' She bustled off to speak to her.

Meanwhile I thought fast. I really had no alternative but to clear the building, but to close it was not an option, not if I wanted to keep our parents onside – which in these days of expensive and elusive childcare was vital. It was a miserable day, with no sign of the rain abating, so having a whole day in the playground simply wouldn't work. Sadly, this village had neither church nor village hall, nothing but a rusting Nissen hut that housed the few remaining Scouts. But Wrayford had a village hall, which had once provided us with a safe haven. It was an old building that had been extensively refitted. With luck we could use it again, if, of course, it was free. The bonus was the excellent kitchen, not to mention the closeness of the Wrayford School playground if the weather improved. All we had to do was get there. I reasoned that if we expected even the youngest child to run at least a mile before school each day, we could expect them to walk the three and a half to Wrayford – two and a half if they went cross-country via public footpaths.

Within ten minutes, Ian was in my office, reaching for his phone.

'This is beyond my remit, you know, way beyond it. You need specialist officers to talk to the girls for a start, Ms Roberts – people who are properly trained.'

Like the one who was supposed to be talking to Zunaid.

'And yes, I'm sorry, Jane, you probably do have to evacuate the school. Maybe pronto. In fact, that would be my advice.'

Hazel spread her hands. 'Ian, this is two ten-year-old girls, not members of ISIS or Daesh or whatever they call themselves.'

He looked at us cynically. 'Surely you know that kids are being referred to the Prevent programme as young as four or five? You must have known that when you spoke to me I wouldn't just tell you not to worry.'

Hazel's mouth tightened. 'Indeed, I did not. I expected common sense. We can't disrupt the education of nearly a hundred children just on hearsay. I'm going to talk to those girls now.' She got to her feet.

'That's got to be left to us. Now, Jane, about clearing the school.'

'The evacuation's already under way. Each child has already collected his or her shoe bag, PE kit and lunch box, and their class teacher is checking the content of each – ditto the boxes they keep their workbooks and so on in. I know, I know,' I said as Ian started to protest. 'Should this be a crime scene I've disturbed it. But at least we know that anything left lying around hasn't been checked and maybe that's a job for your colleagues.'

'Two things: what if there'd been any explosives in their belongings?'

'For goodness' sake, Ian, stop fussing: Jane's acted with sensitivity and intelligence, I'd say – and your colleagues can always recheck if they're not happy. But at least we know that each child has been united with their property.'

'Some of which they'll have to carry to Wrayford, where I've booked the village hall for the day. Donna will be there to update parents and field phone calls and emails. My deputy, Jess Rhodes, will be supervising the pupils and her colleagues when they've walked there in a crocodile. Yes, hi-vis waistcoats all round,' I said. 'As they leave the playground in pairs, you and/or your colleagues will easily be able to recheck everything they carry. What was the other problem, Ian?'

He held up his hands in pleasing surrender.

His colleagues – the real police with powers of arrest – might have been less keen on what I had done but were, I suspect, quite happy to ignore the possibility that a Peppa Pig pencil case might have concealed a bomb. Even a stink bomb.

With nothing obvious lying around, the officers turned their attention to the less accessible areas, which is where, after all, Kayleigh and Cecily claimed to have put – whatever it was. But there was nothing under or behind cupboards, nothing in walk-in storerooms, which were always out of bounds anyway and kept firmly locked. When I'd shown them round and produced keys to order, the only use they could think of for Hazel and me was to make tea, a career opportunity we were quick and firm to decline, though I told them where to find everything they needed.

I had probably scored a diplomatic own goal, because at this point they told us to vacate the building because, amazingly, it was the turn of the army to arrive, in the form of a bomb disposal unit. I didn't need Hazel, still stomping doughtily beside me despite the now driving rain as I walked round and round the building, to say it felt like overkill. But all their electronic and chemical analysis brought up nothing, and we were allowed to return to the building, where we did make tea and coffee, graciously sharing it with the disconsolate officers. We were soon joined by their colleagues whose interview with Kayleigh and Cecily had come up with the same big round zero. There had been a lot of giggles, a lot of face pulling – and a claim from the allegedly responsible adult with them that they weren't old enough to be treated as criminals, which I should imagine was swiftly refuted. Meanwhile, any computer they might have used in their search was going to be forensically examined – including those in the school, of course.

The hot drinks thawed relations sufficiently for the officers to start talking to, as opposed to at, us. In response, I mentioned the fact that it was lunchtime and though most of the ingredients of the school lunches had gone by car to Wrayford village hall, I should imagine that we'd find the wherewithal to make sandwiches. A tiny silence was filled by Ben, the forensic team's leader, who said he was a dab hand at buttering bread if someone else could slice it. Hazel volunteered to do that, and Theresa – one of the two women who'd been questioning the girls – and I found ham and cheese to complete the job. We sat round in the hall, suddenly relaxed and at ease. Over coffee, Theresa brought us back to the work in hand: did I think the whole thing could have been a double bluff, the equivalent of kids in secondary schools pressing the fire alarm to get out of maths tests.

'I've been worrying about that myself,' I admitted, setting down my mug. 'It might be helpful to talk to Lulabelle Petrie, the kid who snitched on them to me, but she's in a very fragile state and you'd have to tread with maximum caution.'

'She wouldn't be lying herself?' Theresa asked. 'Trying to get them into trouble for what they put out about you?'

'Do children's minds work like that?' Hazel asked, rhetorically, I thought.

But I answered her seriously. 'They can. They might. But Lules'? I don't know. I might have wondered myself, especially as she's been a very edgy pupil, and of course she has been bullied herself by girls she considered her friends . . . But on the whole I'd exonerate her. Especially in the light of what you said about Kayleigh and Cecily's response to your questions this morning.'

Which had been nothing: they were entirely innocent, guv.

'Let's talk to her,' Theresa's colleague Charlotte said, putting down her mug with an assertive tap and getting to her feet. 'Falling down and breaking your collarbone's not that traumatic, is it?'

Hazel coughed. 'It was rather more than that, my dear.' She looked sideways at me. 'She . . . she found a woman's body.'

'Even so—'

'A woman who'd been tied to a tree with her own intestine – while she was still alive,' I added, the words coming flatly out of my mouth of their own accord.

Funnily enough I'd felt very little as I spoke. But my words couldn't have had a more dramatic effect if I'd tried. Theresa dashed for the loo. Charlotte's eyes filled. Two hardened officers. I even found myself apologising. I was aware of Hazel putting her arms round me, and leading me somewhere.

At last I realised we were in the playground again. I was kneeling by a drain.

'We all knew it must have been bad, my dear. But not the full extent of . . . the circumstances. And yet you're here working? Or is it better to work?'

'Absolutely. The therapist tried to get me to describe what I'd seen and I couldn't. And then—'

'Better out than in,' Hazel said firmly, mopping my forehead and setting us in motion. 'Whoops – that doesn't look safe at all.' She pointed to the cast iron coal-hole covers. Coke chute, to be more precise. If I could get the term right maybe my teeth would stop chattering. I followed the line of her finger. Yes, there was a crack running across one of what were effectively a pair of iron doors in the ground, like those you see outside old pubs relying on deliveries of barrels. I'd walked in perfect safety across thousands in my life. I'd probably walked across this. But I wouldn't now. Though the crack only ran about a third of the width of the right-hand one, and the split was only a millimetre wide at one end, it widened to about a centimetre. To my shame my first thought was that repairing it would be another drain on our exhausted budget.

Hazel was far more on the ball. 'I don't suppose they could have slipped something through that crack?'

I squatted, though she didn't. 'You could only slide coins through, or maybe at a pinch a squashed pea!'

'Or SATs test or one side of a sandwich!' she responded.

The more we tried to be sensible, the harder we found it. But eventually, still giggling intermittently, we reported it to Ben, who eyed me warily. 'Are you OK, Jane? We—none of us realised just how bad . . . No wonder you're having counselling.' He touched my arm in awkward sympathy.

'Thanks.' If I wasn't careful I'd find myself in very public tears, so I pulled myself up, straightening my shoulders as if Melanie was watching. 'The chute goes right down into the stokehole, where, in the days of caretakers, you'd find the boiler.'

He pulled a face. 'Can you get access any other way?'

'Actually, there is a route. You have to go into our current boiler room, then through a narrow door and down a steep set of steps that would have Elf and Safety in hysterics. But one of the first things I did when I arrived here was to have both doors equipped with touch pad locks. And the main door is behind one of the bookshelves you had to move.'

'So it's unlikely the girls could have got in that way?'

'One way to find out,' I said, determinedly gung-ho and positive. 'You move the bookshelves and I'll tap in the codes.'

They were wearing paper suits and paid to do dirty work; Hazel and I chose to stand and watch. We did succumb to more giggles when a blue-gloved hand flourished their only find, half a crust of bread. But nothing else.

'So, I can get a builder in to make the chute safe?' I said, as they emerged. 'There are times when I take Elf seriously,' I added.

'No problem. Now, before we sign off is there any other conceivable hidey-hole?' Ben asked.

I pointed solemnly upward. 'The loft. With its own touch pad.'

'We'd better find a paper suit for you.' Ben said.

So there I was, sitting on the tongue-and-groove floorboards that covered the majority but not all of the loft floor, marvelling that someone should have gone to so much trouble when these days some sheets of contiboard would have been considered adequate. With the torch on my phone I pointed to the repair that we'd needed after the big storm but had only been completed a few days ago because all the local workmen had been working on bigger repair jobs: the slate was a slightly different colour from the old ones.

'Pity that the flooring doesn't cover the whole space. They knew how to do things properly in those days, didn't they? I bet they thought the place would stand till Domesday, and never dreamt it would be pulled to accommodate an estate full of ticky-tacky houses,' said Ben.

'What?'

'That's the rumour, anyway. And God knows we need the houses. My son'll never get his own place, what with raising a deposit and paying off his student loan. Whoever thought they were a good idea?'

'No one in education that I know, anyway. Tell me about this housing development. Who's behind it?' How on earth had I missed that? Or was it something to do with that secretive activity of Brian's?

'Someone with more than enough money anyway, I dare say – and what's the betting they've got an offshore trust so they won't have to pay tax on their profits? OK, let's see what we can find . . . No, to move all this insulation we'll need proper kit. And we could do with better lighting.' He looked at his watch. 'Tomorrow is another day, as they say. Not that we'll be here tomorrow. This isn't high priority enough for us to apply to work paid overtime.'

'Not high priority enough – a hundred kids' education? I really can't shift an entire school out for another day.'

It seemed I would have to.

CHAPTER TWENTY-FIVE

I hurtled across to Wrayford village hall at the end of school to thank the parents for their cooperation and understanding and to explain that we'd have to use the same building on Monday. Not all had been pleased, of course, to have had to add a couple of miles each way to their journey, but only one got really vociferous. When no one supported her, she piped down and joined the other mothers in the traffic chaos resulting from having two schools finish at the same time.

The staff looked understandably tired: improvising is more stressful than having plans you've prepared in advance, but also ultimately far more fun. I thanked them all, including Donna, of course, and the cooks.

'Pam's dinner tasted even nicer cooked on the stove here,' Zunaid declared, which prompted a round of applause for her and her colleague.

I waved them all off, including Jo, who said she'd have invited me round for supper only they were off to a dance to practise their ballroom skills. She'd text me about what we could all do over the weekend – 'You can't work all the time,' she said.

There was too much adrenalin (and perhaps caffeine) coursing through my system for me to settle for dear old boring admin at either school. After the day's activities, I needed a shower, but the central heating had yet to come on, and it was a short, businesslike affair, still too cold in the bathroom for me to relish giving myself a much needed pedicure. I was also low on fresh food, so although I knew I'd tangle with early rush-hour traffic, I set out for Ashford Waitrose, where I knew from experience I was likely to meet fewer of my pupils and their parents.

The person I did meet was Joy, sleek in appearance as ever, but with a weary droop to her mouth. We adjourned swiftly to the cafe area for our free drinks – yes, in my case, a virtuous green tea – a cake and a natter. Ken was planning yet another trip with Tony: 'Already! And at the weekend too, just when I'd hoped for a bit of company. I'm getting a bit sick of Tony, to be honest. I know I should be grateful to him for providing a roof over our heads, and a very nice one it is too – but he seems to be expecting payment in time, Ken's at least. But he'll never tell me what they get up to – just that it's to do with his damned toy boats. A grown man – I ask you. Him and Tony both.'

Did I dare float the notion that Tony wasn't universally admired and liked? Kent's Croesus? Well, she'd know about the money, and know from experience that he didn't

233

care to throw it in the direction of people he employed or, more accurately, got his friends to employ.

'Anyway, he needed me to pick up some dry-cleaning for him for the do in the evening – and of course, he's too busy tweaking the damned boats to come himself. Oh, Jane – are you free this weekend? Let's do a mini spa break, shall we? Oh, come on – a massage, a facial and a manicure, with a champagne lunch thrown in? Do let's! My treat – no, Ken's actually, because he gave me his credit card by way of an apology.'

'You know what,' I said, casually wiping out a whole day's planned work, not to mention a ball-skills session with the women's cricket team, 'I'd love to. But it's pretty short notice to get in anywhere.' Not much time to find me a substitute for tomorrow, either.

She flourished her phone. 'I'll call the Mondiale down in Hythe right now.'

I flourished mine, too: yes, if necessary, the captain of the cricket team would take my place.

I had some pride. So did my car, and it was damned if it was going to sit in its present state in some upmarket hotel car park next to Joy's gleaming Merc. So when I saw another abandoned petrol station offering hand car washes I pulled in. And wished I hadn't. The thin, hangdog men were the ones who'd cleaned it before. If anything the night air was colder. If it was possible, they looked even more emaciated. And when I produced the top-end biscuits and crisps I'd bought, not to mention packs of oranges and apples, they fell on them, one guy older than the others insisting on sharing them into pitiful heaps while the younger ones toiled. By chance I'd got a few pound coins too. As I drove away, I think the old guy blessed me, but I wasn't sure in what language.

'Language, schmanguage!' Elaine declared, two minutes later when I pulled into the first lay-by I found and yelled into my phone. 'We're on our way.' I could actually hear her breath change as she started to run, throwing comments to people I couldn't see. 'You can stay where you are, Jane, if you insist, but I'd much rather you hopped it straight home.'

Those were her words. What I heard in my mind's ear continued: *And locked you and your car in – especially your car. Because the villains will have CCTV at that garage as sure as God made little apples, and probably illegal access to a number plate recognition app.*

'I'll keep you briefed, don't worry. For Christ's sake get moving!' she yelled, probably not to me – but it might as well have been. I got moving.

As I pulled rather too hastily on to my drive I came uncomfortably close to Enid and Dolly, the former obviously prepared to be outraged. But when I steamed into the garage, erupted from the car and yelled to her to follow me, she obeyed, her expression as alert as Dolly's, who led the way as if scenting an adventure – or possibly a few messages Geoffrey might have left.

The door rolled calmly down.

'I'll just put the kettle on and you can tell me all about it,' she said, as I fumbled the house door open.

I dragged in great gulps of air. 'The tea bags are still in the car,' I managed as she peered into the empty caddy. 'Give me two minutes. And I'm afraid I gave the biscuits away,' I added, dumping the first two bags on the floor. I mustn't explain, must I? Elaine had told me nothing lest I blab. 'A homeless guy.' That sounded quixotic enough to convince her.

It did. She gave me a tolerant smile and a kindly shrug. 'It's the wrong time of day for bikkies. And for tea, come to think of it. Let's get this lot put away and then we'll nip back to mine. I always treat myself to a glass or two of wine on a Friday night, and a nice movie too. Have you eaten?'

The little stack of ready-meals rather gave the game away. 'Have you? If not we could share a couple of these.'

'How lovely. I do love these Charlie Bigham lasagnes, don't you?'

'I've got some salad too. And some wicked garlic bread.'

'Bring that too! What's the matter, dear?' She pushed me gently on to a kitchen stool. 'Put your head down if you feel faint.'

It took me a couple of minutes to work out what to say. I ventured, still censoring as I went, 'I annoyed someone on the road back there. Long story. That's why I drove like a bat out of hell. And I'd hate it if he did follow me and – you know how dangerous that bend can be when you're crossing the road . . . Maybe we should stay here to eat. If you don't mind.' I closed my eyes again, trying to shut out a spurious image of Dolly being thrown into the air or even mown down and a less spurious image of a dead woman. I found I was shaking as well as sobbing. All the time I was dimly aware I was being stupid, but I couldn't find a sign of my common sense.

'What I mind is someone frightening you like this. Let me go and draw your curtains before we switch any more lights on. Dolly, you stay here – I don't want you under my feet.'

'But—'

She fished in her pocket and came up with a house key sharing a ring with a tiny torch. Touching her nose meaningfully, she set off through the house.

Dolly whined a bit, but when I stooped down and petted her she responded with her usual wet affection. I gathered her on to my lap.

'Oh, you naughty girl – you know Jane doesn't like having her face washed, don't you? Jane, I really think you're worrying unnecessarily about crossing our quiet little road.' She pushed my hair out of my eyes, then took my hand, which clutched hers convulsively. 'In fact, I'd go further: I'd say you're having a panic attack of some sort. So I'm going to put our supper into this shopping bag, and I'm going to carry it across the road, and then – when I can see perfectly well in both directions – I'm going to call you across. Then when you've fought your demons, we can have a nice drink and watch a bit of something silly.'

'I can't – I really daren't.' I was sobbing helplessly.

'You can and you will. And you can sleep at mine like I said the other night. Come upstairs with me and we'll shove your things in this, for all it's just a carrier. Hasn't it improved things, this charge on plastic bags . . . ?'

At one level I was sensible: despite her gentle objection, I would take my own duvet, pillow and towel. But I doubt if I'd have got across that road if Elaine hadn't phoned just as I was stowing Nosey and Lavender in the carrier.

'Well done, you, saving those poor bastards!' Elaine said, her voice almost as loud as if I had the phone on conference. 'We've picked up the lot and stowed them in safe accommodation while we mop up the scrotes who were – well, their slave-masters, not to mince matters. We got two straight off. Now we're off to Stelling Minnis to find the rest. You did the sensible thing and went home, I gather? Well done.'

To my amazement, quiet gentle Enid took the phone. 'Elaine, you don't know me but I'm a friend of Jane's. She's not too well – she's having a bit of a nervous turn. I'm trying to get her back to my house just across the road.'

'Excellent. Hang on, what do you mean, trying? And nervous turn – what's that?'

'I think she's afraid of someone attempting to take revenge. Someone might drive at her, that sort of thing. She got very upset.'

Enid held the phone where I could hear it but there was a long silence. 'Put her on, will you? Maybe I can reassure her. Jane? You're safe. I promise.'

'What if someone tailed me?'

'Did you see anyone? Of course you didn't. And we didn't either. Listen, you're safe. Now go over to your neighbour's like a sensible woman. Get pissed. Watch a movie. Try *Mamma Mia*. You'll enjoy that!'

Funnily enough, I did.

And apart from a brief and hair-raising serenade from a vixen, I slept – slept, to my acute embarrassment, till the smell of bacon woke me next morning.

CHAPTER TWENTY-SIX

Enid was full of apologies for waking me so early – not that I considered seven-thirty early! – and explained that Dolly was going to have her nails clipped at half past nine, a procedure that apparently she never enjoyed, but she did like a general grooming. Enid seemed tickled that I was to have the same procedure. 'That's just what you need. Not that you ever look other than well turned out, but pampering always does a woman good, doesn't it, Dolly? Sets you up for the week, I always think. Now, are you sure you're all right going back to yours? Do you want us to come too?'

I would have loved them to, but it was time to take control of myself again. 'I'll be fine. You've been more than kind, Enid—'

'Nonsense: I really enjoyed myself last night, far more than sitting on my own – not that I would have been on my own with Dolly, would I, precious? Look, you can't carry all that yourself. In fact, you could keep your duvet here, until all this business has been sorted out and you feel safe. Oh, very well.'

We set off in stately procession, the three of us, Dolly on her lead. As I put my key in the lock, Joy said, 'Oh, I'm so sorry! I shan't be in tonight – bridge club supper – but I can give you a key if you think you'd feel safer at mine.'

In mid-reassurance – the house was exactly as we'd left it, thank God – I stopped. 'What will Dolly do while you're out?'

'What she always does. She lies in front of the TV and is uppity with me when I get back.'

'Maybe she and I could have a girlie evening over here in front of my TV.'

'Lovely! But she may need a comfort break . . .'

'She shall have a walk, she and I – Girl Power!'

My phone prevented any argument. Another determined woman. 'Lunch?' Elaine asked, without preamble. 'I need to talk to you about something – very unofficially.'

'Just hang on a second, Elaine. Bring her round whenever you want, Enid – right?' I blew Dolly a kiss as Enid led her out. 'Sorry about that, Elaine. And I'm sorry I can't do lunch. I'm booked for a day-spa session at the Mondiale. In fact, I've got to dash or I shall be late.' I ran upstairs, still holding the phone. Where on earth were my swimmies? 'But tomorrow?'

'You couldn't postpone?'

'I'm going with someone – Joy Penkridge as it happens.'

'Are you indeed! How did you manage that?'

'No time to explain!'

'All right – call me when you've finished. Listen a lot and say very little – OK?'

So much for my plans for a day of unalloyed indulgence.

But it's hard to think when the woman massaging you seems to be using a rolling pin to attack the knots in your back and shoulders. Even harder, you'd have thought, to fall asleep while she was doing it. But I did. Then came a facial, and with it more sleep.

The champagne with our lunch (taken in bathrobes and slippers) might not have been the best idea, but Joy implied it was de rigueur, so I didn't argue. I don't recall talking about anything in particular, and she was too busy spotting celebs (some of whom I'd never heard of) to engage in a proper conversation.

A dip in the hydrotherapy pool. Pedicure. Manicure.

Still in bathrobe and slippers, afternoon tea. You get rid of all those toxins and replace them with refined sugar, refined flour and saturated fat. And you risk another glass of champagne.

I said casually, 'You must wish Ken was away every weekend.'

'Why should you say that?' she asked sharply.

'No reason at all – except that this is such a wonderful way to pass the time.'

'Well, it is of course.' She didn't sound entirely mollified. 'More shampoo?'

'Best not: I'm light-headed enough as it is. But please – you go ahead.'

She did. She was obviously less worried about her licence than I was. After a swig, she leant forward confidentially.

'Actually, he's really touchy these days, Jane. He can be quite nasty and sarcastic. That's why we've had all these treatments on his card. To teach him.'

No need to say I didn't follow her logic. 'Joy, I'm so sorry. Is he unwell, maybe? Worried about something?'

'How should I know? He's never there to ask. And if I try he snaps my head off. We've been married forty years, Jane, and suddenly I don't know him.'

'Could it – could it be an age thing? He's older than you, isn't he?'

Her eyes widened. 'You think I should talk to the doctor?'

'If that's what you've been thinking anyway.' I hesitated. 'He's never been . . . unkind . . . to you? Stopped you seeing friends or neighbours?'

She snorted. 'He seems glad to be rid of me. But he's never . . . they say your husband – ex-husband . . . hit you. He's never done that. It's just that he's so absorbed in his boats it's as if I don't exist any more.'

'I'm so sorry. But if you talk to anyone it ought to be to him first, oughtn't it? And then you can decide what to do. But – and I'm sorry to sound so headmistressy – if you want any more champagne, I can run you home so you don't have to drive.'

She giggled. 'I don't want to be pulled over and breathalysed, do I? Actually, you know what, Ken was the other night. We're on the way back from some Masonic do and there's this blue light and suddenly Ken's pulling on to the hard shoulder. He just about passed the breath test. Goodness knows how. And guess who the policeman was? The one who fancied you. Eoin. Eoin – what's his other name? Connor, that's right. I did wave' – she demonstrated a little twiddly finger gesture – 'but he didn't seem to recognise me. Blanked me, more like, actually. Anyway, that was that. He and Ken shook hands and that was it. Imagine if he'd been banned from driving! Ken, I mean. All the publicity.'

'Awful.' My personal view was that drink-drivers should be put in the stocks, but perhaps I shouldn't share it just now. As for the handshake, I just didn't want to speculate.

She waved away the offer of a top-up from an assiduous waiter and ordered coffee – yes, and green tea for me.

It was only when I went to change and see what I might be able to do with my hair, left in lank rat's tails, that I could check my phone. Two texts from Elaine, the first asking me to call her, the second telling me to call her.

Can't – still being pampered.

OK, Meet me for Turkish at 7.00. Will get you home if you want to get pissed. x (Park in our car park – security are expecting U. x)

Who could resist an invitation like that? I responded.

But I had to send another text, this one to Enid: *Dear Dolly, so sorry I won't be back to share your supper this evening. But I promise to bring back any juicy bones I can lay hands on.*

By the time I'd sent that another arrived from Elaine: *No. Use public car park. I'll see you at the Turkish. 7.30.*

Since I had time to kill, and couldn't be bothered to go and shop for England at Ashford's Outlet shopping centre, I took myself to see Will. I obviously wasn't the first that day: Eeyore, still wearing the medal, sat out of range, but Pooh was propped at the end of the bed, with that rather vapid smile on his face. I straightened his t-shirt and, propping him on my lap, sat on the visitor's chair. He smelt of perfume: presumably one of the women from Will's past had recently hugged him. It would be good to meet her, all of them in fact, because what they told me about him in his prime would help me to work out what I felt should happen next – please note the euphemism. What would happen to Eeyore and Pooh when he didn't need them any more? I found myself weeping into Pooh's fur – it was much easier to be sentimental over him than over Will.

But it was time to talk. No, I wouldn't worry him with any serious news: instead I tried to give a very upbeat account of my time in the spa, with a decidedly exaggerated version of Joy's tipsiness. But my heart wasn't in it. She was doing her best to be my friend, and her long marriage was in an unhappy phase. That was certainly no laughing matter. It was, as I told Will, time to meet up with Elaine.

I was paranoid enough to suspect I was being followed from the multi-storey car park I'd chosen as being nearest to both Ashford police station and the Turkish restaurant. If I was, whoever was tailing me was good – changing pace, walking on the opposite pavement, heading quite deliberately towards the police station were all in vain. In my mind's ear I sensed inexorable footsteps. Eventually I gave up the game and simply strode out – courtesy of all those pre-school runs! – towards the Turkish restaurant, where the handsome waiter greeted me as if I was an old friend and pressed a large glass of red wine on me as soon as I was installed at the table Elaine had reserved.

Lloyd Davies had once passed on an old police trick: you sit with your back to the wall and face the door because it's better to see any danger than have it creep up behind you. There was a nice buzz about the place, and the tables were already filling up so well it looked as if Elaine had been wise to make a reservation, especially if she had planned to turn up late. Fifteen minutes drifted into thirty, and thirty into forty. My phone calls went straight to voicemail and she didn't respond to any texts. I'd have quite liked to stalk out in fury, but that would have involved walking on my own back to the car – which I wasn't in a fit state to drive, anyway, not with all that heavy-duty red wine, though I had consumed a fair amount of bread and a lot of huge juicy olives. I had a frisson of anxiety – what if Elaine had to scrub the whole meal and had forgotten her promise to get me home?

After an hour, I was just about to bail when Elaine ran in, almost knocking a tray of meze out of the waiter's hands.

'Have you ordered? Why in hell not? I texted you . . .' In response to my bemused face, she grabbed her phone. 'Er, I saved the bloody text in drafts, didn't I? Shit. Look, it seems I'm going to be working late, very late – so yes, please, a nice fat kebab to take out,' she told the waiter. 'My usual. Usual before the diet,' she added with a grin. 'You want one too, Jane? Put everything she's had on my bill, please. No argument, Jane. Where's your coat?'

We'd actually got outside, clutching our cholesterol kit, before I managed to ask her what she expected me to do now. 'I've drunk too much to risk driving,' I pointed out.

'Hell, and I said I'd get someone to drive you back. And now we're as busy as shit. Where are you parked? No, you can't leave it there all night or you'd have no wheels in the morning – only joking, but it's not the best lit car park in the world, is it? Tell you what, I'll walk round with you to pick it up and I'll stow it in our car park, after all – that'll have to do. And you'll have to get a cab home. Sorry.'

'And a cab back in tomorrow,' I pointed out dryly. 'This isn't working out very well, Elaine, is it? OK, let's go. Can't you talk as we walk? Because there's also stuff you maybe ought to know – about Ken Penkridge.'

'Sorry – you'll have to slow down. I don't do power-walking. And I'm sorry to have messed you about. As for tomorrow's cab, come in early and we'll go and have breakfast – my shout – and I can pick your brain and maybe by then I'll have stuff I can share with you.'

'That'd be great.' We were almost by my car. I handed over my keys. 'There you are. See you tomorrow. And I'm sorry to have snapped: I'm very hungry, that's all.'

A figure turned towards me. 'Hungry? Jane? Well, so am I. I came in to get a takeaway. Lules is at her godmother's for the weekend – yes, I had to take Snowdrop too! – and I didn't fancy anything in the freezer.'

Elaine asked briskly, 'Will you be going straight back to Wray Episcopi, Mr Petrie? Cos if you wouldn't mind a short diversion, you could drop Jane off. I might as well take that kebab too, Jane.'

A distant but embarrassing recollection darted into my mind of that scene in *Persuasion* when Anne Elliot, walking in Bath with Charles Musgrove, suddenly finds herself forced into the company of Captain Wentworth. On the other hand, they were in love with each other, so there were no parallels at all.

'Elaine! Honestly!' My expostulation sounded like that of a fifteen-year-old.

'No problem,' Petrie declared as quickly as if he was embarrassed too. 'What shall we do about food, Jane?'

'That table at the Turkish place is reserved till nine,' Elaine declared helpfully, getting quickly into my car and shutting the door rather too firmly. She didn't lower the driving window. I never drove that fast in a car park.

I hope the wave I gave her was ironic. I was angry, but tried not to show it: after all, Petrie had even more reason to be annoyed. For Elaine to transfer me to the care of a man about whom I really knew very little, some of which wasn't at all good, was outrageous of her. It might even have put me at risk. Or did Elaine know good things about him she hadn't deigned to share with me? 'I really do apologise for my friend,' I said.

I expected a shrug. I got a smile. 'Don't. It's nice to have a bit of adult company.'

'But not necessarily to have it wished on you in that high-handed way. I'm more than happy to take a taxi. Sorry – that isn't very gracious, is it?'

'Not really. I take your point, though.' He gave a formal bow. 'Jane, I'd be delighted if you would eat with me and accept a lift back to Wrayford. In whichever order. The thing is,' he added more normally, 'I don't want to get back home too soon. Irana's girlfriend has come over for the weekend and I thought I'd give them some space. The . . . bedroom noises . . . are pretty loud. Thank goodness Lules isn't there! Actually, there's a nice pub a couple of miles south of Wray Episcopi where I sometimes take Lules as a treat. Or would you really prefer Turkish?'

A load of very laddish lads came bundling towards us, already stroppy with booze.

'You know what,' I admitted, 'towns like this might not be the best place to be on Saturday nights.'

He opened the passenger door for me and then paused to make a phone call before getting in himself.

'Table booked,' he said, easing out of the car park. Looking at the groups milling round, he added, 'I think it was a wise decision to get out now. I just hope the Green Grass is OK tonight.'

'The Green Grass?' I squeaked. It was regularly judged as one of Kent's top-three gastropubs. 'It's amazing you got a table at such short notice.'

'The landlord's a mate of mine. He's very fond of Lules, too. She's even had sleepovers with his daughters there. Nice girls – not like the ones she seems to have fallen in with recently.' He snorted. 'You try to do what's best for your kids, you know. And I didn't see Lules as the sort of high-achieving kid who'd do well at a hothouse private school. Anyway, I guess there'd be cliques and bullying there.'

'And no Snowdrop to snuggle up to when things got bad,' I said.

'Right. I just wish Snowdrop was a hamster or a guinea pig. The way she rides – madness. I get so cross with her – well, you've seen. Tell me, how do you get kids to obey without yelling and swearing and letting yourself down?'

'A degree, a post-grad course and a job title giving you authority. And the weird thing is, parents have the toughest, most demanding job in the world – and they get no preparatory course for it.'

'I suspect it's more than that, you know. I gather you're a

really firm cricket umpire? Oh, you hear everything in a village.'

Should I take a risk? 'Maybe if you're a native. It takes a long time for gossip to filter through to incomers. I don't even know what you do for a living.'

'You didn't look me up in Lules' file?' It was hard to tell if he was pleased or disappointed. 'Though it's not as if you had a lot of time, is it? What with one thing and another.'

I took another risk. 'I do rather hope you're not one of the Mr Biggs of the criminal world who seem to have settled in half of Kent. Whoops! Sorry, I sank a glass of wine while I was waiting for Elaine and it might be the alcohol talking.'

'Jane, I'm so law-abiding I've never had so much as a parking ticket and I even fill in my tax returns on time!' he said, full of self-mocking righteous indignation. He added, 'Actually, if you don't you get fined. No, I work freelance in the arts world.'

'Oh, you're not Banksy? No, wrong part of the world, I suppose.'

'Not art, arts. Music, actually. Music production, before you ask if I'm a secret pop star.'

'I thought you had to be a "yoof" to be one of those.'

'Touché!' He parked neatly in the last space outside a picture-book pub laden with peg-tiles. 'Anyway, here we are. I'm afraid we may have to make a run for it,' he added, as a gust of wind hurled rain at us.

CHAPTER TWENTY-SEVEN

Inside was as cute as the outside, with rough plaster and swags of hop bines and old wooden agricultural tools. We had a table tucked into an alcove, which he said was Lules' favourite. His constant references to his daughter kept the key low – but there was a frisson, I was fairly sure of it. Was it welcome? Until I knew more of what Elaine had found out – and of course Lules' grim discovery had been on her father's land – whom could I trust? My instincts seemed to have deserted me and though common sense told me that Elaine wouldn't have entrusted me to a possible murderer or accomplice, I told myself to be cautious. Unsurprisingly the silence that had drifted over us while we looked at the fairly short menu seemed hard to break, even when we'd placed our order – guinea fowl for both of us – receiving apologies that for once the vegetables weren't home-grown because of the bad weather. We agreed what we'd drink with the meal, and that we might as well start on it now. And I asked for a jug of tap water. I'd drunk my units for the day already, of course, but didn't want to sound too pious.

At last he said, 'Actually, I was a bit embarrassed by DI Carberry. Elaine. I'd have preferred to do the inviting myself, because I . . . I had thought of inviting you to dinner before, but . . . Circumstances have been very strange, haven't they? Apart from anything else, you've been under so much pressure, and Lules has had to be my main – my only – priority.'

I nodded. 'Absolutely. I'm really glad you spared her Irana's sound effects.'

'I was worried about you, too, actually – there's only so much anyone can deal with. But you look much better tonight.'

'So I should hope,' I said, laughing. 'I've spent a whole day at the Mondiale being tarted up.'

His face fell. 'So, you were going on a date with her?'

'Elaine! No! She's got a very tolerant husband who is presumably used to being abandoned at restaurants and then having his meal and his car confiscated. I just had a girlie day out at the Mondiale being pampered. I think Joy had had a row with her husband and wanted to take it out on his credit card,' I added unnecessarily. 'Sorry. I shouldn't have said that, and especially shouldn't have mentioned any names.'

He looked at me seriously. 'Given where you live, that wouldn't be Joy Penkridge, would it, and Ken?'

'Forget it. Please. I was wrong to—'

'No problem,' he said dismissively. 'I know them

251

both reasonably well – and I'm actually quite concerned about Ken.'

'Look, Rufus,' I said slowly, 'Joy's done me nothing but kindness.'

'Recently, at least,' he corrected me quickly. So he knew about their quite valid complaints about my garden – and maybe something else? Before I could ask he continued, 'But I take your point.'

'Another point is that I don't want to say anything I shall regret when I'm sober.'

'Do you ever? Sometimes you give the impression that you take words out and look at them before you utter them. Which is not a criticism. And there's always a wariness about your eyes. And I wondered . . . Another thing rumour has told me is that things have been . . . very tough . . . for you. An ex-husband in jail. And a child by someone who should have been looking after you but who scarpered.'

My face felt stiff as I smiled. 'Five out of ten so far. Yes to the ex-husband; absolutely no to the second. If you're referring to Zunaid, I love him dearly but not because I'm his mother. In fact, the ex-husband made—made it impossible for me to have any children of my own.' Why was I telling him something I never, ever mentioned? I said more firmly, before he could start sympathising, 'But shit happens. And it happened once more when a guy I was beginning to like ended up in a PVS.'

'Yes. I heard about that too. And that you still visit him.'

'As all his friends do.'

A plate of charcuterie for sharing arrived, thank goodness. It was all getting way too personal.

I waited till we'd eaten half the pate and might need to

negotiate the fate of the third of three gherkins. 'I shouldn't have snapped at you, Rufus, when you mentioned Ken. In fact, Joy's worried about him too. Says he's moody and offhand with her. I said she should talk to him. Maybe talk to the family doctor. Do you know anything I should pass on to her in a kind and very indirect way?'

'To be brutal, I'd tell her to talk to a lawyer. He's up to something, Jane. Looks smug sometimes but scared out of his wits others. If I were her I'd empty their account and talk about divorce.'

'Any idea what the something is?'

He paused while our plates were cleared. 'How much do you know about them?'

I shrugged. 'I'm going to be their new neighbour, once both our houses are repaired. The village grapevine told you about their tree? We'd talked over the fence; Joy came to stay when her house become uninhabitable; Ken, who'd been on a model boat jaunt, came and joined her but was carted away in the night with acute diverticulitis. Then they invited me to a drinkies party at their new temporary pad, in an amazing building owned by a man called Tony Carpenter. Do you know him? No? Anyway, party or not, she seemed very much on edge. But all she would admit to was worrying she wasn't paying the waiters enough.'

'Waiters?'

'I try to be gender-free. Pretty waitresses from Eastern Europe. I think she slipped them some more cash when Tony, who'd recruited them on the cheap, wasn't looking. In other words, she's a kind woman. She kidnapped me wonderfully when—after . . .' For a moment he seemed about to take my hand; he ended up patting my arm, as I would a kid who needed a bit of sympathy. 'And then we had a nice time today, most of the time, till champagne helped her open up a bit about Ken, who's on another of his jaunts.'

'Do you get the sense that his model boat trips are getting more frequent?'

'I've not really known them long enough to know. But you do?'

'I have this terrible fear he's – I don't know – doing something else. Something else as well, maybe. I don't know. I'm not ready to confront him, being a bit of a coward, and I'm certainly not willing yet to take it to Elaine.'

'What do you think the something else might be? Are you afraid it might be connected with . . . ?' I didn't need to spell it out.

'Dear God, I hope not.'

'The funny thing is,' I said slowly, sipping water as if to clear my head, 'that—no, I'm seeing conspiracies where there may be none.'

'But?'

'He seems to have been encouraging my friendship with Joy. I've no idea why – he and I have scarcely exchanged a word. But he's suggested I should stay with her, for instance, when he's been boating – or whatever.'

'Just being a decent husband, maybe?'

'Of course.'

'Come on, Jane, you're very shrewd – I've seen you in action, remember – and something is troubling you, however nebulous.'

It was the last word that clinched it. 'Foxes, Rufus. Do you know anything about them?'

He laughed out loud. 'Er . . . No. Why?'

I spread my hands. 'I lived in towns and cities for years. And though I saw lots I never heard one screaming. I've only seen a couple down here, but they seem amazingly vocal. Allegedly.'

'Aren't they supposed to scream like humans?'

'What if it's humans screaming like foxes?' I asked quietly. But raised a hand to stop him replying. Our food was coming.

It wasn't the young waiter who'd taken our order who brought it, but someone I knew – a tall, heavy, bearded guy in his later forties or fifties; he looked remarkably like the pictures of W. G. Grace.

'Dom,' Rufus greeted him, rising and giving him a man-hug. 'Dom, thanks for fitting us in. This is my friend Jane, who—'

I was on my feet too, being bear-hugged.

'I didn't recognise you in your glad rags, Jane! How are you doing? Last time we met she was disallowing a dodgy catch and letting me get my fifty, Ruf,' he explained, over my shoulder. 'Oh, one of my specials on the house tonight!'

I was laughing: 'The fielder had both his feet over the boundary rope! And in the old days he wouldn't even have appealed!'

'Well, I'm your devoted servant for life. Never got a half-century before and I doubt if I will again.' He pulled the chair out slightly and settled me back in. 'And here's Karen with your veg. Enjoy while it's still hot.'

'Just before you go, Dom – what do you know about foxes?' Rufus asked.

'There are more of them than before the ban, I'm told –

not that I have any opinion to offer about hunting, of course,' he added with an air of conscious virtue. 'I've seen the odd corpse on verges, but that's all.'

'You've never heard them?'

Dom looked blank. 'Doing what? Singing the "Hallelujah Chorus"?'

'Barking?' I said vaguely. 'Calling to each other in the mating season?'

'They do it with eHarmony these days,' he declared.

'Of course,' I groaned. After a decent interval I continued, 'Screaming? I've heard them back in Wrayford – seen them once or twice. And they sound horribly like humans, to be honest.'

He narrowed his eyes. 'You're thinking about that bad business the other day?'

Rufus replied, 'It was Jane who carried Lules away from . . . it. So she saw everything.'

'So you're doing a little sleuthing. I'd say I didn't blame you, but if anyone's asking questions, Jane, let it be the police. Just in case. What I will do is ask the kitchen staff if they've heard any screams. Or even done any screaming when they've been arsing around. Now, I don't like seeing good grub go cold.'

Although we both picked up our knives and forks, Rufus asked, 'Am I guessing you really think what you heard were women's screams? Why should other people assure you that they were just animals on heat? Who told you it was foxes?'

'One of my neighbours – she actually threw water over them. And Joy – no, she didn't throw water over her. Joy said it was foxes screaming, not women.' Letting that stone sink into the pond, I applied myself to the guinea fowl. 'Let's talk about her later,' I said. 'This is food heaven.'

'There's one thing I want to ask first: the night you were staying with Joy and Ken—'

'Not Ken – he was away.'

'The night at Joy's – did the neighbours mention foxes the next day?'

My fork returned to the plate as if by its own volition. 'Yes. And shouting and door-slamming. But no sighting of the vixen.'

'Ah. Any moment now I can see you wanting to tell Elaine about this. But not until we've eaten, maybe?'

'Maybe not until tomorrow morning.' The ambiguity of what I'd just said! 'I'm so sorry! I didn't mean—It's just we're having breakfast tomorrow, aren't we? God, it's getting worse! Elaine and I are having breakfast tomorrow.'

'What are you expecting? A takeaway McMuffin? On tonight's evidence she might eat yours too.'

'I wouldn't offer odds against it.'

'Given the not at all remote possibility that she will forget or be tied up, perhaps I might just tag along. How would you feel about breakfast at the Mondiale? Or brunch?'

I think my flush went from my navel to my neck. 'Just now I don't know what I'd feel,' I said when I could speak.

'Let's talk about it later, then,' he said lightly. 'How do you like Dom's special secret recipe?'

'Excellent.' But I ate in silence: I was too busy inventing little speeches in my head to say anything aloud. Speeches about – well, one woman, one man. Do the maths. But I'd no idea what they might add up to.

* * *

257

When our plates were clear, Rufus coughed gently. 'When she was in her teens – no, early twenties – my sister was raped. There were – internal injuries. For years she couldn't face the idea of sex, and she'd tear me to pieces if she knew I'd just made what I can see was a crass bit of innuendo. Except it wasn't innuendo. What I really meant was that I will take you to your house and pick you up at a prearranged time to take you to see Elaine and maybe do breakfast, brunch whatever later. But she also said that what she did miss was normal non-invasive human contact – being cuddled, that sort of thing. Something else occurs to me – that you may not feel you're safe in that house of yours. Not with women or vixens screaming round you. Not after all you've been through. Sorry – long speech.'

'Kind speech,' I said. 'I think I'd like your sister.'

'I hope you'll meet her. Lules' favourite aunt. And I have to say you're not the only one with hang-ups. I'm a widower whose wife died in stupid circumstances and whose daughter matters more than the world. God knows when I last dated anyone – I guess I've forgotten how.'

I tried a dry laugh: 'Dating? What's that? Actually, I did nearly go on one last summer only my date got himself arrested instead. Dom will have played against him, if you ever want to ask him.'

He took my hand and squeezed it lightly. 'I did get round to taking this woman out not so long ago. Then she offered me a line of cocaine. Over. After Lules' mum . . .' He shook his head, removing his hand to make a slicing gesture across his throat. 'So you can see employing a gay assistant, no matter how vocal in the bedroom, makes sense.'

'Screaming again, is she?' Dom asked, collecting the

plates himself. 'Like those vixens? And no, none of the team reports seeing any, not live ones. Henry's dad is the master of foxhounds somewhere – he'll ask him when he gets home. I'll let Ruf here know, Jane, don't you worry. Now, dessert, or are you ready for my special?'

CHAPTER TWENTY-EIGHT

Police scene-of-crime tape still garlanded the paths into the woods Rufus owned.

'Just close your eyes,' he suggested as kindly as if he were talking to Lules.

'I'd better just avert them,' I said. 'If I close them I'll go to sleep! Goodness knows how much alcohol W. G.'s special contains,' I added with pleasurable guilt. Then I succumbed to silence: what happened next was a topic we'd not got round to pursuing again.

'A lot. Hello, what's that?' Pointing, he braked sharply.

'Looks like – yes, it's a woman.' I was out and running towards her before she staggered to a halt.

'Help! Please – must help me!' she panted.

'Of course!' I waved Rufus over.

'No. No car. They'll stop you. Punish us all.'

'Car as far as my school. You'll be safe there.' Between

us we more or less frog-marched her to the car and shoved her into the back footwell.

It only took a minute or so. 'Get her out. I'll open the door ready!'

In fact, we had to carry her. She'd lost her shoes somewhere and her feet were bleeding.

'Can't risk putting any lights on. Just follow me.'

'They search!'

'They won't search here. Rufus, can you shift the car – anywhere but here! – and call the police.'

She grabbed his arm. 'No. Not policeman.'

'Policewoman,' I said. 'Elaine. Probably still working. Just go.' I gave him two things – a kiss on the lips and a shove. Then I locked us in. 'I'm Jane. I'm the head teacher here. I know a very safe place. Oh, dear, this'll hurt your poor feet, I'm afraid,' I said, opening the roof-hatch and pushing the ladder in place. Thank goodness I didn't have to faff around getting the key from the safe. 'Get up there. I'll bring you water. No lights still.' A bottle of fizzy juice someone had confiscated and – yes – a bucket. 'Here you are. Take them. And though it's hard, pull that ladder up. UP!' I gestured. 'Don't open the hatch or let the ladder down till I come back.'

The Audi stopped beside me. 'You've locked the door again?' Rufus said, hauling me in beside him.

'Automatic. Key code, remember. Just drive. Pull into that lay-by by the tape if you want.'

He kept on in the opposite direction, U-turning and pulling up in a gateway. 'Now what?'

'Pretend you're snogging me. Just do it!' Dear God,

Will and I had once done just this. And he'd kissed me, but never again.

'What idiot designed great consoles between the driver and his snoggee? Hell, we'll switch on the satnav if we're not careful. Shit. Company.'

Company indeed. White van man. The one who'd smashed the Speed Watch team gear. Window-dressing time: I unzipped my trousers and pulled my top awry. I grabbed Rufus's hand and laid it on my thigh.

By now white van man was out and banging on Rufus's window. Yes, the central locking was on.

'What the hell do you want?' Rufus demanded through the half-open window.

The voice that replied was remarkably accent free. 'My girlfriend and I had a tiff. She ran away. I want to make sure she's safe.'

'Sorry, mate – we've not really been in a position to look at anything. So just push off and let us be, will you?'

'You've seen nothing? No young woman? Oh, get back to your fucking whore.'

Up went the window. 'You better had, you know, just until he drives off,' I said in my most headmistressy voice. But I did remove his hand.

'But I'd better stop when the sixth cavalry arrives, I suppose?' He leant over me, tidying my top for me as he did so. 'What a shame – sounds as if they're here now.'

I wriggled my trousers back to decency. 'Who is it?'

'Ms Matchmaker herself, I'd say. Yes, she's erupting even now.' He was up and out, perhaps to intercept her. I followed a moment or two later.

'This had better be bloody good,' she was saying.

'And you'd better have armed backup,' I retorted. 'I don't think white van man there was carrying a pea-shooter. He's after a terrified woman – at a guess, one of the women from the close.'

'Why the hell did she come here?'

'Does it matter? I've locked her in the school in the cold and dark and the sooner we can safely retrieve her the better. And I meant what I said about extra bodies.'

'God – now I know why I always hated teachers,' she grumbled. 'What a good job I've got a few grey cells of my own. The close is sealed off. Armed response is on its way – split in two, sadly. Why she didn't have the decency to turn up at your other school God knows – it would have made our life a lot easier.'

'I'm sure you can put that point to her later.'

She surveyed the rapidly assembling vehicles. 'Which door will you bring the woman out of?'

'Whichever you can get a car closest to.'

She put a hand on my arm. 'You really are dead serious about all this, aren't you? OK, I'd say we can take a unit into the playground if there's a handy door there.'

'And no one can take potshots at us from there?'

'*Us?*'

'I've told her not to come out for anyone else but me.'

There were times when I could wring her neck, but this wasn't one of them. 'Let's kit you up before you even think about trying to get in. Rufus, you too – but you stay exactly where I tell you. Ah, here's the super. Jane, stay here while I brief him.' She pointed to a spot two inches from her feet.

A hand took mine and squeezed it lightly – very asexually,

in fact. As if he was thinking about Lules. I squeezed back, equally lightly.

'Are you sure you're OK with this?' he asked.

'Got to be. I can't imagine I'll be allowed to go in on my own: heavens, it looks as if I'm getting body armour and a helmet. Oh, and you too! Very fetching.'

I also got a hug from Tom Arkwright, looking every inch a chief superintendent, who asked me the same question in the same words.

My answer was more succinct. 'Yes.'

'OK. Then this is what you'll do . . .'

I was picking my way through the still dark school using the light on the helmet. Idly I wondered what other gizmos it might have – I should have paid more attention, shouldn't I? Then I heard what I was sure was a shot. Please God, let Rufus be all right. Heavens, didn't all the others deserve equal protection? And let me be all right too, I added.

Although the young woman let down the ladder, she wouldn't come down: she was too afraid of heights, it seemed. So I went halfway up, using the torch on my camera to light the way down. First, though, she passed me the bottle – empty, and the bucket – also empty. And still she didn't want to come down. I went up myself. There was a hint of a sweet smell in the loft I'd not noticed before. Her fear, perhaps. This wasn't the time to speculate, though.

'You have to turn round. Come down backwards. I'll make sure you're safe.' So I grabbed an ankle and placed it safely before reaching for the next. At last she was on terra firma. This time it was her wrist I gripped, leading her through the kitchen. I tapped the door gently.

'OK, Jane.' Tom's voice. 'You can open up. Push her out first.'

'No! No men! No policemen!' she screamed. 'You promised no men.'

'Sorry,' I said – to both of them. 'Tom's my friend. Let me just open the door.'

She threw her weight against it. 'Bad man! Very bad.'

'I'll get Elaine,' Tom called.

By now the woman had moved from the door, but not for a good reason. The helmet light meant she could see parts of the kitchen I'd rather had remained in the dark – like the knife rack. She seized a kitchen knife, which she flourished. 'I kill if that man comes.'

Kill him? Kill herself? Hell, the way she was crossing the kitchen, she could have meant me.

All I could think of was to tell her, as if she was a five-year-old, to put the knife back before one of us got hurt. 'Look,' I added, 'there are thirty officers here to protect you, half of them women. This is Saturday night. You're ruining my date with the guy who helped you. Look, I even had my nails done. What do you think of the colour?' I lifted them so the beam shone on them. 'Tell me,' I said, edging closer to the door, 'which policeman are you afraid of?'

'No. If he's listening at door?'

It only then dawned on me that I'd forgotten the very first, most basic rule of any human interaction. I'd not asked her her name.

I asked it now. Getting no response, I continued, 'I'm Jane, by the way. I told you that I'm the head teacher here. And at Wrayford school too. I live in Wrayford. In Little Orchard Close. Where are you from?' Wrong. I should have asked the question I now put, 'Do you know Wrayford?'

She snorted. 'Wrayford? One room, one house, I know that.'

'A house near me? Tell me, what can I call you?' I knew the police had training courses for hostage situations, which this was rapidly becoming. So far as I knew, there weren't any for teachers. Not yet, at least. 'I'd like to call you by your name.'

'Men say that.'

So her name was all she had left that was hers?

The kitchen was suddenly flooded with light. What the hell was going on? Arc lights outside, that's what.

She blinked, eyes darting round the kitchen. Now she could see a whole lot more knives. But she didn't move towards them. She jerked the one in her hand in my direction.

'Why police clothes?' she asked suddenly and reasonably.

Reasonably I replied, 'Because my policewoman friend, Elaine, who is out in the road there, was afraid that whoever was searching for you might have a gun and try to shoot people – including me.'

'Searching for me!'

'The man you were running away from,' I suggested, 'when we brought you here. Please, tell me your name. And please put that knife down. The sooner we can join Elaine out there the sooner we'll be safe. Look, if you don't want any policemen around, let me phone Elaine and tell her to get rid of them.' But now my phone was a problem.

'You phone that man?'

'Why on earth should I?' Helpless, I sat down, hard on a stool. 'I want you to be safe. I want me to be safe. Elaine, my friend, will keep you safe – protect you. Look after you. Arrest

266

the man with the gun. Only please put down that knife.'

My phone rang. We both jumped.

'Can I take it?' Assuming it was safe, I reached for it.

The knife was an inch from my hand. 'Not that man.'

I shook my head as if I was safe back in my office. 'Most unlikely. Elaine, I should think. Can I look? Yes.' With one finger I pivoted it so she could see. 'Yes? OK? I'll put it on speaker so you can hear.'

'What in hell are you waiting for?' came Elaine's voice. 'We're waiting for you in the blasted cold here by the back door. Not a bloke for miles.'

Casually I picked up the phone. 'I hope we're on our way now. But promise me – and this is a matter of life and death – no men. Not even Rufus. Not even a male doctor. A woman doctor. Promise.'

'You're dead serious, aren't you?'

I tried for a joke. 'Better serious than dead.'

God knows what the woman made of the conversation, especially my flippancy. But at last she nodded, gesturing – with the knife – towards the door. 'OK, you go first.' The knife was so close to my throat I could feel how cold the blade was. 'Go. But no men.'

CHAPTER TWENTY-NINE

There were no men. None visible, at least. And Elaine, hectoring, edgy, irritating Elaine, stepping forward with a kind, almost motherly smile on her face. It might have been a social meeting: she looked ready to shake hands. 'I'm Detective Inspector Elaine Carberry: I'm here to see you're safe and sound. We want to talk to you about the man who was chasing after you and then we'll take you to a safe house – one specially for women. Look, give me that knife and come into the van – you too, Jane – out of this cold wind.'

The young woman got into the people-carrier but still clutched the knife like a talisman. What if she used it on herself?

'There you go. Sit yourself down. This is Sergeant Sue Beard. I'm sorry we all look like astronauts, but you'll be seeing us properly once we know there's no one with a gun going to take a potshot at us. Now, just remind me of your name, will you, love? Oh, and put your seat belt on, there's a good girl.'

To do that, she had to put down the knife, which disappeared into a cardboard tube as easily as if it had never been anywhere near my jugular. She fumbled with the buckle. I helped. She was dithering. I took her hand and squeezed it, smiling at her as if we were friends.

It was all so normal.

The drive wasn't. We hurtled through the lanes as if the roads had been cleared for us. It occurred to me that perhaps they had. Or perhaps there was a mighty whiffler, in the form of another police vehicle, preparing our way. Funny how Shakespeare comes in useful when otherwise you might be in hysterical tears. Or weeing yourself.

Actually, finding a loo took precedence over everything.

Elaine greeted me as I emerged to wash my hands: it felt a bit as if we were in a clip from the classic TV series, *Cagney and Lacey*, with me as the Sharon Gless character. Until I saw myself in the mirror. All my carefully applied make-up had disappeared or streaked and my hair, not at its best after all the oils and water it had been involved in, looked as if it had been sat on.

'Wash it all off. Start again. Here.' To my astonishment Elaine shoved a make-up bag into my hands. 'Come on, you've got this gorgeous guy kicking his heels and you want him to see you looking like a wet weekend? Rufus, of course,' she said, not quite patiently.

'Rufus? What's he doing here?'

Arms akimbo, she gaped at me: 'Maybe he tagged along

just for the fun. Actually, Jane, he's a witness, isn't he? – he might even have been a victim of the white van man had things gone badly.'

'Oh. Of course.'

'Don't sound so damned enthusiastic. And get some of that slap on. You really do look gross, you know.'

I obeyed.

'If only I knew that girl's name! She's still not telling us.'

'The poor kid seems frozen inside,' I said.

'Hm. Hope it's not Stockholm Syndrome. No, she doesn't like men, does she? Hang on, your eyes are lopsided. That's better. I'm in a huge battle, Jane: she's a sex worker and is almost certainly here illegally. That means some of my colleagues see her as a law-breaker. I see her as a victim, and want to find out who trafficked her. But her pulling a knife on you doesn't help.'

'It was just lying around. Once it was in her hand it seemed to hypnotise her.'

'Make sure you put that in your statement. Come on, never heard of a comb? Appearance is all to do with morale, see. Or do I mean the other way round? On a regular basis my colleagues see things – well, like that stuff in the woods . . . One of the things that helps them keep going is putting on a good front. I'm sure you've done it times out of number yourself, what with Simon and now this job of yours. That's better. Come on.' She was halfway out of the door.

I was still staring at the mirror. 'What now?'

She looked at her watch. 'We get a very quick statement from her – and her name, with luck. Not my job – I've got trained interviewers on to it. Sooner rather than later she'll need a medical examination, but as I told her I'm in favour of getting her to a women's refuge or a safe house for a few hours' sleep. You look as if you could do with the same once someone's jotted down your immortal words. There's a B & B we often use but it's a bit late for them.'

'I'll sleep in a cell if you want.' Actually, the way the adrenaline was pumping, I might never sleep again.

'I think Petrie might have a few words to say about that. Come on: someone's organising coffee.'

All this about Rufus was confusing me. We'd had a nice meal. We'd talked. We'd got involved in a charade that with hindsight was deeply embarrassing. It might have saved our lives, though. I must think of it as mouth-to-mouth resuscitation. No. Not after what mouth-to-mouth had done to Will.

The room rocked.

'OK – my office now.' She grabbed my elbow and propelled me to her goldfish bowl. She dug in her desk. 'Here – this is strictly against the rules, but you need something.' The something was a glug of whisky in a disposable plastic tumbler. 'Fire-in-your-belly time. And one of these.'

A KitKat bar. Was I to take the lot or just one of the four fingers? I halved it and pushed the other half towards her. 'Thanks. Elaine, what in hell is going on? I feel as if I've found one piece of someone else's jigsaw and don't know what to do with it.'

'Join the club. Actually, you've been supplying us with quite a lot of pieces without necessarily knowing what they were. Sometimes I didn't know which puzzle they fitted either. I need you to go through everything with me but maybe, for both our sakes, not tonight.' She glanced at her watch. 'After seventeen hours at work, your brain starts squeaking.'

I made a few mouse-like noises. 'Mine too.'

'Quite. OK, fifteen minutes max with Jason so he can record your thoughts while everything's fresh in your mind, and then you and Rufus can go – wherever you and Rufus want to go. Now, the guvnor – no, not Tom, but the Lord High Executioner – wants to talk to me now. Ten minutes ago. Whenever. Come on: I'll introduce you to Jason.'

Jason had been quick and efficient, as befitted a man with a first in English from Manchester, information I gleaned as he took me to where they'd lodged Rufus, in a soft interview room. He wasn't pacing up and down cursing the fact he had to wait for me. He was sprawling on an institutional sofa deeply asleep. There was nowhere else to sit except on the same sofa. I sat – collapsed – beside him and, despite my misgivings, was asleep within moments.

So we did have breakfast together, in the romantic setting of McDonald's. If Elaine had hoped we'd be engaging in deep and passionate conversation, she'd have been disappointed. For a start, we were all too aware that we'd woken with foul mouths and cricked necks and stiff limbs almost entangled with each other and not known how to deal with the situation. Knowing it was all recorded on CCTV didn't make it any better, and it was hard to believe that no one was sniggering at us behind their hands as we asked to be released from the room.

But now the prosaic, even mundane, conversation was actually quite intimate in its own way. Some of it involved his deciding what to tell Lules when he phoned her. Yes, we'd had supper together after a chance meeting. No, to anything else – not until she could see and feel he was safe, I suggested.

'You could come with me to collect her? I'd really like that,' he ventured over his second horrible coffee. He added, as if groping for a plausible excuse, 'So she can see you're safe too?'

'Of course,' I said a little too briskly, perhaps, adding truthfully, 'I'd love to.' Or did that sound as if I was making unwarranted assumptions? And then I realised it wasn't assumptions about Rufus and me I was making. 'How would Lules feel about it, though?'

He looked puzzled. 'How do you mean?'

'I'm not thinking very clearly, I'm afraid.'

'Who would, after last night?'

'The thing is, Lules doesn't know anything about last night until you tell her. She might violently object to your having anything to do with me outside school.'

'No. She's very fond of you.'

'But she *loves* you. Oh, I know you get all the sulks and tantrums, but that's *because* she loves you. And when you love someone you don't necessarily want anyone else muscling in.'

'So you think – you think I should *consult* her before I take someone out for a meal? Come on, Jane!'

'I didn't quite say that. But she's been through a lot recently. She might need the status quo just as it is, at the moment, at least.' I folded the paper napkin with stupid precision. 'Conversely – and I'm just looking at scenarios here – Lules might get the notion that just because we get on well she'd love me as her new stepmother. And she might' – I paused awkwardly – 'want to push things along too fast? Or if things didn't work out well between us, she could feel betrayed.'

'Lots of ifs, Jane! But you're right – on all counts. But one thing I must say – I haven't enjoyed a meal out with someone so much in years.' He gave a questioning smile.

'Me neither! I'd love another soon – one that didn't end quite as last night's did.'

'Though of course we did sleep together,' he pointed out.

We were in no hurry to get back to the police station, talking idly as if we'd suddenly become old friends.

'See you later?' he asked as we slowed to a stop outside the entrance.

'Only if you wait a long time,' Elaine declared cheerfully as she came up behind us. 'Jane and I have a giant jigsaw to put together. I could probably manage without her, but I doubt if she'd ever forgive me if I even tried. Oh, and there's a small matter of going through your statement, Jane – there are bits that didn't make complete sense, which young Jason should have spotted at the time, to be honest.'

'I'm surprised she made any sense at all,' Rufus observed. 'I wasn't particularly coherent and she had much more trauma to deal with than I did.' He looked at his watch. 'I'd best be off then, Jane – one thing Lules hates is when I haven't shaved. I'll call you – right? Early this evening, provided Elaine's finished with you by then,' he added dryly.

We kissed socially, left, right and then added one on the lips for luck. As we parted I saw mirrored in his eyes my hopes and fears. But we both managed a smile and a casual wave.

As if that could possibly fool Elaine.

At least I could divert her. 'That poor girl – the one who

rather interrupted our evening: how is she? And do you know her name yet?'

She signed me in and gave me a name tag. 'She's very traumatised, isn't she? They've messed with her head even more than they messed with her body. Which is a lot, believe me – she may require surgery. The problem is she'd been trafficked from, we think, Albania. As I said yesterday, in some people's eyes she's an illegal immigrant who's been doing illegal things and therefore deserves everything she gets. You'd be amazed how few prosecutions have been undertaken under the Modern Slavery Act. Sometimes I think my colleagues lose sight of people as people! Women, more particularly. Those guys washing cars – their story is being believed, of course, because they're men doing manly things. Hey, remind me to show you the pics of where they were being kept.' She punched the lift button as if it was personally responsible. 'As for women – oh, there are always excuses. Lack of evidence. Trails leading nowhere. Leaky borders – well, that's one excuse I do understand. But I want that woman to be recognised as a slave and I want the guys who trafficked her and used her put away for a very long time.' The lift doors closed gently as if reluctant to inflame her anger further. 'The doctor says she's twenty at most. Hard to tell exactly because of poor dental health, poor diet, drug use. But she won't give her name in case – in case of God knows what. She's afraid of giving anything away in case the traffickers take it out on her family. In fact, she insists she'd rather die than go back. She's on suicide watch at the refuge,' she concluded, breaking off to check her texts. 'Blast! Now I know I said you had to go through your statement with Jason again, but it seems he's not going to be in for a bit yet. '

'What about that giant jigsaw we were going to fix?' I asked quietly.

'Might have to delay that too. Do you fancy a bit of retail therapy while you wait? The Outlet?'

Any moment I might scream. But I kept my voice under control. Just about. 'I might fancy it but I'm not going to shop. I've got an enormous amount of work to do to prepare for another day away from Wray Episcopi School. The forensic guy couldn't work overtime because of the budget – where have we both heard that before? – so we can't use the school. Again. So when Jason eventually rolls up, then, and only then, will I come back. And maybe then we can talk about the bits of jigsaw.'

'It's not like you to take that tone!'

'I'm not taking any tone – I'm simply saying I'm as overworked as you are. But I just want . . . a bit of space, Elaine. My own space. Even if it's bounded by a car.'

'Shouldn't that be "bounded by a nutshell"? So long as you don't get bad dreams. OK. I'll authorise security to let your car out.' She handed over the keys without enthusiasm – or more as if she half-wanted to say something.

'You know I'd stay if I could be of any use. But I'm not one of your team and I know there's information I can't be privy to,' I offered, as a verbal olive branch. 'But there is a lot of stuff – maybe no more than gossip – that you might want to hear. About Ken and Joy, for starters.'

'I'll shout you lunch. Scout's honour,' she added over her shoulder as she dashed off.

This week or next?

CHAPTER THIRTY

I really didn't want to go anywhere near Wray Episcopi in general and its school in particular, but felt honour-bound to do what I'd said, in my strop, I was going to do. It was a nice enough morning anyway, which was an excuse for taking a slightly longer way round to give me time to get my courage up. And to summon up a smile. A car I was sure was Ian Cooper's outside Donna's house. How lovely to be free enough of baggage to do exactly what you wanted to do when you wanted to do it. Though I wasn't so sure what Donna's nan would make of the situation.

I also passed the van belonging to young Aaron, the builder who'd repaired the school roof. It was parked outside a cottage about the same size as Donna's. Something pinged in my head. What if he knew Kayleigh and Cecily and the tweeting sister and one of them had got him to leave something behind when he repaired the roof? What if the forensic examiner and I had actually been sitting on the problem? Wasn't there some movie where a character put shrimps on a curtain rail? Could that be all the problem was? Heavens, why hadn't it occurred to me when I'd caught the whiff of something last night?

Luck might be on my side. He emerged, blearily.

I pulled over.

We exchanged greetings, breezy on my part, cautious on his.

'Aaron,' I said, my smile the sort a pike might smile when it noticed a random minnow, 'I think you might have left something behind when you did our tiling job the other day.'

Got him. He flushed deeply.

'You know what,' I continued, 'the police are pretty well taking the place apart at the moment, looking for something that shouldn't be there. They'll be looking at the loft tomorrow. I wonder what they'd say if they found – whatever it is you left there.'

He writhed as if it was now an alligator smiling at him.

'You've still got your ladders on the roof: do you fancy coming straight up now and – just to make sure there's nothing lying around where it shouldn't be?'

A couple of cars went past. He looked at them as if they might provide inspiration. Another couple came towards us – it was a pity the Speed Watch team wasn't around.

'Don't worry – I'll step the ladder for you.'

'Best get—' he muttered, disappearing into the house. In seconds he was out again, clutching a Tesco carrier bag.

We processed to the school. Without hesitation he parked on the zigzag lines, which I regarded as sacred even at weekends. I parked demurely in my usual spot.

'It's easier to get the ladders down that side,' he announced, pointing.

'You don't want to get access from the inside?'

'All that insulation – you'd need a mask and stuff. And crawling boards. Easier to take a couple of tiles off.' Stuffing the carrier bag in a back pocket – it pulled his jeans down even lower – he marched off, carrying the ladder as easily as I would carry a pencil.

Having set it in place, he paused, one foot on the bottom rung, and said, 'It was only for a laugh, like. I didn't mean it to cause all what you said. And she and I broke up too!' he added bitterly, as slightly to my surprise he pulled on blue gloves. 'Last night, like.'

'I'm sorry to hear that.'

'Just wish it had been last week.'

I couldn't have put it better.

'Just hope I didn't miss any,' he said, five minutes later, passing me the carrier, now holding a few smelly prawns. 'Sorry. Do you have to tell the police?'

'It wouldn't do your business any good if you had a criminal record, would it?'

'You can say that again.' He looked back up, frowning. 'That'll be OK, miss. And any other jobs – well, let's say mates' rates. One thing – what's with all those boards? Why not do the whole lot? Doesn't make sense, does it? You know what, I'd have put the prawns under there if I could have reached,' he added, disarmingly.

'Just insulation, I suppose.' But there was soft fluffy insulation everywhere, and only that one area boarded. Odd.

'Never looked? Fancy looking now? Got my chisel and stuff in the van. Hey, what was that?'

I'd hardly registered anything, but now heard a slight whimper or moan. 'A cat stuck somewhere?'

He abandoned the ladder. 'Best have a look.' He set off the other side of the school, the canteen side, which I'd been quite happy to avoid earlier. 'My God! Oh, my God!' He came running back. 'I think she's still alive.'

A girl. Yes, still alive – but not for much longer.

She was nailed, hands and feet, in a parody of the crucifixion. She was gasping for breath – hadn't enough to scream, though the pain in her hands must have been excruciating as the weight of her body pulled against the nails, leaving trenches in the flesh.

'Just hold her up! Yes, take her weight! Well done.' I could hardly work my fingers to dial 999. 'Ambulance! Police! Desperately urgent!' Somehow I had to calm down enough to give details. The despatcher wanted more details of the girl's injuries than I had time to give them. 'We're holding her so at least she can breathe.'

Aaron glanced at me. 'You strong enough to hold her? Got to get those nails out before they tear her hands and feet in half.'

I took his place. 'Got your phone, Aaron? No? Mine's in my pocket. Take a couple of pics. Evidence. OK. Well done.' He shoved the phone back in my trousers, but in his haste he missed the pocket and it slithered between the fabric and my skin.

But he was dashing off. I talked rubbish to the girl – anything to keep her alive, it seemed. How long was he gone? What was he doing?

No, he hadn't scarpered. He was back with his tool box. Tears were streaming down his face. 'Really need to lever them out. Those nails. But I gotta pull them straight and I don't know if I can.'

'You can. Listen to me. You can.'

I've no idea how we did it. Somehow I held her upright and also gripped her wrist so she couldn't pull away as he worked. One out. Now what was he doing? He was tearing off his shirt to make a bandage.

Now the next hand. More bandages.

Could we manage her poor feet? We had to. Thank God she'd passed out completely. Aaron was grunting in the effort to do her as little harm as possible; I was trying not to collapse under the dead weight

Was that the sound of a car? The police!

But even as I realised there'd been no siren, that there were no reflections of a flashing light, Aaron grunted and slumped back on top of me. And then all went dark.

There were green-overall trousers not far from me. My legs – something heavy was holding me down. There was conversation over my head. More like urgent talk. And some instructions. Fragments of dialogue began to make sense. They were going to lift Aaron – something to do with keeping his head still. 'No! I don't want those wedge things. I'm fine,' he was muttering. 'Just let me sit up. What in hell's been happening?'

'Aaron – he's called Aaron. That's his van parked in the road,' I said; to my shame I was keener that they should move him than that they should take any notice of his protests.

'There's been an incident—' one of the paramedics began.

They shifted him enough for me to speak. 'Too damned right there's been an incident. How's the girl? Is she going to make it?' There was a pause, as if glances were being exchanged.

'There isn't a girl, Jane.'

'There was. There was a girl nailed to the door. Wasn't there, Aaron?'

He groaned assent. 'Jesus, Jane – I don't know what the hell's going on!'

'You were heroic, Aaron – just hold on to that. I don't know anyone else who could have done what you did.' I turned my head slightly. 'If it wasn't for Aaron, the girl would have died. Crucified.'

'There's no sign of a girl.'

'In that case whoever did this to us abducted her. Her or her body. Look – you'll see bloody nail holes. Get a police officer here, for Christ's sake. Now!'

'Concussion,' someone muttered, as if that explained my weird fantasy.

'Police. Now. Please.' And suddenly I added, 'A woman, for preference.'

'We need to get you to A & E, Jane.'

'Take poor Aaron, but I'm going nowhere till I've spoken to a woman officer. It's a matter of life and death.'

As if simply to humour me a young woman approached, squatting beside me. 'PC Dale. Kim. We can talk as soon as they move this young man.'

'This might hurt you too, Jane,' a paramedic warned me.

'That's OK. He's a good kid. He didn't deserve this.'

He cried out as they shifted him. I tried not to – there was no point in worrying him. 'Good luck, lad: see you soon!'

He flapped a hand.

Ignoring PC Dale's patent disbelief, I told her what Aaron had found.

'You're right – there is blood. And some nails. My God!'

'There's photos of her. On my phone. Which I'm lying on.'

'Don't move!'

'If I don't move I can't reach it.' Hell's bells! 'There.'

'Jesus God! And you say you and Aaron tried to free her?'

'Succeeded. Only if she's been abducted, it might not have been the best thing. Look, on my list of contacts you'll find DI Elaine Carberry. Send her the photos. If there's no immediate response, then use any means you have to tell her to get down here. Oh, and anyone else from the serious crime people. Tom Arkwright. Someone as senior as him.'

'There's a rapid response team already on its way, Jane.'

I'd have liked to be heroic, and leap to my feet and organise everything. But the pain when I'd wriggled round to get at the phone suggested that such a burst of energy wouldn't be wise. So I lay where I was, and next time someone suggested taking me to hospital I wouldn't argue. Once I knew Elaine was on to it, that is.

PC Dale – Kim – was back beside me. 'I can't reach her. I've left a message.'

'Did you send through the photos?'

'Did you really see her – like that? So there was a body—'

'No. There was a young woman. Alive. Just about. That's why we tried to get her down. And they say there's no sign of her. Can you get the image out as widely as you can – she may be lying dying in a ditch or something.' Was it surprising the poor woman looked taken aback? 'Look,

I've been helping DI Carberry with information about . . . a case she's working on. And – goodness, why have I only just thought of this? – I've got CCTV images that will help you all. Just get someone to help me into my office – yes, I'm the head teacher. I'm sorry. My brain seems addled.'

'They say you've probably got concussion – I can't see them letting you go anywhere except in the next ambulance to A & E. In any case – sorry, Jane – someone's smashed the CCTV lens,' she pointed out.

'Not a problem,' I said. 'There's a backup system. OK, if I have to get into my office without the medics' permission, I will. Give me a hand up, will you?' As I moved, I swore. More than I would in a whole year. Kim was clearly taken aback. 'Sorry. Just keep me steady and I'll show you everything you need.' We made very slow progress to the main door. Heavens, my hand was shaking too much to tap the keypad. Eventually Kim had to do it for me.

'Straight through here. Do you mind if I sit down and tell you what to do? The plan is we use the other CCTV camera, the one no one knows about. Security issues with my ex-husband,' I said. 'That switch there, please. And move the joystick a bit closer to me. We'll need to wind the footage back a bit: sometimes it needs a little time. Do you mind if I check that text? Probably nothing.'

Lovely surprise, Jane! Ken's just phoned to say he's whisking me off to the Continent for a few days as a sorry present! Off to Ashford NOW!!!

'Get me Elaine Carberry or Tom Arkwright now. Just trust me. Do it.'

'Call for you, sir,' she said doubtfully after three or four rings. 'A Ms Jane—'

'Jane Cowan, Tom,' I finished for her. 'That case Elaine Carberry's on. I think one of her suspects is heading for Ashford, not for the Outlet but to go to France. Next train. Ken Penkridge,' I added with a bit of a gasp.

He whistled, deafeningly. 'OK. I'm on to it. Stay where you are.'

'Don't cut the line. There's more – CCTV pictures you really need to see. I need to send them through to your mobile or computer or whatever.'

CHAPTER THIRTY-ONE

It was as if my body had kept going as long as it needed to, and then decided it had had enough. Standing was impossible. Thought hurt. My mouth wouldn't move properly. I wanted – needed – to sit still in the quiet. How likely was that? There was an unbelievable amount of action in my tiny office: Kim yelling down her phone, screaming at me, me trying to explain how to download the images but probably failing, and suddenly paramedics turning the room green. At one point I know I told them if they'd give me a shot of morphine I could keep going, but I don't think anyone took much notice. In any case, I couldn't shout at them because to do so I'd have had to breathe deeply and to breathe . . . No thank you.

It must have been quiet in A & E because there was no hanging round in the ambulance waiting to be handed over,

286

no queuing on a trolley in a corridor – just a very swift progress through triage to the company of medics. X-rays; blood tests; all sorts, including, oddly enough, the removal of what the nurse said looked like a bit of gravel from that bit of the back where you can never scratch properly. But it was hard to be a model patient when I still had things on my mind. I demanded news of Aaron, who was, I suspected, far more seriously injured than I was. The nurse cited patient confidentiality and walked away. I would have snarled, but there was a lot of movement and some raised voices in the corridor. Presumably they had a sudden influx of emergencies.

Then it went quiet.

But not for long. Elaine erupted into the room, fist clenched and pumping the air as if she'd just taken a vital wicket.

'Well done you!' she yelled. 'Hang on, we can't talk here. I'm having you moved to a single-occupancy room. Now.'

'But—'

'They're going to keep you in for observation, they say. Possible concussion. No broken bones, though – just a lot of bruises. No kidney damage. All in all you got off comparatively lightly. Unlike the kid who was with you. Concussion for sure; possible damaged spleen. Definitely a badly broken hand – boot marks on it. Anyway, they might as well move you sooner than later because they need the space here. Then I can tell you what I've been doing and who we're talking to right now. No, my team don't need me just at the moment– we've got a tranche of PCs specially trained in interview techniques. Ah! Looks like you're on the move.' She turned to the porter, a smiling lad in his twenties who looked like a young Imran Khan. 'They've checked your ID? Excellent.'

287

'What do you mean, checked his ID? It's on his scrubs, Elaine. Ahmed.' I smiled at him.

I expected a simple trundle, with perhaps the odd ride in a lift; what I got was a veritable procession – with armed officers fore and aft. And Elaine walking beside me, holding my hand as if I were her sister.

'Is it medically necessary for me to stay in, Saira?' I asked the woman – she might have been Ahmed's sister – who told me she was to be my dedicated nurse.

'If they want you here, it must be,' she said. 'You need to ask the doctor questions like that. Why didn't they explain before you were moved up here?'

'My fault,' Elaine declared, bouncing back in.

'Heavens, Winnie-the-Pooh and Eeyore at another room in this hospital, and now I've got Tigger!' I wasn't sure if I said it aloud, however: certainly Elaine didn't react.

'It'll all become clear, I promise, Jane. Meanwhile, I've brought some overnight stuff and a change of clothes – what a good dodge, your system of keeping a bag packed ready at school: it's in case you ever needed to make a rapid exit, I suppose? Oh, and there are some green tea bags for cuppa time: I know you won't want hospital brew and I'm sure they'll find you some hot water. Someone'll bring you some proper food later: meanwhile, have a bikky.'

Saira and I shared a smile and a shrug. And a biscuit. Elaine waited rather too pointedly till she'd left the room before she began, 'It's either here or a safe house. We need to keep an eye on you. Two birds, one stone. OK, so you went to solve the mystery of the item designed to close the school ad infinitum?'

'Exactly. But Aaron more than paid his debt for that bit of silliness: a quantity of raw, shell-on prawns. He scattered them in the loft space when he repaired the roof. It was he who heard the girl – moaning. It was he who – God knows how he did it – pulled out the nails that were pinning her to the kitchen door.'

'You managed to hold her up while he did this? Those mile runs must be good for you.'

'And then someone came and disturbed us, didn't they? I wonder why they were so vicious with Aaron and not so bad with me. Maybe they just heard the ambulance siren and scarpered. With the girl, of course.'

Elaine reached for a biscuit. 'It's OK. I've not really fallen off the wagon. I missed lunch. We think they put the girl in Aaron's van because it was found abandoned. Empty.'

'Where?'

'Do you remember we were mopping up the bastards who'd enslaved the car washers? And we went to Stelling Minnis to do it? Well, the hamlet – it's not really big enough to call a village – gets its name from a tract of open land. A common. It's one that escaped enclosure, somehow or other. They still use it to graze cows, I gather. Anyway, we found the van there. Blood inside it, which is obviously pretty useful. There's the sort of massive search for the girl you see on TV. More likely for her body, I'll admit.' She peered at me. 'I reckon your concussion is worse than they say.'

'Why?'

'Because you've not asked an obvious question. Or two. First, do you recall looking at the CCTV footage in your office? Whom did you see there?'

'The guy who hassled Rufus and me – wasn't it?'

'Right. A particularly unpleasant Albanian. It seems he's got a taste for more esoteric punishment and deaths. A woman in Dorset was pressed with huge heavy stones, like the Elizabethans did to prisoners when they wanted to inflict a slow, vile end. What you saw up in those woods was like a Druidical punishment, according to one of the team's quiz buffs. Apparently, any stray Romans who they caught had that coming to them. I suppose there's a certain abstract justice, given what the Romans did to Christians and gladiators to entertain themselves. And, of course, crucifixions . . .' She shrugged. 'Anyway, we presume it was this charmer who nicked the van and dumped the girl. But you never asked who might have helped him – because if it took two of you to release the poor creature, how many do you think it took to put her up there? And then to drive away the Albanian guy's vehicle when he took the van?'

'Ah,' I said. I looked at her sideways. 'And the answer to the second question is? Oh, bloody hell, Elaine! No!'

She'd only left the room clutching her phone. She returned a minute later with a grin that was strangely sombre. 'That bit of gravel the nurse found: didn't you wonder how it got in such an inaccessible place?'

'You said it earlier – my brain's got a tendency to go AWOL.'

'Obviously. Well, the gravel wasn't gravel.' She paused, dramatically, as if waiting for a drum roll. 'It was a chip. Not just any chip. An electronic chip. The sort someone had implanted in the woman you and Lulabelle found in the woods and in the girl you rescued last night. You know we can't tell you everything, and the less we talked to you about the – the first woman – the better. What a way to treat your sex slaves – to fit them with a tracking device! As if they're wild animals on some David Attenborough documentary.'

Eventually I found a thread of voice. 'And me? Someone to deal with later?'

'Couldn't have put it better myself,' she declared breezily. 'Which is why you've got two of our brightest and best outside your door, and why I'm fussy about ID. Meanwhile, I'm going to sort out somewhere for you to lurk a bit – not a safe house, don't worry about that. I know they give you the heebie-jeebies.'

'But if I'm no longer . . . chipped . . . then surely there isn't a problem?'

'Your chip will be going on a little journey, don't you worry. One or two of my team with quite infantile senses of humour will be on to it within the hour – or at least once it's been cloned. Clever devils, our techies. Imagine long, expensive rail journeys to far distant parts of the UK, for instance. And everywhere it goes there'll be an equally amused colleague waiting to intercept any would-be pursuers. I'll be off now: try and get a bit of shut-eye.' She headed purposefully for the door.

'Hang on! Joy. Joy and Ken. I grassed them up. She's my friend. Was my friend.'

'Still is, probably. All she'll know is that they missed the train they wanted because of a computer glitch – and it affected other people, poor lambs, too. So they found themselves en route to Waterloo for a later train with, incidentally, a complimentary upgrade. But – guess what – their car is still in the Ashford International multi-storey. Car? Did I say car? It's like the monster that tried to flatten you last summer. Strange choice. I'd have seen him in a Merc, somewhat superior to his wife's, wouldn't you?'

'Do I gather that the other people with booking problems and upgrades might be some of your people?'

'Ah! You're obviously feeling better! Now – close your eyes and sweet dreams!'

She missed my snort of derision. But then, closing my eyes didn't seem such a bad option.

The sweet dreams didn't come, however, just a jumble of incoherent thoughts. Some were quite constructive, to do with managing the problems of being unable to use Wrayford Epsicopi school: I couldn't imagine the police letting us have it back very quickly, and even then, how many parents would want to let their kids go anywhere near such a horrible crime scene. Staff too – all women. And me. Could I ever—? No, that was a thought I'd better suppress.

Easter holidays – that would be what my therapist might want me to imagine. If I ever had a chance to take Easter or any other holidays, of course . . . I was to open a catalogue, and look at the pictures of beaches and hills and blue skies and . . .

Someone was towering over me. I awoke with a terrifying start.

'Goodness,' I said as brightly as I could. 'Superintendent Arkwright in person! And in uniform, to boot! Tell me, Caffy, should I stand to attention? At very least sit to attention?'

'You can shut up and have a hug,' Caffy said, 'so long as you tell me where the bruises are.'

'Chiefly to my ego – at being discovered snoring and dribbling,' I said.

She passed a cup of water and a bunch of tissues. 'There. That's better. When I heard Tom was coming in person I thought I'd tag along – though it's highly irregular.'

'That's Caffy for you,' Tom said, moving a couple of chairs nearer the bed. He took the high-backed one meant for patients. It might suit his long legs, but I wondered if we'd ever prise his shoulders out of it. 'We're here to ask what you'd like us to bring in for your supper.'

I had a sudden, horrible frisson of disappointment. I hated to admit it even to myself that the 'someone' bringing in food might be Rufus, with or without Lules. 'Elaine would bring in Turkish,' I said, as if I'd just been hesitating over my choice of cuisine. I doubt if I'd fooled Caffy for a minute.

'If that's what you want,' Tom said doubtfully. 'Meanwhile, I've brought some of my auntie's best cake.'

I spread my hands with pleasure. 'Wow: what a treat! Thank you! About supper – if after all this I've got any room – can I text you? I've really no idea what I fancy.'

Caffy took my hand. 'You can *tell* us, when you're ready, that is. We're not going anywhere yet. Elaine reckons you're ready for any information she or Tom can give you without compromising the investigation or the trial. Elaine's pretty well asleep on her feet—'

'I've stood her down till tomorrow morning,' Tom put in. 'Oops. Sorry about that. I only make puns when I'm pleased with our progress, just so as you know. But you've been through a lot and I wanted to tell you it isn't all in vain. I'd like to begin at the beginning, but in all honesty, like you, I suspect, I'm not sure where that is. We could do with a giant whiteboard, but we'll have to manage without till we can get you out of here, although Elaine and I officially advise you to go into witness protection—'

'The answer is no!' I said, revolted. 'I've been on the

run a third of my life, Tom, because of my ex. I'm not changing everything again – not sacrificing everything, not changing who I am, ever again. So please let there be an alternative! Hey, Elaine said something, didn't she?' I genuinely couldn't remember.

Caffy smiled. 'There's actually battle royal going on between us and Jo and Lloyd about which is the best place for you to stay, my place or theirs. They're both secure, with CCTV and entryphones. Not quite up to police standard, but pretty good. The upside with ours is the swimming pool, the downside the fact we can't be there all day to keep you company. With Jo's you'll have her popping in from time to time, and of course there'll be the kids bouncing around. Problem?'

I was rigid with doubt. 'I don't want to bring trouble to anyone's door.'

'You won't. No one will know where you are,' Tom said. 'OK, I have to make this clear. You'll be incommunicado until we've dotted every last "i" and crossed every last "t". We'll get you another phone – OK, we'll download your address book for you. You'll use another computer. We'll get you new clothes. Nothing that can be identified as yours. What have I said?'

I suppose they'd been lurking for some time, but suddenly the tears flowed as if I was four. And what I said could have come from the mouth of one of my reception class kids: 'Oh, Caffy – I want my teddy.'

Tom blinked. 'I'll nip down to the hospital shop, shall I?'

'No,' I sobbed. 'Not a new bear. My own bears.'

CHAPTER THIRTY-TWO

Braced by a cup of green tea and some Divine chocolate Caffy happened to have in her bag, I tried to redeem myself, to prove myself an adult once again. Questions. Of course I had questions. And Tom had explanations.

'We can get anything you really want, Jane – I promise. Your bag, which you'd left in your car, is safe – as is your car, of course: I think you must have taken the keys with you when you went into the playground. Right?'

I nodded. 'Jacket pocket.'

'So it got towed away. I'll get hold of the keys and someone will pop round.'

'Will they tell my neighbour I'm OK? Enid. Her number's in my phone.' What about Brian? No, he could wait.

'Of course. But we can't tell her where you are or where you're going to be. OK? Now, interrupt if you want: Caffy alleges I talk in paragraphs. You've been a real busybody, haven't you?' he observed, the kindness of his voice belying the words. 'You've certainly kept our control room people on their toes. And fortunately, though they never seem to do anything other than murmur platitudes and promise to record what you've reported, they've actually been pretty meticulous. Especially about what you and your clever neighbours have observed in your close, from foxes upwards.'

'Foxes,' I said, in the encouraging tone I use to pupils reluctant to do their class presentation.

'Which we actually investigated. Like all animals, they leave traces. And guess what, there is evidence that one or two real foxes do pass some of their time in the close, making a great song and dance about it – but our clever little gizmos proved that not all the fox screams emanated from foxes. Some were real human screams. So well done you. Seriously. And well done for spotting that a room in one of the houses, and then one in quite another house – had photographic quality lights inadequately blacked out.'

'Used for—?'

'Bear with me. Because nothing happens just that fast. We get a lot of white vans and indeed other less obvious vehicles hurtling up and down an otherwise quiet residential street. A sudden burst of Amazon deliveries? Could be. Or it could be something else. The fact that some public-spirited soul in Wrayford wanted to set up a Neighbourhood Speed Watch Scheme was a wonderful coincidence. We got an excuse to discuss with some of the drivers that you and your colleagues logged the reason for their haste.'

'Hang on. Eoin Connor told us that the speed merchants just get a warning letter telling them to mend their ways. OK, so I'd guess that in some cases, as if it was normal procedure, your colleagues paid them a visit, and asked a few questions. Especially, I should imagine, those guys who smashed the speed gun and the camera.'

'Yes and no. There are a lot of surveillance cameras around, Jane – even some in the country. Sometimes it's better to track people than to alert them.'

'Of course. But those bright lights, Tom: my God, they weren't making snuff movies?'

'Actually, no. The young women in question were involved in cyber-sex – a so-called victimless crime. The idea is that it's a safe, no-touch form of prostitution – which in some cases it is. The pervy punter pays by PayPal or whatever, she takes the money and she does what he fancies watching. What is totally illegal is when the girl is joined by a sexual partner and they both perform for the voyeur who's paying.'

He was as keen on alliteration as Elaine, wasn't he?

It was time to make an effort: 'And as well as pop-up cyber-brothels, I'd guess there were pop-up everyday brothels – if there are such things. Like the one our anonymous woman was held in. And maybe that house that was deep-cleaned and redecorated.'

He raised his eyes as if surprised I knew about it. But he didn't comment. 'That's still worrying us, as it happens. As is the state the vicarage was in. Not to mention its garden and that interesting bonfire. Thank goodness you persuaded Mrs Vicar (what's their name? West?) to report it – or was it you who actually called it in? At least the house has been industrially cleaned and the garden's been well dug over – in patches, at least. Nothing to show for it all, sadly, except those burnt shoes. We got the wearer's DNA so let's just say the case isn't closed, not by any means.'

I made the words come out of my mouth. 'Do you think she might have ended up like the . . . the body . . . in Rufus Petrie's woods?'

'Petrie? Oh, Elaine was saying . . . No, there's no trace of his ever having done anything you wouldn't tell your grandmother about. Ever. Not to everyone's taste, but a decent guy. Our take so far is that people took advantage of his having public footpaths through his woodland, and the fact that very few people use them in the winter. The undergrowth's pretty dense – maybe he should manage it better or maybe he's one of these re-wilders. Let Nature Take Her Course,' he intoned.

I didn't want to talk about Rufus any more. 'Have the Wests forgiven me yet? People are so funny, aren't they? You'd think they'd be pleased that they were able to provide evidence of what may or may not be a crime, but they seem so resentful. And especially of me.'

'I gather they actually made one of my colleagues suspicious of them at one time.'

'Really? They're decent people, surely – just temporarily homeless. I'd probably have been grumpy in their situation.'

Narrowing her eyes and pursing her lips, Caffy seemed about to say something but apparently thought better of it.

A little silence became a bigger one. I suspected there was something Tom needed to broach; I knew there was something I had to ask. To lighten things up a little, I said, very plaintively, 'You mentioned your auntie's cake, Tom. I'm inclined to think it's a myth.'

I'd once had some before, so I knew it was real, but the quip gave me time to brace myself. 'I don't know if you can answer this, Tom, and I shan't be offended if you can't. But the CCTV footage of this afternoon's – incident – will have shown two people . . . dealing . . . with the poor girl. One of them I know about: Rufus and I sort of met him.'

'And you got away with it, which is something of a miracle! Yes, he's one of them.' His voice was very controlled.

'I'm guessing, since Elaine was at great pains to avoid the issue, that the other one is someone I know. Your face is giving you away, Tom.'

'I'd just rather you didn't have to hear it from me.'

'For God's sake, whisper it to Caffy and she can tell me! OK, let's run through the people I know. Male people. Rufus? You seemed to rule him out a minute ago. Or should I rule him in again? After all, your Albanian had every chance to kill him, and didn't. Didn't kill me either. And funnily enough, the injuries I got this afternoon were minor compared with Aaron's. One theory might be that Rufus was using some leverage – note I used the English, not the American pronunciation, Caffy! – to protect me. Which he could only do if he was involved.'

'It's a plausible theory. One we might have explored, but for your CCTV.'

'I don't see this as Brian Dawes' thing at all. He's a dyed-in-the-wool capitalist, who fails to connect his activities with the social problems he deplores; he's a bully and a chauvinist – but he has a strong sense of right and wrong. Your namesake, Tom, my deputy, works so many hours he wouldn't have time to do anything bad. My ex-husband is still in Durham Jail – yes? Oh, fuck!'

Tom's phone rang. 'Sorry. Yes, he is, but I have to take this.' He dodged outside.

'It's going to be tough, living next to Joy and her husband

299

after this, isn't it?' Caffy observed. She didn't quite add, 'I told you you'd have to sell.'

I managed a grim laugh. 'Joy's a friend. A kind woman. And I've betrayed something she said in confidence.'

'She may never know – if things turn out all right for Ken.'

'But I will. She said he'd changed – she didn't know him any more. And by coincidence, Rufus said I should tell her to leave him.'

'You like this Rufus, don't you?'

'Cautiously.'

She took my hand. 'Can you ever imagine falling head over heels with—? Oh, no! I've been trying to avoid that. And out it comes.'

'After Simon, any man has to come with a cast iron warranty – ideally I'd want him to go through the disbarring inspections teachers and volunteers submit to,' I admitted, forcing a laugh. 'Rufus has the complication of a daughter whom I teach. We did talk – was it only this morning? – about the implications.'

Before she could respond, Tom burst back into the room. To my amazement he cupped my face in his hands and kissed me on both cheeks. 'Got him! Ken Penkridge. That great beast of a vehicle – he may have bought it to transport his yachts, but he's been carrying humans too. They've found human hair, some blood and cloth fibres. As yet, we don't know if his passengers were willing or unwilling, living or dead.'

'Neither do you know if Ken was willing to carry them: don't forget his landlord was Tony Carpenter, someone Joy really didn't like. Carpenter could have been putting him under pressure—'

'Which is something he's got a name for. It isn't just us who've had our eyes on him, Jane – a lot of other unpleasant people are after him too. Don't worry – we're not leaping to any conclusions about Ken. We'll just follow the trail of evidence and see where it leads us.'

'Does it lead you to the conclusion that it was Ken who beat up Aaron and implanted that bug?'

He shook his head, sitting down again. 'No. The CCTV cameras have him on the M26 at that point.'

'So . . . OK, I'm trying to employ a little logic here. Stop me if you don't want to hear what I'm saying because it concerns one of your own.'

He said nothing, but nodded, rather sternly.

'I must still be concussed because I can't remember how long ago this was: it could have been yesterday but equally last year. When Wrayford and Wray Episcopi set up the Speed Watch team. I went along – with Joy, as it happens. There seemed to be an immediate rapport, an attraction, I'd say, between me and the officer running the scheme. Yes, Caffy, immediate. Weird. Anyway, he joined me and Joy for a pub supper, and came back with us to check out the close and its goings-on. But he shooed us back inside almost immediately – said it wouldn't do us any good to be seen with an officer in uniform. Then Joy did a really stupid thing.' I told them about the Amarula moment.

Caffy fell into an attack of giggles.

Tom didn't. 'What a totally crazy irresponsible thing to do. Why the hell?'

'You know what, I think she might have been attempting to do some matchmaking.'

'Does that usually involve getting someone drunk and

putting their career at risk? Imagine, a man in his position getting done for driving under the influence. My God!'

'All was well that ended well. He left his car on my drive – it was an unmarked one, maybe even his own – and took a taxi home. End of flirtation. But he did come with me to check out a site where one of my pupils heard a woman scream. No, we found nothing wrong. But curiously he popped up at the same place when our school secretary had an accident in the same woods: did she fall or was she pushed? One of your PCSOs, Ian Cooper, was concerned enough to check hospital records to see if there were any signs of violence. I think there was a problem with her records, or maybe my head's too fuzzy to remember.'

'I can check, anyway. Go on.'

'Two more odd things. I didn't know that traffic police responded to 999 calls, but when I heard what I thought was screaming – though Joy and my neighbour assured me it was probably foxes – I called it in, only to have Eoin turn up, again in an unmarked car.'

Tom's face was increasingly grave.

'Then Joy said something weird, when we were in the spa – was it really only yesterday? She said Eoin had pulled Ken over on a motorway the other day and breathalysed him. She expected Ken to fail, but Eoin waved him on his way with a friendly handshake. Tom: I'm not making accusations. But it should have dawned on me earlier that Eoin and Ken were . . . acquainted.'

'No reason why it should.'

'The only other thing is that when . . . No, this is really tenuous.'

'Go on.' His voice, his face, showed that he was used

to deploying this calm, compelling authority.

'I wish I knew her name! The girl Rufus and I rescued and stowed in the school loft. She was absolutely emphatic that she wanted nothing to do with male officers. Any at all.'

'That's right: I got sent away with a flea in my ear.'

'So you did. Does this suggest she'd had a bad experience with a male officer?'

His face was stern. 'And one in particular? Is this what you're implying?'

'I told you you might not want to hear it. And I'm not *implying* anything, just stating facts that may or not be connected.'

He eased himself out of his invalid chair and came to sit on the edge of the bed, taking my hand gently. 'Do you still like him, Jane?'

'I think that was only for one evening, and I had had red wine on an empty stomach.'

'Good. And thank you for spelling all this out. Because I'm sorry to say it confirms what your school CCTV suggests. And, to be honest, what the team are beginning to find evidence of – that at least one officer connived in the apparent escape of some of these trafficked women. They thought they were running for their lives to escape their slave master – in fact, they ended up as prostitutes in Wrayford and Poole and Wellington and other places. Betrayed, in other words. And after a week or so would be moved on. You can almost trace their movements via social media – their adverts, if that's what you can call them. Poor things.'

'Criminals or victims?'

'Victims, Jane – always victims. Now, I think we should push off now. Let you rest.'

'If you give me your house keys I'll go and get you some clothes and stuff. And your bears. No?' Caffy looked at Tom and frowned.

And she didn't argue when he said baldly, 'I think you should leave that to my team.'

CHAPTER THIRTY-THREE

I refused to leave hospital without speaking to Aaron, who told me with a grin he felt much better than I looked. 'They say they'll get rid of me tomorrow or the day after. Where there's no sense there's no feeling,' he added, patting his head.

'How will you manage?'

'Well, I was worried about that. I've got the van to finish paying for, and a queue of people who need jobs doing like yesterday. But that weird woman who's repairing your house came to see me yesterday and only goes and tells me I have an armed guard outside my room.' I nodded. He grimaced. 'Anyway, she says she and her team will pick up my jobs while I'm off. And give me a percentage, so I can keep up my van payments. And if necessary, if it all takes longer than it should, they'll put me on a contract for PACT or whatever they call themselves, those women, doing estimates and such. Do you think she's having me on?'

'If Caffy says she'll do something, she'll do it. I'd trust her with my life, Aaron – in fact I'm going to. She's found me somewhere to stay – until all this blows over.'

'You won't be going back, then – not to the school? I tell you, I wouldn't want to – except to see what's under them floorboards. Come on, I'm dead nosy, me. Bet you are too. Aren't you?' I didn't tell him what one of my bears was called. 'Fuck, I hope someone put my hammer and chisel in a safe place – don't want to lose them.'

'I owe you, Aaron – I'll buy you replacements if necessary.'

'No need. Caffy – is that really her name? – says if you're beaten up by a criminal trying to save someone you eventually get compensation. So you and me both, eh? Except if the school sacks you, you may be in deeper shit than me.' He lowered his eyes. 'All that social media stuff, miss. Stupid cow. I don't know why me and her ever got together.'

'Stuff happens. Tell you what, I'll send you some pics of what we find in the school loft.'

'Shit! No! You won't fucking do it without me!'

Nor would I.

I also looked in on Will, as immobile and unresponsive as ever. As always, I held his hand and talked to him, explaining I was in a bit of a crime-related pickle and might not be around for a few days. As I kissed him goodbye, Martin, his designated nurse, popped his head round the door and mouthed that he'd like a word. Interestingly, he led me well out of earshot when I joined him, as if he too accepted the remote possibility that Will could hear and process information.

Putting his hand on my shoulder, he said gently, 'There's going to be an approach to the High Court for permission to withdraw all the support systems that are keeping him going. You know there are a couple of Will's exes at loggerheads about his – possible – future. This is the only way to sort it out. I'm so sorry. I can't imagine there'll be a speedy decision, of course. They'll probably take months, and there'll be an appeal, probably. You know how the law takes for ever. The thing is, Jane, if life support were to be withdrawn, would you want to be present? No need to tell us now. Just something to ponder . . .'

Something amongst a whole lot of other things to ponder.

Caffy's apartment was very quiet, as she had warned it might be, and it was all too easy to dwell on what Martin had said. But the garden that her living room opened on to, and the grounds that surrounded the house, were very noisy – with birdsong, every note of which was promising spring and new life. I discovered gloves and tools in a shed and tried to dig and weed myself back to some sort of normality.

The main worry was about the two schools, and my place in them, especially after Aaron's comment. Using my new pay-as-you-go mobile, I had phoned Hazel on Monday morning to tell her I needed a couple of days' sick leave. Her response had been more guarded than usual – none of the unequivocal support I'd hoped for.

'The thing is, Jane, that I'm already getting phone calls from parents who don't want their children ever to have to pass that kitchen door – and I can't say I blame them.'

'Me neither. And I can see the children can't use the Wrayford village hall for ever. But the problem isn't insuperable: Grenfell Tower showed how quickly a substitute school can be put together, using upmarket Portakabins, and there's enough room in the Wrayford playground. I bet it could be organised and set up within the week. I have every faith in Tom Mason and Jess being able to come to an arrangement about sharing facilities.'

'Your deputies? Not you?' She sounded horribly relieved.

'As I said, I need a couple of days at least . . . If the parents don't want their kids to pass that door, Hazel, you can imagine how I must feel about seeing it. And recalling what—I'm sorry.' I swallowed hard. 'If you need to parachute in a head to cover my absence, I shall understand.' My voice must have sounded as forced to her as it felt to me. 'Can I ask who's talking of withdrawing their children?'

'I have to tell you some have already, I rather think as a result of that tweet. But Mr Petrie, whom I thought was rather an ally of yours, has emailed Donna. He says he's sure you'll understand.'

'Of course.'

She listed a couple of others – I'd miss them, but they wouldn't leave a hole in my heart like Lules' leaving.

It was only as I made myself a coffee that I realised that Rufus couldn't have contacted me in person: he didn't have my phone number. But it still hurt. What did Lules think about it? Possibly I'd never know.

'Come on, miss – I'm bored out of my skull and I really want to see,' Aaron insisted, his voice tinny down the phone.

To be honest I was getting cabin fever too. I might have more books at my disposal than I'd ever had in my life, there might be a wonderful music library, I could even use the Daweses' home cinema if I wanted – but I couldn't concentrate on anything for more than a few minutes, even assuming I could make the effort to choose and then open a book.

'If the police will let us,' I said, 'and you're sure you can manage the loft stairs—'

'You make me sound like my granddad. They only stood on the one hand, didn't they?'

My therapist thought it might be a good idea to see the school again. 'If you don't now, you won't ever manage it,' she'd said. 'Always get back on a horse the moment you've been thrown.'

No doubt Lulabelle would have agreed.

So on the Friday afternoon, Elaine, who was taking a proprietary interest in Aaron, on the grounds, she claimed, that you always needed to be on the right side of an odd-job man, picked up first me and then Aaron himself, and drove us both there. She parked outside the main entrance, only moving when a cough from me drew her attention to the yellow zigzag lines.

We couldn't have seen the kitchen door even if we'd wanted to – it was still hidden under a police tent. I let us in via the front door: the school smell was familiar, but the silence deeper than I'd ever known it, even though I'd worked there alone many a time. It was as if the school was already dead.

Even one-handed, Aaron was up the loft stairs like a monkey, his hammer and chisel tucked into his jeans' pockets. 'Come on. Got to see.' Then he added, almost in tears. 'Can't do it, Jane. You'll have to.'

Obeying his instruction to the letter – he didn't need to know I'd met such tools before – I inserted the chisel just where he pointed and hit it. And moved along and hit it again. Soon we could ease the floorboard out.

'Fucking hell!'

I couldn't have put it better myself.

'What's all that lot, then?' He pointed to decaying heaps of newspapers, tied with brown string. Twine. Elaine produced a camera, snapping from every angle. 'Go on, get one out.'

In response, though she left the parcel in place, Elaine eased away some of the paper, stroking away layer from layer till she stopped. 'Wood. Or something like it. No, look – it's paint. Oil paint.'

'Lady Preston's pictures,' I gasped. 'No: leave them as they are. We need art specialists to deal with them now.'

She snorted. 'Oh, they'll be Victorian crap!'

'Look at the dates on the papers: just at the end of the last war. They've been hidden from sight ever since. Elaine, I know I've got a suspicious mind, but I wonder if these got here legally?'

'You mean we're not going to see anything? Come on, miss!'

Elaine was worrying away all the paper from one, meanwhile. Colour shouted from the oil below. She froze. 'Does that say Vincent? Looks like you've found the school a Van Gogh, Jane!'

And we had. Assuming they were originals, we'd found one Van Gogh, at least, and a Seurat. I stopped them

310

opening anything else. In those two alone there was enough money to build a new school – to build new schools in every village in Kent. A new hospital or two. To change lives. Since there were at last half a dozen more waiting to be unwrapped, miracles were possible.

Or not.

'There's a body called the Commission for Looted Art,' I said, my mouth almost numb. 'They'll know what to do with them. They'll know who owns them. But then, the owners might have died – might have been killed in the war.'

'So that means you get to keep them?' Aaron yelped.

'It means someone will trace their families and return them.' I managed a grim smile. 'No wonder Lady Preston wants to get her paws on them. The only consolation is that if we don't get them she doesn't either.'

It wasn't much consolation, actually. Theoretically it was good knowing justice would be done, even if it was over seventy years later. In fact, I was, as Aaron elegantly put it, gutted. Museums had managed without them quite well; they had other pictures. At least, however, the public would get to see them, I told myself. But some, eventually, would go back to private owners and never see the light of day again. That was the worst scenario.

'They might give us a reward,' Aaron said hopefully.

'They might. But I wouldn't hold your breath.'

My therapist had been concerned by what I freely admitted were still negative feelings about the school, but more about my anger that our amazing discovery

311

would do no one any good. All that the media had been told was that an anonymous workman had found the pictures during routine maintenance. The village was awash with cameras for a couple of days. I didn't find it hard to stay away. Elaine reported that she'd spirited Aaron off to his granny's in Dartford, under the strictest instructions to keep his lip buttoned, because if he said anything the villains who'd hurt us would know where to find us and might return to finish the job. I backed her, wholeheartedly.

Late the following Sunday afternoon, Tom, finding me in Caffy's garden leaning idly on a hoe, once again floated the idea of the thing I really dreaded, witness protection. 'We've mopped up as many people as we could,' he said, throwing a worm towards an impatient robin, 'but gangs like these have long tentacles. You live a very public life – well, you're a biggish fish in a very small pond, what with your work and your umpiring – so it's very hard for you to hide. If only you had a great aunt in Australia who's longing to see you . . . No? Well, I promise you we'll do all we can to protect you – yes, both me officially and me as a friend – but you know that we're under as much financial pressure in the police as you are in education. If you mess up, kids fail exams. If we mess up . . .' His shrug said everything. 'Anyway, Caffy's roast lamb requires mint from the greenhouse. I'd best get it.'

'I didn't know mint had to be kept in a greenhouse,' I objected, as much to prolong the conversation – any conversation – as long as possible.

'Apparently if you dig some up in the autumn, pot it up

and keep it warmish, it flourishes while the stuff left in the garden is still lying dormant. There – you learn something new every day. By the way, Caffy says the pool is lovely and warm and if you have a swim now you won't be so stiff tomorrow.'

On the grounds that Caffy was usually right, I cleaned and put away the tools. I'd managed thirty lengths yesterday, so I'd try forty today. After all, the pool wasn't full-size and normally I was a strong swimmer – these days I was unaccountably weak. But I wanted to swim further and further because if I thought about anything except breathing and co-ordinating my limbs, I sank, ignominiously. And it was good not to think.

I was so intent on reaching forty it came as a shock to realise I wasn't alone. Someone had taken a seat at the far end of the pool and was nursing what looked like a G & T. He flapped a hand. I swam painfully back, and heaved myself up the steps. He got up, yanked me upright and passed me one of the giant fluffy hooded robes.

'Todd Dawes,' he said, with a smile to die for, now shaking my still dripping hand as if it was some social occasion. He must have been in his sixties. His face was well lived in, but it radiated intelligence and kindness in equal measure. 'I'm the reprobate many-times-removed cousin of your respectable friend Brian.'

'And Caffy's adoptive father. Married to . . . Jan?'

'Well done – you've been doing your homework. So have I. Come over here and sit down for a bit. Brian tells me you run two schools admirably, with fewer resources by the day.'

'That's what every head in the state sector does.'

'But it's tough?' He moved his chair slightly so he could see my face.

Surprising me probably more than him, the words poured out: 'It's tough having to sack your colleagues, manage without textbooks, rely on people's generosity for things like music and drama you know are essential, but can't fund without cutting other vital things.'

'And you feel you should go back and carry on fighting?'

'Of course. But my GP won't sign me off – says I'm not ready yet.'

'And are you?'

I dropped my gaze. 'I could be. Should be.'

He shook his head. 'Tom says you should never send in an injured cop to stop a fight. I'd have thought that applied to you. You need to get well, surely?'

Again words came out of their own accord. 'That could take a long time. To get over this properly. In fact, despite what I just said, I've tried to tell the governors they need someone who's on top of their game. I've told Brian and Hazel, his opposite number, told them straight. And they won't accept my resignation.'

'I don't know about this Hazel, but Brian's a stubborn bugger when he wants to be. He's feeling a lot better after his bypass, he says to tell you, better than he's felt for months, although he's still recuperating. He says you saved his life.'

'I didn't, but as you say, if he gets an idea in his head it stays there.'

'I gather you and he aren't together – or likely to be?' He grinned. 'No, of course not. Though some women might – certainly in the past – have been attracted, not least by his bank balance. You know there's to be a new pop-up school building to replace Wrayford Episcopi until the police have finished there? In the Wrayford School playground?'

I nodded.

'Actually, didn't you suggest it? Yes, of course you did – he almost admitted that. Almost.' We shared a grin, a bit feeble in my case. 'But I bet you didn't know that Brian's funding the move out of his own pocket? Don't say I told you. In fact, don't mention it. But it seems both schools need a protector – some big building firm's circling, I gather?'

'Brian would know a lot more than I do, I'm afraid.'

'Let me get you one of these.' Getting up easily, he strolled off in the direction of an unobtrusive cupboard, which he opened to reveal a fully stocked fridge.

He came back with two glasses; as if on cue his female equivalent came in, as attractive as he, with bones that would still be beautiful if she lived to be a hundred. She gathered me up as if I was Caffy, not a stranger.

'Jane, I'm Jan. Sorry to be so alliterative.' She hugged me again.

She picked up a glass; I didn't. I had this theory that it was fine to drink if you were happy, but positively dangerous if you were sad.

'Have you asked her yet?' she asked, toasting us both and sitting down elegantly.

'*Your* job, my love.'

Asked me what? To leave? It was true I didn't want to be here but suddenly I didn't want to go.

'OK. Here goes. Jane, you know Todd and I have used his ill-gotten gains to set up this trust. We work in various parts of Africa, with, for instance, children who are former child soldiers, or rape victims – kids who have suffered even more than their peers, though God knows things are so bad in so many places. We give them the best education we can – or that they're capable of dealing with. My special brief is girls. If a girl wants to keep goats, really wants to keep goats, that's fine. If she wants to become an eye surgeon, and has the work ethic and the ability, we can put her through medical school. Currently we're working alongside another charity, which we think might be close to your heart.'

For the first time I managed a real smile. 'Chance to Shine?'

'A smaller one, Cricket without Boundaries. It's committed to work with African kids exposed to AIDS, in particular. And we understand that you love your cricket. Our current liaison officer's on maternity leave, and we'd like to replace her. With you. Just for six months – though if she chose not to come back straightaway, the post would last longer. Or you could move across and concentrate on something else. Say yes, please.'

Yes, please! But I couldn't say it, could I? What about supporting Joy, now things were going truly wrong – though she might not want anything to do with me, of course. And what about fundraising, and protecting the school, and the women's cricket training, and my umpiring? And Zunaid? Who would speak up for Pam fostering him? Desperate for a stern, unanswerable excuse, I spread my hands. 'I'm used to a much more open selection process.' Did that sound as priggish to them as it did to me?

'Of course. We sometimes forget about equal opps, and you're right to remind us. In fact, I respect you even more. OK. We can advertise, shortlist and interview. That takes time. Can you come in as a stopgap while we do that?'

Todd grinned. 'It'll annoy the socks off Brian, which shouldn't of course influence you either way. You need both a rest and a challenge, Jane. According to Tom, who, incidentally is the only man we've ever thought remotely good enough for Caffy, you'd be better off out of the country for a bit. Heavens, you haven't even got your own house to live in! Even if you did, Caffy says it's too remote for you to be there on your own. So you can live in our place – it's just on the edge of a game reserve so you can have unusual company sometimes.'

'Have you ever met warthogs?' Jan put in. 'The silliest, sweetest creatures.'

'You can come back for Caffy and Tom's wedding, of course. And maybe come back altogether when everything's calm again, especially if that guy Petty realises what an idiot he's been.'

'Petrie. And I'm not sure I do reformed idiots.' I managed another weak smile. My God, I was tempted. Surely doing something useful was better than sitting moping. But in my bleak depression, I might more easily have opted for a task in a hopeless war zone: even the prospect of sun and kind people made me teeter towards guilt. I shook my head, trying to clear my thoughts: I'd never met a *deus ex machina* before. Or a *dea ex machina* for that matter. Now I had one of each, beaming intently at me.

They must have sensed I was weakening.

'About Petrie, time will tell,' Jan said, putting her

317

arm round me again. 'More important, time will heal. Sun will heal. Cricket and kids will heal. Oh, do stop tormenting yourself, Jane, love, and say yes, because Caffy's already got the champagne on ice.'